I0667542

The Echelon Mind

A Rory Mack Steele Novel, Volume 7

Eugene Lloyd MacRae

Published by CreateSpace, 2013.

THE ECHELON MIND

First edition. December 11, 2013.

ISBN: 1927767075

Written by Eugene Lloyd MacRae.

Chapter 1

THE WOMAN WAS TOTALLY NUDE and shivering in the cool night air. Her pubic hair, head hair, and even her eyebrows had been shaved completely off. The only hair on her entire body were the blond eyelashes.

The sounds of her bare feet crunching on the gravel sounded as painful as her raspy breathing. She ignored the small stones biting into the soft flesh of her soles and toes as she desperately fled across the open compound under the harsh lights. She had no idea what was in the darkness far ahead of her. But it had to be better than what she was leaving behind.

After two hundred yards of running, her lungs were starting to burn.

The darkness at the far edge of the compound seemed to stay in the distance, no matter how long she ran.

Fear of capture began to enter her thoughts. Her legs were heavy and burning but she willed her body to keep moving. The alternative was unthinkable.

A shadow loomed ahead in the distance. It was a fence!

She desperately pushed her weary legs harder.

The fence grew taller, beginning to look impossibly high.

No matter, she told herself, keep running. 75 yards away now...50 yards...20 yards...it was a high, chain-link fence with curly, barbed wire across the top.

In the back of her mind, she wondered if it was electrified. She pushed the thought away. Barbed wire or electricity didn't matter. She would rather die than stay inside the compound one more minute. She kept running and leaped as high she could, ramming her fingers and toes through the diamond-shaped holes in the galvanized wire mesh and began scrambling higher.

The wire at the top ran across the length of the fence in barrel-sized loops.

But that didn't stop her.

She grabbed the curly wire and cried out in pain as the sharp razor-like attachments cut into her flesh.

But that didn't stop her.

She stayed focused on getting to the top of the fence. She *had* to. Lifting her leg up, the woman straddled the wire. The sharp edges continued their assault into her feet, her legs, her arms and her groin. Her naked stomach screamed in pain from the slashes as she climbed over the vicious wire to begin her descent to the ground on the other side. Blood flowed between her fingers as she climbed down from the roll of razor wire to the wire mesh.

A flash of light caught her attention and she stopped. Through her bloody fingers clutching the fence, she caught sight of several vehicles rushing her way back inside the compound, their lights spearing their way towards her. Fear struck her heart.

Lights began flashing on the poles high above the wire fence.

Sirens began wailing.

She must have triggered an alarm.

They knew she had escaped!

Only halfway down the mesh fence she desperately jumped to the grass, tumbling onto her back. The naked woman rolled and jumped to her feet, running across the soft, open ground. Dark trees loomed two hundred yards ahead and the smell of pine needles beckoned her.

Halfway across the open ground, she could hear someone behind her yelling, telling her to stop. She heard herself curse and she pushed on, her lungs searing. Stopping was *not* an option.

Finally reaching the tree line, the naked, bleeding woman plunged into the darkness. Branches and pine needles scraped every part of her naked body. She ignored this pain as well and kept running. Something caught her right foot and she fell forward. She found herself rolling downhill, could feel the leaves, exposed roots and stones on the forest floor as she passed over them. Suddenly the smell of mud filled her nostrils and then her body plunged underwater.

Panic filled her heart as she thrashed desperately. Her feet found bottom and she anchored herself instinctively, pushing upwards. Her upper body emerged from the water but she found her feet slide out from under her and she went under again. Emerging the second time, she widened her stance and stayed upright, choking from the water that had gone down her throat. Wiping cold water from her eyes, she peered around in the darkness. She was waist deep in a ten-foot wide creek, the trees dark and foreboding a dozen feet up the sloped bank on either side.

Something in the back of her mind told her to stay in the knee-deep water. In the darkness ahead, she could see the stream turning to the right and moving away from the compound. If they tried to track her or they brought dogs, moving downstream should help to hide her escape.

She didn't know where this idea had come from.

It didn't matter.

It had to work. It *had* to!

She moved as quickly as she could, slipping every now and then on smooth, slimy rocks on the bottom of the stream as she fled the nightmare on the other side of the wire fence.

Chapter 2

PEACOCK POINT, Haldimand County, Ontario, Canada

RORY MACK STEELE took a sip of his coffee as he stepped onto the front porch of his log cottage on Peacock Point. The deep, rich smell of the earth and trees around the cabin mingled with the scent of his coffee. He loved getting up well before dawn like this and watching the sun rise over Lake Erie. The air was a bit chilly right now but once the sun rose it would warm up quickly.

The moonlight outlined a 1,000 foot long Great Lakes freighter moving slowly across the distant horizon. Rory wondered what she was carrying, and where she was headed. He cocked his head. It appeared to be angled on a heading that would take it to the long pier in front of the Nanticoke Generating Station. That was where they used to offload tons of coal to be burned to generate electricity for two million homes in the province. But the station was all but closed as part of the Government of Ontario's commitment to eliminate coal power. Rory chalked it up to his imagination.

A cricket chirped somewhere off to the right. Rory remembered reading that crickets had four different chirps. One particular sound was made right after mating and this one sounded happy to Rory. He smiled. Lucky little bugger.

Rory stretched his left arm over his head and then froze in position for a brief moment. His peripheral vision had picked up movements off to the right in the trees. He slowly brought his arm down and lightly scratched the back of his head, trying to be nonchalant. The movement wasn't that of an animal, that he was sure of. He slowly brought his left arm down to his side, nonchalantly took a sip of coffee and turned his head slightly to the right. Whatever it was, it was moving through the trees towards the back of the cottage. His baby Eagle handgun was hanging in its shoulder holster on the back of the door just behind him. As he sipped his coffee again, he turned slowly to the right. Rory got a glimpse of someone's bare back in the moonlight just before the figure disappeared around the corner. He assumed it was some shirtless, homeless guy looking for food. Rory didn't mind sharing, but he preferred people walking up and asking. That way no one got hurt by accident. Rory moved quickly through the front door and set his coffee cup on the little table to the right. Closing the door silently but quickly, he reached up and pulled his Baby Eagle handgun from the shoulder holster. At 6'2" tall, athletically fit and militarily trained, Rory could take of himself. But he also wasn't a fool.

He knew every squeak in the floor and Rory avoided each one as he moved quietly towards the kitchen at the back of the cabin. Moving carefully to the end of the hallway, Rory caught a glimpse of something moving in the dark inside the kitchen. He squinted at a small, dark form and watched for the glint of a weapon.

A soft light began glowing in the kitchen. The dark form had opened the refrigerator.

Rory took the last two steps, slowly reaching inside with his left hand towards the light switch. He flipped the light on and stepped into the kitchen, "Freeze!"

A figure screamed, slammed the refrigerator shut and moved to the left. But there was no way out that way. The figure turned and cried out in a whisper, "Please don't hurt me!"

Rory stood in place, shocked.

It was a woman. And she was totally naked.

The nude woman backed up against the wall, her hands up, her face filled with fear.

Rory was speechless.

Chapter 3

IT WAS IMMEDIATELY EVIDENT that the woman had no hair anywhere, not even eyebrows. Rory had seen women with shaved heads and shaved privates before. That wasn't unusual in this day and age. But what caught his attention...was the blood. There was blood splashed or smeared on her face, her body and her legs. Rory glanced down and saw partial bloody footprints on his floor where she had walked from the back door. Rory first wondered if she had murdered someone. He looked back at the cowering woman...and realized the blood had come from dozens of cuts on her hands, arms, breasts, stomach, and legs. This hadn't been caused by someone just running through the bush. Something had happened to her. And from her fear, it wasn't a good something.

The woman was shaking and she slowly slid down the wall to a crouch, her hands up in surrender. "Please don't hurt me," she whispered again. "Please don't. Please don't." Her voice tapered off in fear.

Rory realized he was still holding the gun straight at her face. He quickly placed it in the waistband of his jeans in the back and then held his hands up, "It's okay. I'm not going to hurt you."

The woman was immediately up and running for the door.

Rory stepped forward and caught her in the crook of his right arm, pulling her gently back against his body.

The naked, bloody woman screamed.

Rory draped his left arm around her shoulder as he talked soothingly in her ear, "It's okay. You're safe. You're safe here."

The woman began pounding Rory with her fists, desperate to escape.

"It's okay, you're safe. You're safe," Rory repeated gently.

The fists swung slower. The woman's body sagged after a few moments and she broke down.

Rory gently led her towards the spare bedroom as big sobs racked her body. Moving her through the open doorway, he quickly pulled the bedspread off the bed with his left hand. He draped it gently around her, covering her nakedness. Rory saw blood staining the sleeve of his shirt. "Maybe we should get you to a doctor," Rory suggested.

The woman shook her head emphatically no.

"But you're bleeding–"

"Please, I'll just leave. I won't bother you anymore," she said softly.

"You're not bothering me. I just want to make sure you're okay," he said gently. "How did you get those cuts?" he asked as he looked at the two on her neck. The blood was coagulating and partially dried so he assumed it had happened within the last hour or so.

The woman remained silent as she looked down at the bed. She looked exhausted.

Rory didn't want to push her. From his days in the Canadian Army, Rory thought the cuts were from razor wire. That was a bit disturbing. Why would she be climbing over razor wire? "Okay.

I've got some Band-Aids and bandages," he said. "Why don't you take a nice hot shower and then we'll fix those cuts up."

The woman looked around the room. She wasn't really focusing on anything. She turned her head quickly, looking at the open doorway as if she had heard something

"It's okay," Rory repeated again. "You're safe here. Whatever hurt you, I won't let it happen again, all right?"

She finally nodded her head just slightly a couple of times.

"Good. Let's get you to the shower," Rory told her. He slowly guided her into the hallway and into the bathroom next door. "Once we get you cleaned up, then we can have something to eat."

The woman nodded her head slightly again.

Rory discreetly backed out of the bathroom and pulled the door partially shut. There was no window, so there was no way for her to climb outside and run. And Rory had no doubt she would, given the chance. But that would mean she might be running right into the hands of whoever she was running from. But he doubted she would think about that. He opened up a small closet door across from the bathroom and gathered up his collection of bandages and assorted first aid equipment. He heard a slight squeak from the bathroom door.

The woman's bloody face peeked around the door as she opened it a little wider. She looked apprehensively out at him.

Rory simply nodded and gave her a smile.

The woman pulled back inside and Rory saw the bedspread fall to the floor. He heard the shower start and after a few moments, he heard the shower curtain being pulled across.

Rory opened the door just a bit and placed everything he had on the counter inside. Then he slipped back down the hallway and into his own bedroom, pulling out socks, underwear, an extra pair of jeans and a red and black, flannel lumberjack shirt. He set his Baby Eagle on the top of his dresser, gathered up the clothing and went back to the bathroom. Rory knocked gently on the still open door, "I'm bringing some clothes in," he said in a soft voice. Then he stepped inside and set the clothes down on the counter.

The shower turned off.

Rory grabbed a couple of the big fluffy towels off the shelf over the toilet and draped them over the shower bar, "Here are a couple of towels." One of the towels disappeared quickly. After a few moments, it was thrown back over the bar, wet. Then the other one disappeared. "Once you get out we'll clean up your cuts –"

The shower curtain slid back. The woman stepped out with a white towel draped around her body. It was like a little white miniskirt on her, extending from just above her nipples to barely below her crotch.

With all the blood gone Rory had his first real look at his visitor.

She was exquisitely beautiful. Her eyes were a deep blue and her features were like a fine porcelain China doll. She wasn't crouched now and she stood about 5'-10". Her body was well proportioned and she had the look of someone who kept herself fit. And there was something else behind those eyes besides the fear. He had the impression that she was extremely intelligent.

Rory took some cotton balls and antiseptic and knelt in front of her. He began gently working on the cuts that were on her legs and feet. He put a flesh colored band-aid on each one, working up to her thighs.

The woman was silent and began shaking.

"Are you cold?" he asked as he looked up.

She nodded yes.

"Turn around and we'll get these cuts fixed up quickly."

She looked down at him for a moment and then complied, turning slowly.

Rory saw only a couple of cuts near the back of her knees. He applied a band-aid to each one and then he stood up and took care of the two he had looked at before on the side of her neck. Then he worked to take care of several severe cuts on her arms. He noticed blood spots on the towel where she had held it against her body. "How about your hands?" he asked gently.

The woman held the towel under her arms as she opened her left hand and then her right.

Rory gently applied band-aids to the numerous cuts on the palms. "Do you have any on your back?"

The woman turned and the white towel dropped away in back while she held it tight to her front.

She had a couple on her back and Rory quickly took care of them. He stepped back. The towel had ridden higher as she had moved around and he saw traces of blood inside her legs below her butt. He wasn't going to touch those. He stood up and placed everything back on the counter, "You can take care of the cuts on the front of your body yourself...and anywhere else you might have them. Then you can get dressed in those clothes. I'm afraid it's all I have. But they'll keep you warm. I'll get the fireplace going in the front room to warm you up. Then we can have some hot coffee. Deal?"

The woman turned to look at him, nodding slightly as she held the towel tightly against her.

Rory left and got a roaring fire going in the front room. He kept an eye on the hallway, making sure she didn't make a run for it.

She didn't.

Rory walked back to the kitchen and got his Keurig Platinum coffee maker going. He had two big mugs of coffee in hand as he headed back down the hallway. "Ready?" he asked outside the bathroom door.

The door opened slightly and the woman peered out.

"Follow me," Rory said as he held a mug up before he headed for the front room. He glanced back and saw her cautiously slip into the hallway. Giving her an assuring nod, he continued on.

The woman walked slowly behind Rory towards the front room. Her eyes darted back and forth, taking everything in and watching for danger.

Rory moved softly across the front room towards the stone fireplace, not wanting to spook the woman with any loud noises. He set one coffee mug down on the small table beside a large easy chair to the left of the fireplace. Then he walked over and sat in the easy chair on the right.

The woman tentatively entered the front room. She hesitated for a moment and watched Rory sipping his coffee. Then she walked over to the empty easy chair and sat down. She picked up the mug of coffee and took a sip. Her left hand rubbed the roundness of the mug as if the heat soothed her wounds under the Band-aids. The crackling of the fireplace caught her attention and she stared at the dancing flames for a moment before she took another sip of coffee.

"My name is Rory Mack Steele."

The woman just stared at the crackling flames. She took another sip of coffee.

"Can you tell me your name?"

The woman shook her head no.

Rory didn't push.

After a moment the woman stared into the leaping flames and said in a soft voice, "I can't tell you my name."

"You don't have to be afraid—"

The woman looked at him with hurt in her deep blue eyes and spoke in an anguished voice, "I don't know it."

"Pardon?"

"I don't know who I am," she said as tears filled her eyes.

Chapter 4

RORY LOOKED AT THE WOMAN sitting in the easy chair across from him. The flickering firelight reflected on her face and emphasized the anguish and despair he could see. "You have amnesia?"

She looked into the fire for another moment. "I don't know," she finally answered in a quiet voice.

"What have the doctors told you?"

"Doctors?" The woman opened her mouth to say something and then stayed silent. Her blue eyes focused again on the dancing flames.

Rory had the impression every question he asked would be answered in the same way, 'I don't know.' Something traumatic had happened to her. The cuts and the blood and the fear had been genuine. He wasn't a psychiatrist and he didn't know how far he could push his questioning before he affected her adversely. He set his coffee down gently and sat forward in his easy chair, "Can you tell me what you do remember? Can you tell me where you got those cuts?"

The woman looked down at the coffee cup for a moment and then looked up and to the left. Then she looked down at the floor and fear showed in her face.

"It's okay," Rory said softly. "You're safe here. No one can hurt you."

The woman nodded after a moment. Then she looked back at the coffee cup, "I... I remember escaping over a fence. It had...sharp pieces of metal... "

Rory nodded, "That's razor wire. That's consistent with your cuts. Where were you escaping from?"

The woman narrowed her eyes, obviously thinking, "It was...a large place...a lot of open ground before the fence... and after...."

Rory nodded, "That sounds like a large compound surrounded by a security fence." Rory wondered if she was an escapee from a maximum-security prison. But there was nothing nearby that would fit the bill. Escaping as a prisoner being transferred from one lock up to the next didn't fit either. "What do you remember about where you were being held?"

The woman was silent, her eyes dancing back and forth as she peered into the past, "I remember... I remember sitting in a chair...naked. It was...humiliating."

That surprised Rory, "A chair? What kind of chair?"

The woman shook her head, "I don't know...I remember something being strapped on my head...but I don't know why."

None of it made any sense to Rory.

Her hand went to her head and her fingers brushed across her scalp, "I...I remember being shaved." She looked at Rory, humiliation showing on her face as she whispered, "I was shaved...someone shaved me...everywhere...even down there." She looked away, staring into nothing.

"What else?" Rory asked, fearing what he might hear.

"I think I was drugged," she said as she looked at Rory again. "I'm not sure why, but I remember being drugged most of the time. I was kept in a room...I think I was there for a long, long time." Then she looked back at the fire and shook her head, "I don't remember anything else."

Rory didn't know what to make of the story. It sounded like she had been held by some kind of sexual predator. He clenched his fists and wanted to find the pervert and rip him apart. "Can you remember how you got here, to my place, from where you were being held?"

The woman looked at him, "I remember trees...and I was in water...in a stream of water that I followed for a while...and then I went across some fields... But I don't remember much. It's all a blur...like a long nightmare."

Rory wanted to find the place but he didn't want to push her too much right now. Then he remembered the reason why she had showed up here in his cottage in the first place, "Are you hungry?"

The woman looked at him and nodded.

Rory got up, picked up his coffee mug, then went over and held his hand out for her mug, "Why don't you and I go into the kitchen. Hand me your mug and I'll make you more hot coffee and something to eat."

The woman looked up for a moment before she handed over her coffee cup. There was still a lot of confusion and worry in her eyes.

Rory left the front room and headed for the kitchen, fully expecting her to follow him. It didn't look like she would run right now. Rory placed the two mugs in the sink and then flipped the Keurig Platinum coffee maker on again. As he was pulling two fresh mugs from the cupboard, he heard her softly pad into the kitchen behind him. "What brand of coffee do you like?" he asked her without turning.

The woman didn't answer.

"I have these little K-cups in different blends of coffee," Rory said as he held one up at his shoulder. He wondered if he could stir her memory this way. "I can make the same thing as a Tim Horton's coffee...McDonald's, Timothy's...I have The Original Donut Shop blend, Newman's blend, green mountain coffee—"

"McDonald's...I think," she said.

Rory glanced around at her and nodded. That was progress. His jeans and lumberjack shirt were big on her. She had rolled the pant legs and the shirt sleeves up and she looked like a lost soul.

The woman glanced around the kitchen and then she sat in one of the chairs at his small wooden table on the right side of the kitchen.

While he waited for the coffee maker to get hot, Rory got out the eggs and bacon. "A couple of fried eggs with bacon and toast is about all I can handle. Is that okay with you?"

The woman seemed to shrug and nod all at the same time.

It wasn't long before they were sitting across from each other, the smell of bacon, eggs, toast, and coffee filling the room. Rory watched her dig into her breakfast, obviously hungry, but the way she held her knife and fork told Rory something about her. She had manners and seemed well educated. Rory got up and got something he had forgotten about, a couple of paper napkins. He placed one beside her plate and the way she used hers confirmed his thoughts. A well mannered, educated young woman, who had lost her memory somehow, was sitting across from him.

"Would you like some more?" he asked as she cleaned her plate.

She shook her head no and dabbed the corner of her mouth with her napkin, "Can I use your bathroom for a minute again?"

"Of course," Rory said. He stood up and started to gather up the dirty plates. He watched her walk away. Just the way the light illuminated her as she turned into the hallway revealed something on the back of her head and he froze in position.

She walked down the hallway and disappeared into the bathroom.

A moment later, Rory put the dishes in the sink, adding the dish soap and water as he contemplated what he had seen – and wondering if he should bring it up.

The woman came back into the kitchen ten minutes later as he was finishing up.

Rory placed the last clean plate back in the cupboard. "More coffee?" he asked.

"Yes please," she replied as she sat down.

Rory brewed her another McDonald's blend. He set it down on the table in front of her, then went back to make one for himself. Once he was done, he took his own mug back to the table, "Can I ask you another question?"

The woman took a sip of coffee, looked at him and then nodded apprehensively.

"I noticed when you were walking away, you have a couple of very fine scars running up the back your head. Were you in an accident? Maybe that's why you can't remember anything."

The woman looked up at him in surprise. She felt the back of her head. "Nothing I remember," she said.

Rory nodded, "Do you mind if I take a look? Maybe it's nothing."

The woman thought about it for a moment and then nodded her okay.

Rory went around behind her and placed his fingers gently on the area near her right ear. There was another fine scar over by the other ear, "Definitely scars. They're very, very fine. And very hard to see unless the light hits them just the right way. They run from the base of your skull all the way up to the top of your head. Maybe that explains your amnesia."

The woman placed her hands on the back of her head, feeling for the scars.

"Here, Rory whispered. He gently guided her fingers along the scars on both sides.

"I can't really feel anything," she said quietly.

"As I said, they're very, very fine," Rory said gently.

The woman's fingers continued to feel along the back of her head.

As she turned her head, a chill ran through Rory's body.

Chapter 5

RORY DIDN'T SAY ANYTHING, but when the woman moved her head, Rory could see the full extent of those scars. They actually went right across the top of her scalp towards her forehead. He angled his head and could see the scars followed along her hairline at the front and met in the middle. Rory imagined someone peeling the skin back, sawing through the skull on the top of her head and working on her brain inside. Had she been in a hospital? No. There was a security fence of some type. That didn't make any sense...unless she was being held someplace for the criminally insane!

The woman was still feeling along the scars at the back of her head. "I don't remember anything about an operation or anything," she said softly.

Rory walked back around to his chair, keeping the full extent of the scar to himself. He sat down, "Maybe—"

There was a loud pounding on the front door of the cabin and someone yelled, "Open up in there."

The woman got up to run.

Rory put a hand on her shoulder to stop her and put a finger to his lips, cautioning her to stay quiet.

There was someone tramping around the back of the cabin in the dark as well, just outside the kitchen door.

Rory guided the woman to the left where there was a pantry that she could hide in.

Her eyes were wide open in fear and her body was trembling as Rory placed her inside the pantry.

He put his finger to his lips again and then closed the pantry door gently. Turning quickly, he headed down the hallway towards the front room. He stopped along the way to grab his Baby Eagle from the top of the dresser in the bedroom. Through the glass in the front door, Rory could see several men standing on the porch outside. He saw a rifle in the hands of one of them. Not one of them was wearing the uniform of the local law, the Ontario Provincial Police. This didn't look good. Rory opened the door and made sure they saw him holding his Baby Eagle up by his shoulder.

"That isn't exactly too friendly there, buddy," said the one closest to him. He was a burly guy dressed in hunting fatigues, his rifle pointing towards the floor of the porch. There were two other men behind him, at the bottom of the stairs, dressed exactly the same. They held their rifles across their chest.

"Oh," Rory said, "everything will be nice and friendly as long as you keep those guns pointed to the ground."

The two men on the ground drifted left and right and the man on the left sneered "And what if we don't, pal?"

Rory looked at him and raised an eyebrow, "Just keep moving and you'll find out."

The lead man held a hand out and gestured to the men behind him as he kept his eyes on Rory, "It's okay, boys. Stay in place. And lower your weapons."

The two men behind stopped their drift and lowered their rifles.

His eyes flicking to the handgun and then back into Rory's eyes, the lead man smiled, "We don't mean no harm, mister. We're just wondering if you saw somebody skulking around out here."

"Just you three," Rory answered.

The man on the right gave Rory a sullen look, "Now listen here, mister–"

"No, you listen," Rory said in a low, even voice. "When three men come to my door carrying rifles, in a country where we don't normally do that, I have a very good reason for concern. And you're not the police, yet you pound on my door and yell open up—"

The man on the left swore and made a slight move to lift his rifle.

Rory held a finger up in caution, "This handgun has a premium, aluminum trigger...finely tuned for a number of quick, accurate pulls. No matter what happens, I should get *one,* if not two of you."

The three men stiffened just a little.

Rory looked the lead man in the eyes, "And if one of your men down there so much as twitches again, I'll make sure *you* are the first one that I take down."

There was silence.

"And I'll tell you what," Rory added, "if your man prowling around in back of my cottage doesn't get his ass back here now, I might just consider that as good as a twitch."

The three men stood there for a moment, considering their next move. Then the lead man nodded his head slightly, leaned a bit and yelled, "Caleb. Back here. Now!"

A few moments later, another man carrying a rifle, came from around the right side of the cottage. The leader indicated for him to keep the rifle down.

The man complied. He blinked twice when he saw the handgun at Rory's shoulder.

"Now," Rory said in an even voice. "I would suggest you leave. And don't come back. If you do, I'll consider that as being unfriendly."

The three men held their ground for a few minutes, then the lead man backed slowly off the porch to join the others. The fourth man joined them and then the group walked sullenly off into the darkness of the trees on the right.

Once they disappeared from view, Rory moved back quickly through the house to the pantry, snapping off lights along the way.

The woman was shaking when he opened the pantry door.

"It's okay. They're gone. But I think it's a good idea if we do the same."

The woman nodded her understanding.

Rory gently took her arm and led her towards the back door, grabbing his ring of keys off the counter as he passed. If the men were still prowling around out there, he and the woman only had a few seconds to get away. He picked up a pair of boots for the woman, "You'll need these. But we don't have time for you to put them on, okay?"

The woman nodded, taking the boots in her hands.

Rory flicked the lights off, then stepped across to the back door.

The woman followed closely behind.

Rory slowly opened the door and peered into the darkness. He didn't spot any movement in the trees. Taking the woman by the elbow he guided her outside.

His Jaguar XKR-S was parked off to the right of the cottage and he guided the woman through the darkness, keeping his Baby Eagle at the ready.

Guiding the woman around to the passenger side, he whispered, "Get inside."

As soon as she opened the car door, the interior lights went on, illuminating them both.

Rory moved swiftly around to the driver side, watching the trees for movement during this most vulnerable moment. Switching the Baby Eagle to his left, he pulled open the driver's door, slipped inside and pressed the start button, all in one motion. The 500 hp V-8 engine roared to life as Rory pulled his door shut. He kept the gun up at the ready as he put the Jaguar in reverse. Cranking the steering wheel hard, Rory stepped on the accelerator and backed up quickly.

There was movement in the trees from the right of the cottage.

Rory put the car in drive, jammed down the accelerator and the tires spun through grass and gravel. The Jaguar fishtailed to the right, then they shot quickly away from the cabin and up the long, gravel driveway. As they headed for the main road, Rory glanced over at his passenger.

The woman was shaking like a leaf, still holding the boots at her chest.

What in the world was happening here? There was no doubt those men were looking for this woman. The question was why?

The sun was just peeking over Lake Erie as they left the cottage behind, making a run for it.

Chapter 6

INTELLIMAX INTERNATIONAL Branch Office, Toronto, Canada

BROAD-SHOULDERED United States Brigadier-General Bryce Taylor pointed a beefy finger and his voice boomed, "Mr. Brecc, my aides tell me we have been receiving information far below the standard that you normally delivered to this point." He had refused to sit when shown into the office. Instead, he stood side-by-side with his counterpart in the Canadian Army, Brigadier-General Mac MacGillivray. In fact, both officers had preferred to stand to look down on the white-haired man on the other side of the large desk. They were using the psychological ploy to intimidate him. It wasn't working.

Maxwell Brecc merely steepled his fingers and looked up at the two officers. Brecc had the look of an elderly statesman, but his hard, dark gray eyes revealed an unforgiving nature. He lowered his white eyebrows as he spoke in a low, even voice, "And that is precisely the reason I flew here from my Washington offices this very morning. I wanted to personally address your concerns, gentlemen–"

"We're not gentlemen. We're your bosses," MacGillivray said forcefully. He puffed his chest out.

Brecc raised a white eyebrow as nodded his head once, "That you are. But I can assure you that my capable staff is working around the clock in order to fulfill our obligations–"

"Work harder," interrupted Brigadier-General Taylor. He tapped a finger hard on the desk several times, "We are paying you millions of dollars to feed us information. If we don't get that information *and* in the quality we expect, don't expect the money to keep flowing."

Maxwell Brecc nodded again.

"Damn it, Brecc," Taylor thundered, "our arrangement has worked well for both sides to this point. Don't screw this up any further. Mac and I have had a lot of heat put on us and we'll do whatever we need to protect our own interests. Do I make myself clear?"

Brecc placed his hands on the desk, caressing the wood for a moment. Then he stood up and slowly buttoned the front of his Alexander Amosu suit, "I can assure you both, that we will do our utmost to return our supply of information to its previous quality. And if you feel we need to make restitution for that which you deem of dubious quality, please have your staff supply Mr. Foxen here with the amount we need to repay."

Bartlett Foxen stepped up beside the two officers. Foxen was a former member of MI5 in the British Intelligence Agency and the man who coordinated IntelliMax operations around the world. He addressed the two Army officers, "Sirs, all you need to do is supply me with–"

"Look Brecc, just give us the damn information we need and stop the nonsense," Taylor said curtly without acknowledging Foxen.

Foxen narrowed his eyes and gazed at the Army officer. His fingernails bit into the palms of his hands as his fists tightened.

Brigadier-General Taylor made a gesture with his head to his fellow Brigadier-General that they were leaving. "Let's go get one of those smoked meat sandwiches again, Mac."

MacGillivray nodded his head once. "As he said, do your job Brecc," was his parting shot. He turned in quick, military style and the two officers headed across the large plush office to the exit door without another word or any acknowledgment towards the two men left standing behind them.

Maxwell Brecc watched as the two Army officers walked towards a large security guard standing in front of the closed door.

The security guard looked directly at Brecc, not budging from his position as the officers approached.

Brecc paused for a moment, then gave him a nod of his head.

The security guard opened the door, letting the officers out and followed behind them.

When the door closed, Brecc spoke firmly, still glaring across the room, "Mr. Foxen, do we have much on our two *friends*?"

Bartlett Foxen replied in his clipped, British accent, "Yes sir. Brigadier-General Royce MacGillivray has solicited ladies of the evening wherever he has traveled. I took the initiative of paying a number of the young ladies very well and we have several digital photographs. Many of them taken quite recently, in fact. I can always get more, of course. Brigadier-General Bryce Taylor...well, he has *also* enjoyed the company of young ladies when overseas. However, in his case, I have to stress that these were very young ladies, sir. *Very* young."

Brecc nodded as he slipped a hand into each side pocket of his suit jacket, "Good. If you get any more push-back from these two clowns, we will, no doubt, have to act in an appropriate manner."

"I understand, sir," Foxen replied. "I will have our people create additional information along these lines. And our technicians can filter for anything shady in their work."

"Do we know everything else necessary if we have to take more drastic measures?"

"Yes sir," Foxen replied immediately. "We know everything from their work patterns to home addresses and a full list of their loved ones. If they can't be kept in line...we can simply..." His voice trailed off, leaving no doubt as to what he would do, if necessary.

Brecc nodded, "I'll be returning to Washington on the Gulfstream 550 jet immediately. Keep me apprised of any further actions on their part."

"Yes, sir."

Brecc stroked his jawline as he stared across the room at the closed door.

Foxen waited patiently.

"What about our most important asset?" Brecc asked after a moment.

Foxen put his hands behind his back and shook his head, "I am afraid we have nothing to report yet sir."

Maxwell Brecc calmly sat down behind the custom made Carpathian elm and ebony desk. Then he exploded and banged a fist on the customized glass covering the desk, "We need more than full compliance with their requirements in order to continue with our project, Mr. Foxen. Use whatever resources you need to return our asset. Now! The asset is vital to our operation. Failure is not an option."

Chapter 7

SIMCOE, NORFOLK COUNTY, Ontario

AN HOUR AFTER SUNUP, Rory pulled into the parking lot of the Ontario Provincial Police station in Simcoe. For some reason he couldn't really explain, Rory had decided to bring the woman to the Norfolk County detachment, one county over from where his cottage was located on Peacock point. The O.P.P detachment in Cayuga may have been closer, but the expression, better safe than sorry, came to mind. He looked over at his passenger.

The woman looked scared and seemed to shrink into her seat. "Why are we here?" she asked. She looked at the four-story, two-tone brown brick building on the other side of the parking lot.

"I'm hoping that the OPP can use your fingerprints to find out who you are," Rory explained. "Is that all right?"

The woman sat there, thinking about it.

Several people stepped out of the building under the concrete canopy on the right.

The woman slipped lower in her seat. Her eyes darted to each one as they walked to a car a few parking spaces down. "What if I turn out to be a criminal? What then?" she asked finally.

"Those men looking for you last night weren't the police. And since we don't have licensed bounty hunters in Canada, I doubt the law is after you," Rory reasoned. "Although, they could be trying to kidnap you and bring you back to the United States," he admitted.

She looked over at him, her eyes wide in fright, "Do you think that's possible?"

"Look, your recollection of being held naked in a chair doesn't sound like you were being held by any police force," Rory said. "And you escaped from some place near my cottage so I shouldn't have said anything about bounty hunters or the US. I'm sorry—"

The woman stared at the dashboard, "What if I was in an insane asylum? What if I'm the crazy woman with a shaved head?"

Rory looked at her, considering the possibility.

She looked directly into Rory's eyes, "With shaven pubic hair. Who does that?"

The comment took Rory by surprise. Then he had to chuckle, "Well, at least you found out one thing about yourself. You normally like to be au-natural south of the border."

The woman just stared back at him for a moment. Then she broke into a smile. Some of the tension seemed to dissipate from her shoulders.

Rory was struck again by the woman's beauty. Her teeth were perfect and white. That told him more about her. She had either taken very good care of herself or was from a well-to-do background. Who was she?

The smile left her face almost as quickly as it had appeared. Tears filled her eyes and her face was filled with anguish again, "I'm scared, Rory," she whispered. "I have no idea who I am.

Where I'm from. Who my loved ones are. Do I have a husband? Do I have children?" She paused for a moment and then whispered, "Do you know how frightening that is?"

Rory could only shake his head, "No. I can't even imagine how it must feel." Then he had held his hand out across to her. As she put her hand in his, Rory gave it a gentle squeeze, "But I'll do everything I can to help you figure it out. Okay?"

"Why *are* you helping me?" she asked as tears rolled down her cheek.

Rory shrugged, "It's what I do for every naked woman who breaks into my cottage."

The woman blushed even as she gave him a half smile.

"Look," Rory said as he changed the subject, "why don't we go inside and see if the police can help us figure out who you are. We may have you back with your family in no time." He gave her hand a squeeze again.

The woman gave him a half-hearted nod. She squeezed his hand back once and then used both hands to wipe the tears off her cheeks.

Rory got out of the Jaguar and waited patiently for her at the front of the vehicle. He wasn't going to push her. She had to be comfortable with every step of their journey.

After a few minutes, the woman slowly made her way out of the passenger seat and joined Rory at the front of the Jaguar. She took his hand like a little child, allowing herself to be led to the police station. She cowered closer to Rory, pressing her shoulder against his every time an individual was near them. It didn't matter if it was a police officer or a citizen. Male or female, young or old, she was afraid of everyone.

They walked together underneath the short, concrete canopy, through a set of glass doors and up seven steps to a small foyer.

An older woman, sitting behind a large desk on the far side, looked up and greeted them with a smile.

A young constable, standing to her right, turned and looked at them. A look of amusement crossed his face as he considered the bald woman dressed in the over-sized red and black lumberjack shirt, the over-sized jeans, with the belt pulled tight to the last notch and the too-large boots. "Yes, sir," he said to Rory, "how can I help you?"

Rory showed him his Private Investigator license, "I'm working with this woman and I'm hoping you can help her."

The young constable barely glanced at the license, handing it back nonchalantly, his eyes staying on the oddly dressed woman. But as Rory explained the situation regarding her amnesia, the young constable's face and demeanor changed to one of concern. He glanced at the woman from time to time and then, noticing of the band-aids on her hands and neck, he asked gently. "Did something happen, ma'am...like...?"

The woman only pressed closer to Rory, mute, silent and scared.

The young officer gave Rory a nod and then quickly led them past the desk and into the hustle and bustle of the station. He took them into the office of the detachment commander and explained the situation. After some discussion, the detachment commander agreed to help with the fingerprint search.

Rory and the woman were led into a back room where the seriousness of the situation was driven home as the young constable printed 'Jane Doe' at the top of the file he started. Rather than using old-fashioned ink, the constable recorded her fingerprints with a scanner and popped them right into the computer system.

From the corner of his eye, Rory detected someone standing just outside the door on the other side of the room. Discreetly turning his head, Rory saw an older officer peering cautiously around the door jamb into the room.

The officer watched 'Jane Doe' intently as the young officer worked with her.

That triggered Rory's radar. Why would a police officer try to be so discreet watching a visitor to his own police station?

After a moment of intense study, the older officer stepped back out of view instead of coming in.

Rory had an uneasy feeling. He addressed the young officer, "We passed a washroom just down the hall when we came in here. Could I use it?"

The officer turned to Rory, "Of course, sir. Go ahead. I'm just getting the search started."

Rory looked at the woman, "I'll be right back, okay?"

The woman looked a little apprehensive but she nodded her head.

Rory slipped out of the room and looked up and down the hallway quickly.

Down the hallway to the left, the older officer slipped quickly into an open doorway on the right.

It was in the opposite direction to the washroom to the right. Rory looked back at the young officer and then turned left, treading as lightly as possible. Stopping just this side of the open doorway, Rory carefully peeked around the door frame.

The older officer stood behind a desk, dialing a number as he looked at a piece of paper in his hand.

Rory pulled his head back and listened intently.

"Yeah, that woman you asked me to keep an eye out for? I think she's here. Yeah, bald as a cucumber. Getting her fingerprints taken. Yeah. She's with a tall guy. Yeah...black hair...yeah, that sounds like him."

Rory didn't wait to hear anything else. He wanted to know more but he couldn't take the chance of delay. Maybe the officer was talking to those same armed men from the cottage. Or maybe it was someone else. It didn't matter. He had to assume whoever had held her prisoner was trying to get her back. And if he didn't act fast, the officer could hold her for some reason until they got here. Rory ran back to the fingerprint room and went inside.

The young officer was sitting behind a desk and a computer monitor, working away at a keyboard.

The woman sat to his left.

Rory grabbed a pen and piece of paper and wrote down a pre-paid cell number he used for these types of situations. He handed it to the young officer, "I just remembered we have a doctor's appointment for some medical advice on her situation. Can you call me if you get a hit on the search?"

The young officer took the piece of paper, "Of course. I understand, sir."

Rory already had the woman halfway to the door as the young officer stood up.

The woman was looking confused and was about to say something but Rory gave her a subtle shake of his head.

"Oh. I forgot to mark down your name sir," the younger officer said. "Sir—"

Rory was already down the hallway, holding the woman's hand and heading for the front entrance of the station.

The young constable popped his head out the doorway and called out for his name again.

Rory hustled the woman outside the police station and across the parking lot to his Jaguar. Within moments they were out of the parking lot and turning right, heading into the town. Rory cursed under his breath. Now he had no way of knowing which police officers he could trust and which he couldn't. This just cut off an avenue of help.

The woman's voice was high and tense as she sat rigid in her seat, "What's wrong? Why did we leave so fast? I didn't know we had a doctor's appointment."

"It's okay," replied Rory, "I just was being cautious—"

"No you weren't," she interjected forcefully. "Please don't lie to me. I have enough problems without wondering who I can trust."

Rory nodded, "You're right. It's just...I heard one of the older officer back there talking to someone on the phone. It appears someone asked to be notified if you showed up at this police detachment."

The woman nodded, fear and anguish mixed on her face, "So...we can't trust the police...?"

"Actually, it just means we don't know which ones we can trust and which ones we can't," Rory said.

"Which means we can't trust any of them, like I said," the woman added.

"Well, I think that young officer back there is okay," Rory said. "But...yeah...pretty much what you said...."

"Great," the woman said as she crossed her arms and looked out the side window, tears filling her eyes. She was silent for a few moments, staring out the window but not really seeing anything. The fear was evident in her voice as she asked, "The people he was talking to on the phone...do you think it was the same men who came looking for me this morning?"

Rory didn't answer because he didn't have one for her. He gripped the steering wheel a little harder. He knew how she felt.

Now what do they do?

Chapter 8

INTELLIMAX INTERNATIONAL Head Office, Washington, DC

"**MR. BRECC**, there is a tremendous amount of concern in America today about the government intrusion into their privacy in the name of catching terrorists. They intercept our emails, know the web sites we visit on the Internet, know what we search for through the search engines. Ordinary Americans are even afraid to simply pick up the phone because the NSA will record the call and know who they're calling and what they're saying. Now that your company is a part of that invasive intrusion, do you sleep well at night?"

Brecc smiled at the attempt to goad him into a sensational answer that would sell a lot of newspapers tomorrow.

Glenn Shartner, the columnist for The Washington Post was well known for casting bait and setting traps in his interviews.

"I sleep quite well at night I can assure you Mr. Shartner," Brecc replied with a smile. A smile that never reached his dark gray eyes. "In actual fact, I feel very honored to be part of the fight to protect the free world. And we don't spy on American citizens. Not as long as I'm leading this company. I can't speak for other firms, of course."

Shartner smiled, "Words are one thing, actions are another, Mr. Brecc."

"And I'm a man of my word, I can assure you Mr. Shartner," Brecc replied.

"Very easy to say," Shartner countered.

Brecc sat calmly, not reacting to the barb.

Shartner's eyes narrowed as he considered the man sitting across from him. "Tell you what, Mr. Brecc? Why don't you simply allow me to see what you do collect–?"

"And I would be thrown in jail by the highest authorities in the land for breaching my sworn duties to national security," Brecc said with a flourish of his hand.

"C'mon, how are they going to know?"

"Why Mr. Shartner, according to you, big brother knows everything."

Shartner had to laugh, "Touche."

Brecc watched Shartner look down at his notes, waiting for the next, probing, devious question designed to unravel him. He enjoyed the cat and mouse scenario. Until he decided to squash the mouse.

The smile left Shartner's face as he looked up again, "But seriously Mr. Brecc, do you really feel we still need to be so draconian in our attempts to gain leads to possible terrorist attacks after all these years? Bin Laden is dead, Al Qaeda is weakened. ISIS is losing territory–"

"How many terrorist attacks have we stopped in the last three months, Mr. Shartner?" Brecc asked him quickly.

Shartner blinked at the question. He opened his mouth but nothing came out.

"You have no answer," Brecc stated firmly. "And I wouldn't expect you too. If we announced every month that we had stopped a major attack, how safe would the public feel? If we told you that we had prevented a nuclear device from being detonated in downtown San Francisco last week, would you want to travel there next week?"

Shartner sat straighter in his seat, "But the people have a right to know–"

"Ah, the proverbial right to know," Brecc said as be steepled his fingers in front of him. "The doctrine quoted by all news sources who want to make money selling the news the public has a right to know. They just don't always have the right to know it for free."

"That's a little unfair, Mr. Brecc," Shartner complained. He shifted a little uncomfortably in his chair.

"Perhaps you're right, Mr. Shartner. The press does do a great deal of excellent work fighting to maintain the freedoms we all enjoy under the United States constitution, including the freedom of speech. But does the public *always* have a right to know?"

"I believe they do," Shartner countered.

"Should leaks revealing intelligence agents and their undercover operations be reported, for example?" Brecc asked him pointedly. "Leaks that put the very lives of those doing that undercover work at risk? As you well know, that has happened in the past."

"Sometimes people get hurt when you try to do what is right," Shartner said smugly.

"Precisely, Mr. Shartner. And there are times *on my side* that we need to do what is deemed necessary as well," Brecc countered.

The look on his face showed Shartner wasn't pleased with where the interview was going. Brecc wasn't taking any of his standard baiting techniques and he complained, "I think you're twisting my words, Mr. Brecc."

"We are all trying to protect the free world, Mr. Shartner. And I said the free *world*, not just the United States of America. As long as I am leading this company, I am quite willing to make the tough decisions to protect our liberties–"

A buzz interrupted their conversation.

Brecc hit a button on his intercom, "Yes?"

"Sorry to disturb you, Sir," a young female voice said. "You have a call from Mr. Foxen on line one."

"I'll take it in the conference room. Transfer it there," Brecc instructed her.

"Yes, sir."

Standing up and stepped around the side of his desk, Brecc said, "Excuse me for a moment."

Shartner looked very concerned and shifted around in his chair, "That wasn't a prearranged signals so you can get out of our interview, was it?"

Leaning and patting Shartner on the shoulder, Brecc said, "Absolutely not. Just give me a moment and I assure you I'll be right back to continue our interview."

Shartner didn't look convinced.

Brecc stepped across the room and went into the conference room next to his office, closing the door behind him. He punched line one and picked up the handset, "Yes?"

"You wanted to be kept apprised, sir," Bartlett Foxen said. "We received a call from one of our sources, a police officer. The asset was spotted inside a police station one county over."

"Do you have her yet?"

"No, sir. She left before our source could put her into custody and hold her for us," Foxen answered. *He hesitated for a moment and then spoke, "She was with a gentleman."*

Brecc stiffened in concern, "Do we know who he is?"

"No, sir. The man left with the woman in a hurry before his name was marked on the file the police started. Our source didn't want to ask too many questions and attract attention to himself."

"I see," Brecc said. His eyes narrowed as he pondered the implications, "Did the source know *why* they were at the police station?"

"The gentleman apparently brought her in to see if she could be identified by her fingerprints," Foxen explained. *"The police constable was told she had amnesia and could not remember anything."*

"I see. Did they leave before or after the fingerprints were put into the system?"

"Before, sir."

Brecc was silent for a few moments. "This man with the woman could prove to be a problem for us."

"I don't see how sir," Foxen said. *"We have more than enough resources at our disposal to deal with him."*

"Think about it, Foxen," Maxwell Brecc said sternly. "He was concerned enough to bring her into a police station to help determine who she was through her fingerprints. We know the search would have come back empty, correct?"

"That's true," Foxen agreed slowly.

"The very fact this man left - *before* he knew that - means he detected a problem that caused him to flee with the woman. This man is too observant and too smart to dismiss. Do not underestimate him, understand?"

"I understand," Foxen replied slowly, giving it some thought. "When they left, the man said they had a doctor's appointment for some medical advice on her situation. It may have simply been a ruse to leave but...."

Brecc understood where he was going with the thought, "This man is concerned with her condition. So he probably *will* take her to a doctor at some point. And he'll be referred to a specialist at some point as well."

"Exactly, sir," Foxen agreed. "*I can have our analysts recalibrate their searches for the woman in conjunction with doctors and specialists –*"

"Have them filter for any references to amnesia, memory loss, head trauma, that type of thing as well," Brecc instructed.

"*Exactly my thoughts, sir,*" Foxen said. "*And we can filter in importance from their last location outward. We can monitor airport feeds using facial recognition software, in case they go that way, but I'm sure they will use conventional transportation for now. And that means they can only travel so fast and so far.*"

"Good, good. I also want you to alert Blayze. And Frost as well. Have their teams at the ready," Brecc commanded.

Foxen hesitated a moment, "Is that necessary, Mr. Brecc?"

"We have a duty to fulfill our obligations to protect the free world, don't we, Mr. Foxen?" Brecc said with a hard smile.

"*Yes sir.*" *The return smile was evident across the phone line.*

"We must return our focus to our special project as soon as possible. This is too important a matter for half measures. You know how to handle any incidents. We've done it before."

"*You are right, sir. We will find where they went and rectify the situation.*"

Brecc's voice was hard, "Make sure you do, Mr. Foxen. Make sure you do."

Chapter 9

SIMCOE, NORFOLK COUNTY, Ontario

THE WOMAN SAT stoically in the passenger seat as they drove, staring out the windshield, not really seeing anything. Then all she said was, "Jane Doe."

Rory glanced over at her, "Pardon?"

It took a moment before she responded, "Jane Doe. That's what they called me. That's what that police officer put on the file. Jane Doe." The fact seemed to haunt her as she stared at the road ahead.

"Well, it's better than *John* Doe. Right?"

His comment didn't register with her right away. Then she turned and gave him a half-smile, "Oh. Right. I didn't get it for a minute."

Rory returned her smile. "The brain is a funny thing, isn't it?" he said after some thought.

"What do you mean?"

"Well...you can't remember who you are...but you can still function. You can recall something like Jane Doe and John Doe. And you can remember about policemen. And how to hold a knife and fork. I don't know. It just seems strange...," Rory said as his voice trailed off.

The woman gave it some thought and shook her head slightly, "I don't understand it either," she said. "And I'm on the inside."

Rory felt sorry for her.

"Maybe that tells us something else," she said. "That means I'm not a doctor. Otherwise, I would understand it, right?"

Rory had no answer. But it gave him an idea. "Maybe we should ask one."

"What do you mean?"

"We ask a doctor," he answered. He hit the call button on the steering wheel of the Jaguar and made a call.

"Highland Investigative Services, how may I help you?"

"Mandy, it's Rory," he said quickly.

"I thought you were on vacation?"

"Tell me about it. I have a client who has amnesia," Rory explained. "Can you pull some strings and get me an appointment with a specialist right away?"

"A female client, I suppose."

"Yes, a Jane Doe. And don't you start—"

There was a giggle on the other end. "I'll call you right back, master." She hung up.

"Who was that?" the woman asked.

"My office. Mandy is a cousin who runs the Toronto location. We have another office in New York and my Uncle Murdock and my sister Skye work out of there," he explained.

The woman looked over at him, "You showed the police a private investigator's license. That's what you do for this Highland Investigative Services?"

Rory nodded, "Yes—"

"So...I'm a client," the woman said as she crossed her arms. "I don't even know if I have the money to pay you...."

Rory looked over at her and shook his head, "No problem. This is for a friend, okay?"

The woman looked over at him and tears filled her eyes. "For a friend," she repeated. "Thank you. It's good to have one. A friend I can rely on, considering the situation." After a moment to compose herself, she said, "And...you've seen me naked...so I guess we're close friends, right?"

Rory returned her smile and gave her a quick wink.

She lifted a tear from her cheek and returned his wink, "So...when is it my turn...friend?"

"Keep your eyes on the road...Jane," he replied with another wink.

A half smile appeared on her lips. Then she looked at the road ahead and grew serious, "Jane...Jane Doe." She nodded after a moment, "Yeah, I can live with that...for now."

Chapter 10

WITHIN TWENTY MINUTES, Rory's office called back. A former client, Dr. Anders Mensen, was the top neurologist at Hamilton University Hospital and had been teaching there for years. He agreed to meet with Rory as soon as possible. The drive to Hamilton would take about an hour but Rory said he would arrive after lunch and Mensen agreed to clear his schedule for the afternoon. Rory wasn't a psychiatrist but he figured Jane Doe would feel better about herself if he got her into some clothes that fit.

Jane Doe wasn't fussy and it only took a stop at one store in a nearby mall to satisfy her. She picked out a blue pantsuit with a white blouse and shoes she said were cute.

They both agreed this was probably another part of her forgotten self.

She also picked out a light blonde wig with a blunt bob cut. Two young ladies took her into the back of the store where they applied some makeup. The 'Jane Doe' that stepped back out was a stunner.

"Thank you for everything," she whispered to Rory as he paid by credit card.

"That's what friends are for," he whispered back to her.

She actually blushed a little.

Rory could tell she felt much better about herself and that was a start. He picked up a couple of light jackets and ball caps at another store on the way out of the mall. After a quick lunch at a McDonald's, they were on their way.

HAMILTON UNIVERSITY Hospital, Department of Medicine, Hamilton

Hamilton University Hospital was a large, imposing building on the main campus of Hamilton University. The place was an amazing hub of activity and Rory had to take a parking spot at the far end of the huge parking lot.

Just like back at the police station, Jane Doe was nervous and wary of every single individual they passed on the way into the hospital. Most of them were young students but that didn't seem to matter to Jane. She treated everyone with suspicion and concern. She was constantly on guard and more than once she pressed herself close to Rory for comfort.

The receptionist behind the large round kiosk in the main lobby directed Rory to the nearest elevator that would take them to Dr. Mensen on the third floor. As they headed across the lobby, Rory noticed Jane Doe wrinkle her nose in reaction to the heavy smell of rubbing alcohol and hospital disinfectant. But there was also a sense of fear in her eyes and she seemed to get lost in some thought. Rory wondered if she was vaguely remembering something that had to do with the scars on her neck and head. As they approached the bank of elevators, a bell dinged and the doors to a large elevator car slid open. Rory put a hand on

Jane's back and guided her inside before he realized it was already crowded with visitors, patients, staff, and students.

Jane immediately pressed herself close to Rory, her eyes darting from face to face.

Rory could feel her body shaking slightly with fear and he felt bad as the doors closed behind them. He hit a button for his floor and then had her face the front with him, keeping her close.

Jane was obviously relieved when they left the confines of the crowded elevator car on the third floor.

The posted signs led them down a long, crowded and noisy hallway and Rory found the door the receptionist told him to look for, the fourth on the right. He pulled the door open and held it for her.

The reception area for the office was large and filled with people of all ages, sitting on chairs lining the walls. Jane took a moment before she moved cautiously inside and stopped until Rory stood beside her.

Rory spotted Mensen on the other side of the reception area.

Mensen was in the middle of a group of young students wearing lab coats. He was a spry man in his 80s who refused to retire and give up guiding research students at the university through their studies.

Rory could see the joy in the old doctor's eyes as he talked to the young people around him.

A moment later, Mensen looked up and spotted Rory. He moved quickly across the reception area and grabbed Rory's hand, "Rory! So good to see you again, my friend."

"Nice to see you again, Dr. Mensen. How is Christiana these days?" Rory asked as the elderly man pumped his hand up and down joyfully. Rory had helped locate the doctor's daughter when a jealous ex-boyfriend had kidnapped her in a stupid attempt to 'get her back'.

Mensen had never forgotten, sending Rory thank you notes every year on the anniversary. "She's good, thanks to you. Married with two beautiful little girls," he said proudly.

"Good. Dr. Anders Mensen, this is...Jane."

Dr. Mensen took both of her hands in his, "Very nice to meet you. You're in good hands with Rory."

Jane nodded and smiled, "I know."

"Come," he said. The elderly doctor guided her across the reception room and down a short hallway to a large examination room, "Why don't we sit down in here and get started?"

"Can Rory come in with me?" she asked hopefully.

"Of course, of course. You're the patient and we'll do everything we can to make you comfortable and secure while you're here," the doctor told her. He motioned for Rory to come with them as he ushered Jane into the room.

Rory followed in behind, closing the door.

Dr. Mensen motioned to an examination bed on the other side of the room. "Why don't you sit on there and we can start?"

Jane slowly walked over to the bed, looking at everything before she turned and sat on the bed. She looked apprehensive, her hands held tightly between her knees, "Do I have to take my clothes off?"

Mensen picked up a reflex hammer and walked over to a chair beside the bed, "No, it's fine."

Jane flicked a hand towards Rory, "He's already seen me naked so...if we have to...."

Amused, Mensen glanced at Rory, "I see."

Rory suppressed his own smile as he crossed his arms and leaned against the wall, "Strictly a business relationship, doc."

"Of course," Mensen said with restrained delight as he moved the chair in front of Jane and sat down, "Nice business if you can get it." Before Rory could answer, Mensen looked up at Jane, " Now dear, I understand you have amnesia. Is that right?"

"I...I think so," Jane said in a small voice, "at least...I can't remember anything..."

Mensen nodded, "Just tell me what you do remember while I do a few tests." He began to use the reflex hammer to test her reflexes.

Jane Doe went through the same vague recollections she had given Rory.

Rory stayed leaning against the wall, quiet, watching Mensen work.

The doctor listened without comment as he retrieved and used various other test instruments, an ophthalmoscope, visual acuity cards and a 256-hertz tuning fork to test her neurological responses. Mensen recorded a few notes on a clipboard as he went through each test.

"Do you have any idea why I can't remember anything?" Jane asked. "Or how I can get my memory back?"

"Well," Dr. Mensen said in the neutral voice, "so far, I don't see any neurological problems." He opened up a small box and took out a small vial, holding it just under her nose, "Can you tell me what that is?"

Jane Doe's blonde eyelashes fluttered as she sniffed and then she glanced across at Rory before looking back at Mensen, "That's...that's coffee...?"

"Very good," the doctor said.

Looking confused, Jane's naked eyebrows knit together, "Why...why is that good?"

"Because that means there's no loss of olfaction. That's why. That little test would seem to rule out a history of head trauma and cribriform plate fracture."

"Whatever that crib-o-thing means," Rory said as he stood erect. "But your mention of head trauma reminds me of something." Rory walked over to stand beside Mensen, "Jane, would you mind removing your wig and showing the doctor the back of your head?"

Jane nodded and carefully removed her blonde wig before turning sideways on the bed.

The doctor stood up to take a look, glancing at Rory before he leaned in. "Oh my," the doctor said as he ran his fingers lightly up the slight scars on the back of her head.

Rory caught Mensen's attention and then placed a finger to his lips to ask the doctor for silence. He then indicated how the scars ran up and across the top of Jane's skull.

Dr. Mensen narrowed his eyes, shifting his place to look closer. Within seconds he turned to Rory, his eyes wide open in surprise.

"What do you think?" Rory asked him.

Mensen looked back at the extent of the scars and then asked softly, "Jane, do you have any recollection of brain surgery?"

Jane shook her head slightly, "No, nothing. Why?"

The doctor didn't say anything for a moment as he looked closer. Then he glanced over at Rory before talking, "I could be wrong. But...this looks fairly recent. Maybe...within the last few months....or at most a few years...."

Jane didn't say anything but she started to tremble.

Rory placed a gentle hand on her shoulder. "It's okay. Let's not worry too much until we get the whole story. All right?"

Jane gave a slight nod but the trembling continued, "I'm just very scared."

"Whoever did this was very skilled, Jane," the doctor said kindly. "In fact, I would say the surgeon who did this, used some very advanced, computer-assisted, laser surgical tools to perform the operation."

"Operation! What kind of operation?" asked a very agitated Jane. The sheet on the bed rustled hard as she turned.

"I'm not sure," the doctor admitted. He put his hands in his pockets and looked into Jane's deep blue eyes, "Some amnesia is typically associated with damage in certain areas of the brain. The medial temporal lobe, specific areas of the hippocampus or areas of the diencephalon–"

"Do you think that's what happened to me?" Jane whispered.

The doctor considered her question for a moment before answering, "The diencephalon is the region of the vertebrate neural tube, the interbrain, which is what I would expect to be the target, considering how the surgery was done. But I would have expected to see optical problems and I don't see any. You're perfectly normal in every way."

"That's good news, isn't it?" Rory asked Jane.

Jane didn't nod in reply. She stared down at the floor instead.

"So what do we do next, doc?" Rory asked.

Mensen ran a hand over his jaw several times before he said, "I would suggest we go with a CT scan. Our computed tomography scanning system produces cross-sectional images or 'slices' of areas of the body, like the slices in a loaf of bread. Would that be all right, Jane?"

Jane looked up at Mensen, "Will...will it hurt?"

"Not at all. Our computer system will simply produce an image of your brain, slice by slice, that the three of us could look at. It will take about twenty minutes. Are you up for that?"

JANE DOE LAY ON A MOTORIZED table. She looked very afraid as she was slowly moved through a circular opening in the huge CT imaging system. Once she was completely inside, the x-ray source and detector within the housing began to rotate around her body.

Rory and Dr. Mensen sat in a white room separated from the CT imaging system by a large glass window. They watched the large LCD screen in front of them intensely as the computer hooked up to the system analyzed the image data being sent. A cross-sectional image or slice of Jane's brain was produced and displayed on the computer screen every second. It was fascinating to see her brain slowly being produced from the neck upwards in a 3D image. Each slice also revealed the internal structure of her brain. Five minutes passed, then ten minutes, and slice after slice of her brain was added.

Dr. Mensen leaned forward, peering closer at the building image. At the fifteen-minute mark, he turned and looked at Rory.

Rory was speechless.

Finally, at the twenty-minute mark, the image was complete.

Dr. Mensen sat numbly staring at the screen.

"What the hell are we looking at?" Rory asked in a whisper.

"I have no idea," Dr. Mensen whispered in return.

Chapter 11

THEY WERE NOW in a large open room that Dr. Mensen used for teaching. More than two dozen of his young graduate students in white lab coats, along with another dozen university professors, were watching a 3D model of Jane Doe's brain rotating on the huge LCD monitor on the wall. The image would disappear, slice by slice as they removed each one, and then reappear as they added them on like thin layers of a cake.

A black, nearly transparent, fabric-like material flowed across the top of Jane's brain, conforming itself perfectly to the convolutions of the wrinkled brain tissue. Rory had heard the term 'graphene' a number of times. It was apparently a form of carbon in which the atoms are arranged in a flat hexagon lattice like microscopic chicken wire, a single atom thick. It could conduct electricity as well as any known material and conduct heat better than any other known material. But it was so new that no one was using it for any purpose other than experimentation. And what was in Jane's head looked a number of generations beyond the experimental stage. That *was* the one thing everybody was able to agree on.

Equally confusing to everyone in the room were the countless numbers of thin, silver-looking nano-wires, extending from the edges of the fabric and wrapping down, around and into the brain matter. It looked like a flat, space-age spider that had the entire brain wrapped in its silvery legs. It fascinated everyone and made them shudder at the same time.

Jane Doe, back in her blonde wig, stood with Rory against the wall in the back of the room. Her arms were crossed defensively across her chest and her blue eyes were filled with tears and fear.

Rory broke into the medical jibber-jabber that was going on between the students and the staff, "Does *anyone* know what that thing is?"

A few turned to look at him, but no one said a thing.

"Does anyone know what it's for?"

No one wanted to commit themselves in any way.

Rory shook his head in frustration. He was getting the feeling this visit to the Hamilton University Hospital had been a wasted trip and a bad idea. All it had done was intensify Jane's feelings of despair and helplessness.

A few moments later, the entire gaggle of doctors and scientists all turned their attention back to the LCD screen, talking in a low chatter of excitement and wonder, peppering each other with theories and questions as if Jane Doe wasn't in the room.

Dr. Mensen walked across the room to join Rory and Jane, a troubled look on his face.

"What do you think?" Rory asked in a low voice as the doctor approached.

Mensen looked back at the LCD screen for a moment. Then turned back and slipped his hands into the side pockets of his white lab coat, "I'm sorry. But the truth is...no one here really knows what the device is. Our best guess...and it's only a guess, mind you...is that it *appears* to be what is called a BCI, a brain-computer interface. But..." Mensen's voice tailed off as he looked back at the LCD image again.

"But...?" prompted Rory after a moment.

Mensen turned back to Rory and Jane, "But we don't see any physical connection placed in the skull itself that would transfer signals outside to a computer system."

"Maybe it's sending wireless signals," Rory reasoned, "like a Bluetooth phone or a wireless remote."

Mensen shook his head, "No. It sounds possible but we don't detect any signals emanating from the device and—"

"Can you take it out?" interrupted Jane anxiously. "That's all I want to know."

Dr. Mensen had a sad look on his face as he shook his head again, "No. I'm afraid not. Without knowing what the materials themselves exactly are, what the whole thing does, how exactly it's even connected around and into your brain.......we have no way of knowing what damage we could do. It's going to take some time for us to study it."

"Is that thing the reason why I can't remember who I am?" Jane asked.

Dr. Mensen opened his mouth to say something and then simply shrugged, "I'm sorry Jane. We have no way of knowing that at this point."

Rory cursed himself, the feeling of this being a bad idea increasing. He had to get her away from this room, even if only for a few moments. He spoke softly, "Jane, it's after six o'clock. Why don't you and I go downstairs to the cafeteria and get something to eat?"

"I'm not really sure I'm hungry," she said as she wrapped her arm tighter and stared across at the images of the thing in her head.

"I know. Maybe just a coffee then. Let's let the doctors do their thing in here and maybe they'll have an answer by the time we get back."

"That's a good idea, Jane," Dr. Mensen said kindly.

Jane nodded a half-hearted okay.

Dr. Mensen placed his hand on her elbow, "Good. And if you don't mind, I'd like your consent to send all your tests, this CT scan and the images we took of your scars to Dr. Hans VanOstrand. He is the Head of Neurological Surgery at Victory Hospital in London, Ontario. It's a large, teaching hospital, affiliated with the University of Western Ontario. He and I have worked together on a number of various projects over the years. I believe, if *anyone* would know what this is, he would. *And* he might know how to deal with it."

Jane nodded her consent.

"Good, good. I was hoping you'd say that and I prepared a package," Mensen said. He turned and stepped over to a young lady who was putting files into a large, pouch sitting on a desk. He pointed to files on another desk, "Susan, I need you to add that set of files as well."

The young lady looked over at the files, nodded as she grabbed them and stuffed them in with the others.

"Hopefully it won't make it too heavy for you," Mensen said.

The young lady smiled and shook her head as she lifted the pouch and slung the strap over her shoulder, "No, I'll be fine. And thank you again for helping me with my project."

"You're very welcome," Mensen said as he smiled in return. Mensen stepped back to Rory and Jane and gestured to the young woman as she headed for the door out, "Susan is one of Dr. VanOstrand's graduate students and she's been working with us here for the last week. She's headed back to London right now and VanOstrand will have the files in his hands in no time."

Jane faintly nodded as she watched the young woman disappear.

Dr. Mensen put a hand on Jane's shoulder, "Now why don't you go and get something to eat and drink? By the time you come back, we may have a few answers for you."

Jane thanked him with a half-smile but she didn't look too encouraged as she walked out of the office with Rory.

Out in the hallway, Rory glanced back through the glass wall at the hub of activity still going on inside the room. It didn't look good for getting the help he had hoped for. He was getting the feeling this had been a bad idea, Yes, she knew something more about her condition but–

"Do you think I could use the washroom before we go down to the cafeteria?" Jane asked.

Rory broke out of his thoughts, "Of course."

A woman with hospital credentials around her neck was passing by in the hallway.

"Excuse me, can you tell me how to get to the cafeteria?" Rory asked her. "And are there washrooms nearby that we could use?"

"Of course," the woman said. She pointed ahead, "Just go down the hallway that way and the elevators are on the left. There's a small cafeteria one floor up."

"Okay, we came up that way."

The woman turned and pointed down the hallway, "And there are washrooms down there to the right."

"Thanks."

Nodding, the woman hurried on.

"Do you really think they'll be able to figure it out eventually? Jane asked as they headed for the washrooms. She sounded pessimistic.

"Dr. Mensen is one of the best in his field," Rory told her. "If he can't figure it out, I know he has a lot of contacts, like that doctor in London he was talking about."

Jane nodded but still didn't look too hopeful.

They turned the corner and found the washrooms thirty feet along the hallway. "I'll use the men's washroom and meet you back out here in a minute," Rory told her.

Jane nodded and slipped into the women's washroom.

Five minutes later, Rory came out of the men's washroom and walked back to the area by the door to the women's washroom. He waited patiently, looking out the windows to the street below. Rory wondered if there was something else he could do to help Jane. His mind worked back through the various contacts and clients like Dr. Mensen that he had helped over the years. Maybe there was someone else he could turn to – a sound broke into his thoughts.

Gunfire?

Chapter 12

RORY LISTENED INTENTLY. What he had heard sounded familiar - like someone firing a Heckler & Koch UMP submachine gun in the distance. He was sure the sound had come from the area where Jane had taken the CT scan. But that didn't make any sense. After a few moments, he relaxed. There must be a medical machine that creates the same type of rapid sound he told himself–

The rapid burst of submachine gun fire erupted louder this time. And it *was* back toward where he and Jane had left Mensen!

Rory's military training from his days in the Canadian army kicked in. He flattened himself against the wall and he slid smoothly but rapidly towards the sounds of screaming and terror mixed with the sounds of Heckler & Koch UMP automatic gunfire. Rory reached the corner of the hallway and peered around. Not seeing anyone, he ran low to the teaching room where the doctors had been discussing Jane's CT scan. Cautiously he peered around the frame of the glass wall into the room.

There were a dozen men, all dressed in black, including black body armor, black ski masks, and tactical headsets. Each man's weapon was an H&K UMP9 submachine gun with a curved magazine.

Rory's blood ran cold when he also saw the white-coated, bloody bodies lying on the floor, blood spatter painting the walls where the staff had been standing. The woman with the hospital credentials they had stopped in the hallway was one of the bloody bodies. If they had gone to the elevators first –

One of the men stepped back from the far wall, tossing a spray can onto the dead bodies. He had just finished spray painting 'Jihad' on the bloodstained wall. A terrorist attack?

"Where is the woman?" demanded one of the black-clad men. He was talking to Dr. Mensen.

The elderly doctor jutted his jaw out. He wouldn't answer.

Rory's blood ran cold.

These men weren't terrorists.

They were looking for Jane.

"Who else saw these scans?" yelled another man. He was pointing at the 3D image of Jane's brain still spinning around on the large LCD monitor.

Dr. Mensen wouldn't reply to him either.

"We'll just kill *everyone* on this floor, including the *patients*, if you don't cooperate, doc," warned the man.

Mensen was visibly shaken at the threat but still remained silent.

The man in front of him raised his weapon and fired.

The elderly doctor's body danced like a puppet as it slammed back against the wall under the hail of bullets.

"Destroy the computer," the man instructed before the body even hit the floor. Then he looked at his watch and issued commands into the microphone of his headset, "We don't have the woman. Repeat, we don't have the woman. Begin the sweep. Find her. Kill everyone else you come across."

Rory was on the run back to the washrooms when he heard more gunfire behind him. He didn't go down so he assumed it wasn't aimed at him. He cursed himself as he ran. He had left his Baby Eagle handgun in the lock box in the Jaguar's trunk. Not planning ahead for all contingencies could cost them their lives. He pushed that from his mind and hit the washroom door hard with his shoulder, pushing it open, "Jane?"

Jane Doe at one of the sinks, rinsing her hands under the tap. She turned and knew something was wrong immediately by the look on his face.

Rory held out his hand, "We need to go."

"What's happening?" Jane asked as she ran to the door and grabbed Rory's hand. She held on tightly as he pulled her into the hallway without another word.

Automatic gunfire erupted again down the hallway.

Jane's eyes widened, "Is that–?"

Rory didn't answer. He led her away from the gunfire and screams.

"What's happening? What about Dr. Mensen?" Jane asked.

"Someone is looking for you. Just like back at the cottage," Rory explained as they reached a turn in the hallway. Being cautious, he peeked around the corner.

Jane started to cry, "Why me–?"

Rory's arm went across the front of Jane's shoulders and he pushed her back against the wall.

"What–!" Her body was trembling.

Rory raised a finger to his lips to shush her.

Two more men, dressed in black body armor, black ski masks, and tactical headsets, were at the far end of the hallway, moving slowly towards them. The exit to the stairs was behind them. The way out was blocked.

Now Rory understood the command to start the sweep. Armed men would be moving inwards from all the exits, while the other men moved outwards from Dr. Mensen's office. Rory and Jane would eventually be caught between the two groups of armed killers.

What now?

Chapter 13

RORY TOOK JANE'S HAND and pulled her quickly back down the hallway. Her body was rigid with fear and her wooden legs stumbled a few times. Holding tight, Rory kept her upright. "Stay with me. Stay with me," he urged her.

Jane's voice was raspy, low and tight, "I'm trying."

Rory swung over to the right side of the hallway, to the line of windows, and took a quick look as he moved with Jane in tow. There was no way to break a window and climb out to safety because it was straight drop to a courtyard three stories below. Moving back towards the center of the hallway, he looked for a set of double doors he remembered passing. There they were, twenty feet ahead. The problem was - he had no idea where they led. It could be a dead end. Or even worse, another hallway with another set of gunmen. But they had no choice. He moved faster. They were running out of time. The men behind them...or maybe the ones in front...would be on them at any moment.

Jane stumbled on her wooden legs, let out a cry and went down to her knees, her hand slipping from Rory's.

Rory turned and reached down to help her, "C'mon, Jane, you can do it–" He glanced back down the hallway.

One of the black-clad men in black stepped around the corner at the far end of the hallway. "Hey!"

Rory grabbed Jane's pantsuit and hauled her to her feet, pulling her through the double doors without hesitation.

A burst of gunfire filled the air and 9 mm bullets ripped through the set of double doors as they swung back out.

Jane screamed and stumbled again.

The gunfire stopped, replaced by the sounds of heavy boot steps pounding out in the hallway, heading in their direction.

Rory struggled to keep Jane upright as he looked to see where they were. It was a surgeon's scrub room, with stainless steel wash stations on the left and shelves and cabinets on the right. Across the floor was another set of double doors. More than likely there was a large operating room on the other side. Rory spotted a number of silver foil packs sitting on a shelf to the right. He pushed Jane and then pointed as he moved to the shelf, "Keep moving. Go through those doors over there."

Jane nodded woodenly, moving across the room as best she could, but it was like her legs were wading through molasses.

Rory reached for one of the silver foil packs labeled #11 surgical scalpels, peeled it open and removed a stainless steel tool. He almost felt rather than heard someone pushing through the double doors behind him and he turned and in one smooth motion, backhanded the scalpel.

The stainless steel blade went through the right eye hole of the first gunman's ski mask.

The gunman screamed and he fell back, his weapon firing and ripping dozens of holes in the ceiling tiles, the slugs ricocheting off the sprinkler heads and the water pipes underneath.

Rory ran across the room and dove through the double doors into the operating room, landing hard on the floor.

Jane was already running low for the far side of the room.

Anticipating what was coming next, Rory rolled to his right while yelling, "Get down, Jane–"

The second gunman was right behind the falling body of the first. He sent a burst of fire low at the double doors on the other side of the scrub room.

The bullets ripped through the doors, gouged into the surgical flooring and ricocheted in all directions off equipment and chairs, penetrating the walls and ceiling.

Jane screamed again as she cowered behind medical equipment in the far corner of the operating room.

The gunman stopped firing and spoke into his headset, "I have eyes on the woman. Converge on my position, operating room four. I'm going in."

Rory heard the command and knew he only had seconds before the gunman came through the doors, no doubt followed by the others. His sense of self-preservation went into high gear but everything played out in slow motion. As Rory rose from the floor, he had already chosen the only weapon close at hand, a machine on the surgical cart.

But would it work?

Could he act in time?

Taking the ten feet across the floor to the surgical cart in two large steps, Rory leaned forward, grabbed the closest handle and pulled hard. The sounds of the wheels moving across the floor echoed off the walls.

The double doors started to open.

As the cart rolled past him, Rory stepped behind it, set his hands on the handle on the other side and pushed it hard towards the doors. As the wheels clacked along the floor, Rory ran to keep up, got alongside, reached down to the machine, flipped the switch on and spun the voltage dial to maximum. The defibrillator began to whine. It was charging. How long did it take?

A gun barrel appeared between the opening doors.

Rory kept pace with the cart rolling cart, reached down and picked up the paddles to strike. He suddenly realized the gunman had his weapon at his shoulder and he had to adjust, taking a step to the side.

The gunman's shoulders pushed the doors open as he moved forward, his weapon aimed and ready. His eyes were looking in the direction of the rolling sound to his left but his eyes flickered when he saw Rory just to his right.

Rory brought one paddle down on the gunman's shoulder.

The gunman reacted, turning to aim his weapon towards his assailant.

Rory dropped the second paddle lower under the man's arms and slammed it upward to hit his lower chest.

Zzzzap!

The gunman emitted a cry of agony as his body jerked. His heart went into cardiac arrest and his finger tightened on the trigger. The machine gun erupted in a loud burst that spit out more than one hundred bullets.

Jane screamed again as those bullets tore into the wall just over her head and then ripped a line of holes upward into the ceiling.

The rolling cart banged against the edge of the open door and came to a halt.

The firing stopped as the gunman's body dropped straight down and he landed hard on his back, his legs bent awkwardly beneath him. The double doors closed partially, coming to rest on the gunman's shoulders as his weapon clattered to the floor back in the scrub room. The smell of gunpowder hung heavy in the air and mingled with the semi-sweet scent of hot metal.

Rory looked quickly through the opening between the doors. He only saw the body of the other dead gunman lying on the floor on the other side of the scrub room. Good thing. He would've been exposed and dead if another man with a weapon had been there. He counted his lucky stars, threw the defibrillator paddles down on the cart and dropped quickly to his knees beside the body, reaching across for the dropped weapon. Holding the H&K UMP9 machine gun in his left hand, he used his right to pull the gunman inside the operating room. The double doors closed and Rory repositioned the cart to impede anyone else coming in. Then he removed the gunman's headset and looked at it. It was a Liberator III Secure Dual-com tactical headset. The evidence was mounting that these guys were professional soldiers or ex-military and well financed. He put the headset on as he rose to his feet and looked around.

Jane was still cowering in the far side of the operating room.

Rory quickly moved across the room to her side and reached down. Taking her by the wrist, he tried to pull her to her feet as he glanced back towards the double doors, expecting more men to come bursting through at any moment.

Jane was rigid with fear and resisted.

Rory slung the weapon over his shoulder and used both hands to pull her to her feet, "Come on, Jane, we have to go." Once he had her up, he placed a hand on her lower back, urging her to move towards the second set of doors on the right side of the operating room. But it was slow going. Jane was totally seized with fear and Rory had to buy more time. He spoke into the headset, "I have eyes on the woman. She is headed back towards the elevators."

A moment later, a voice came back over the headset, "Negative. Unknown voice on our communications. Go silent. Converge on the surgery. Four minutes."

Rory swore as he ripped the headset off and threw it to the floor. Taking the weapon off his shoulder, Rory used the barrel to push open the left double door slowly so he could see what was on the other side. Beyond the doors was a large intake area for the surgery room. It was empty. Rory stepped out cautiously, pulling Jane with him. The double doors closed behind them. There was a long hallway off to the right that met another hallway running left and right. The floor directory on the wall told him the nearest exit was at the end of that hallway on the right. Escape?

No. He could hear heavy boots steps. Which meant another team of men was moving quickly towards them, coming from that direction. They were cut off from all exits.

Now what?

Chapter 14

RORY STOOD IN the intake area for the surgery, trying to figure out what to do as the teams of armed gunmen converged on his position. He could see a door halfway down the hallway and he briefly considered looking to see if it offered a hiding place. But he quickly discarded the idea. The team of men coming this way would be checking each door they went by. Rory cursed under his breath. There *had* to be another way. He closed his eyes, trying to think as he felt Jane's body shaking beside him. He visualized all the equipment he had noticed in the operating room and a plan formed.

It was a risky plan but it was the only one they had.

He pulled Jane back through the double doors into the operating room and had her stand against the wall to the right of the doors.

"What's wrong," Jane whispered in fright.

"I just have to clear the way out," Rory assured her as he slung the weapon over his shoulder. He moved across the surgery floor to a bank of H-type medical oxygen cylinders. There were 18 cylinders in the row, standing upright and tied into a manifold on top. Rory unhooked one cylinder and pulled it out. It was filled with 6500 liters of oxygen and weighed about 150 pounds, heavier than he thought it would be. He carried it across to the double doors, laid it down on the floor and went back to get a second cylinder. Taking it back to the doors, he leaned his shoulder against the left double door to open it and took a look down the hallway. No sign of the men yet.

"Don't leave me!" Jane whispered urgently as she moved to Rory.

"It's okay. I'm just going to set this down in the hall and I'll be back," he said in a reassuring voice. "Just stay against the wall for me, okay?"

Jane nodded but she moved slowly, glancing over at the dead body lying near the other set of double doors.

Rory looked down the hallway again. Still not seeing anyone, he stepped out, set the cylinder on the floor and pushed it hard.

The medical oxygen cylinder rolled with a tinny sound twenty feet down the right side of the hallway where it stopped.

Rory cursed as he realized it stuck out like a sore thumb. He rushed down the hall and set the cylinder upright against the wall. Still not good, but it would have to do. Rory then ran back inside the surgery, picked up the second cylinder and pushed his way back through the double doors. This time he carried the cylinder down the hall and placed it upright against the left wall, across from the other one. He took a couple of steps back, looking from cylinder to cylinder. He just had to hope the men didn't – as he turned he realized Jane was out of the operating room and standing in the middle of the intake room.

"No, no, no," he said urgently as he moved to her quickly and took her by the elbow, "I asked you to stay inside–"

"I don't want to stay in there. I want to stay with you," she whispered and resisted.

"We're both going back into the operating room. Okay?"

"We are?"

"Yes." He moved her back to the double doors.

"But why aren't we escaping?"

"We will. Just do this for me and we'll get out. Okay?" He moved them both back inside the operating room.

"But I'm afraid," Jane protested. "What if those men come in here?"

"Just trust me," Rory said as he placed her back against the wall. He unshouldered his weapon and then pushed the left door open again with his shoulder. He opened it just enough to aim at the H oxygen cylinder on the left.

Boot steps moved down the hallway towards them. The gunmen were closing in. The boot steps were lighter, which meant they knew they were closing in. And probably wondering about the cylinders.

Keep coming, keep coming, Rory said to himself as his finger tightened slightly on the trigger.

The light sound of the boot steps came closer. It sounded like there were two, just like the first team.

Rory waited.

He saw a boot near the cylinder on the left.

Rory pulled the trigger and the submachine gun roared.

There was a flash explosion and the cylinder rocketed into the gunman on the left. He screamed and went down, both legs broken and bent at unnatural angles.

Rory jumped out further to get a better angle to the cylinder on the right.

The gunman on the right had recoiled from the explosion and his gun was pointed up to the ceiling. He tried to bring it down when he saw Rory. But he was too late.

Rory fired and the second cylinder exploded in a flash of light.

The concussive force of the explosion knocked the gunmen against the wall and he crumpled to the floor unconscious.

But the cylinder itself shot in Rory's direction like a Chinese rocket. He barely had time to drop backward to the floor. The oxygen cylinder shot just over his head and hit the slowly closing double door, ricocheting into the operating room.

Jane screamed as the metal cylinder shot across the room, banged hard off the surgical table, hit the anesthesia machine and came back hard to bury itself in the wall just above Jane's head. She screamed as pieces of wallboard and pulverized dust rained down on her.

Rory was up and through the double doors, putting a quick burst of bullets in both fallen men. Then he quickly brought the UMP9 up and scanned for more targets. A small cloud of smoke hung in the hallway but there was no sign of anyone else. He moved cautiously backward, sweeping his weapon back and forth until he moved back into the operating room.

Chapter 15

JANE REMAINED IN HER POSITION, crouched against the wall, trembling with her hands over her head and clearly traumatized by the events.

Rory moved over to her and took Jane's hand as he knelt beside her, his voice soft, "It's okay. It's Okay. We have to move now. All right?"

Jane was slow to respond but finally got to her feet. She brushed wallboard powder from her head and shoulders, whimpering slightly in fear.

Rory pulled her to the doors again and then brought the submachine gun up firmly against his shoulder, ready to fire. "Follow me," he whispered as he cautiously pushed through the double doors.

Jane moved right up behind him, her hands clutched to her chest, her body shaking.

Rory led the way down the hallway, weaving the weapon back and forth as he moved.

Jane made a sound when she saw the two fallen bodies a few feet ahead and pulled back.

"It's okay. They can't hurt you now," Rory assured her as he reached back to keep her moving.

Jane hesitated for a moment, screwed up her courage and then skipped quickly forward between the dead bodies.

Rory kept the submachine gun at the ready as they reached the junction of the next hallway. He pressed himself against the right wall.

Jane moved up close behind him, literally pressing herself against him, her hands still clutched tightly at her chest.

"I'm going to step out and checked the hallway both ways," Rory whispered back over his shoulder. "Stay against the wall."

"Don't leave me!" Jane whispered urgently.

"I'll just be two feet away," he whispered back. He could feel her trembling head nod against his back. Bracing himself, he stepped out quickly and checked in both directions. There was a door to a stairwell far down the hallway on the right. "Okay. Let's go. Stay close behind me," he whispered to Jane as he headed towards it.

Jane moved around the corner quickly and followed closely, checking nervously behind them constantly as they moved down the hallway.

They finally reached the exit stairwell. Rory took a cautious look through the small window in the door. The landing was clear. He pressed down on the handle and then pushed the door open with his shoulder cautiously. The stairwell was quiet.

Jane followed through the door and watched nervously as Rory checked over the railing, looking below.

"It's clear," he whispered, "let's go."

They moved swiftly down the stairs, passing the second-floor landing without incident. As they approached the main floor landing, Rory saw it had an exit door to the outside of the building. There were two large potted planters on each side of the exit.

Standing just inside the exit door with Jane behind him, Rory began wiping his prints from the H&K UMP9 with his shirt.

"What are you doing?" Jane whispered nervously.

"I'm pretty sure the police will have tactical response teams on scene by now. If we go outside with a weapon, I'm pretty sure they'll shoot first and ask questions later," Rory told her.

"But what if those men are out there?" she whispered in fear.

"We'll be okay," he assured her. He wasn't really positive but what were the alternatives? Pulling the ammo magazine from the weapon, he placed it along with the weapon in one of the big planters. "Okay, let's go," he said as he pushed down on the exit bar and opened the door.

Jane followed quickly behind him into the bright sunlight.

Rory could now see they were at the front of the building, with the entranceway they had first gone through far off to their left. There were scores of people streaming out of the building, running for their lives as well. "The Jaguar should be parked that way," he said as pointed ahead and to their left. "Let's go."

Jane didn't wait to be asked again. Sensing they were escaping the men inside the building, she started moving faster.

Both of them ran hard across the sidewalk, then the wide strip of grass just before the entranceway road, heading for the parking lot.

"Look out," Jane yelled as she clutched at Rory's sleeve.

Rory stopped just in time.

A large, black SWAT SUV narrowly missed running over Rory as it barreled past on the entrance road, heading for the front doors of the hospital.

Rory nodded at Jane in thanks and then they began running again across the road and onto the black tarmac of the parking area. After several minutes of hard running, Rory pulled out his keys and pressed the button to unlock the Jaguar doors he could now see just ahead of them. The car lights flashed a welcome.

Jane ran for the passenger side without any prompting.

Jumping in the driver's side, Rory was breathing heavy as he started the Jaguar and pulled out of the parking spot. Then he put the brakes on.

Jane stiffened in her seat, "What's wrong?"

Rory didn't answer. The problem was the jam of cars and people on the exit road that left no way out. Despite the SWAT team that was now on-scene, Rory had no intention of waiting for everything to clear. Glancing around quickly, Rory saw there was a way out. He cranked the wheel hard and jammed his foot down on the gas. The Jaguar accelerated as he took a clear short-cut across the one hundred yards of grass between them and the public road. The Jaguar ripped up grass and dirt as he accelerated across the open space.

Just before they reached the road, Rory caught a glimpse of something leaving the roof of Hamilton University Hospital. It was a large helicopter, designated as a medical unit. But Rory highly doubted it was a medical helicopter. His ten years in the Canadian Army, including Special Forces training, told him otherwise. No doubt the helicopter on the roof was how the men had entered en masse to find Jane. And now it served as their escape route. The whole attack had been set up and timed with military precision. He glanced at Jane. Who exactly was after her? He shook his head as he cranked the wheel hard to enter the main road. And what had he gotten himself into?

Chapter 16

RORY MANEUVERED THE JAGUAR into heavy traffic and continued moving away from the hospital. The helicopter had disappeared beyond the tops of the high buildings but he kept it in the back of his mind as he drove. He had no idea if the helicopter was just leaving or circling around to attack them again so he kept an eye out for any possible escape routes. If it did come after them, they had to be ready.

They rode in silence for a time, Jane's arms tightly crossed over her chest.

Rory's eyes continually flicked from the side mirrors to the rearview mirror and then swept the skies above, watching for another attack

Jane finally spoke, her voice a shaky whisper. "I can't believe we survived. It doesn't seem possible."

Rory nodded as he continued to scan the skyline. Surviving an attack from an efficient and highly trained team like these men *was* almost a miracle. Then the comment from the leader came to mind, 'Find her. Kill everyone else you come across.' Rory realized *he* was the one who had survived. They had wanted Jane alive. But sending a highly trained team of killers to capture her? Who would do that? And why? Another troubling question came to mind. How did these men even know where to find Jane? Rory couldn't help himself; he glanced over at Jane's head.

Jane caught the movement out of the corner of her eye, "What?"

"Nothing." Rory looked away. He steered the Jaguar into the next lane and took the exit to Highway 403 westbound.

"No, it's something," Jane replied. "You were thinking about that thing in my head."

Rory had to grudgingly admit it and he let out a low breath, "I'm just wondering how those men knew where to find you."

"And you're wondering if that thing is sending signals to them. I can't blame you," Jane admitted. "We almost died." She looked out her window for a moment, her knee bouncing until she looked back at Rory, "But didn't Dr. Mensen say they didn't detect anything coming from it? He said that, right?"

"*Detect* is the effective word here," Rory said. "What if they just can't detect it? They admitted they didn't really know what it was."

Jane's voice rose in anger and she threw her hands up in the air, "So what do we do? Make me a tin-foil hat?"

Rory blinked at the comment and then had a difficult time not laughing. This was a serious matter...but still....

Jane finally saw the humor in her own words and she smiled sheepishly, "I think I meant to say aluminum hat. Even without my memories, I know a tin-foil hat is for nut jobs."

"Well...."

"Hey," protested Jane, striking him playfully on the shoulder.

Rory chuckled, then grew serious, "Despite what they said, we have to assume the possibility that device *is* sending signals. I mean there are analog and digital signals, WI-FI, Bluetooth, microwave, different radio frequencies–"

"Fine. You've mentioned everything but smoke signals. The question is, what do we do about it?"

Thinking about it for a moment, Rory shook his head, "I don't know *what* we can do about it. But we have to consider it." Then he shrugged, "That being said...we also have to consider the possibility they tracked my cell phone somehow. Or maybe the Jaguar is bugged."

"When could they have done any of that?"

Rory shook his head in frustration, "I don't know. Maybe they did it back at the police station in Simcoe. Considering what's happening, I guess anything is possible...."

The Jaguar growled as Rory pressed down on the accelerator and they shot up the Ancaster hill. Hamilton lay spread out below them to the right. Rory scanned the horizon over top of the buildings but there was still no sign of the helicopter.

Jane looked out over the city, quiet for a few moments. Then she crossed her arms tightly over her chest again, "So, what do we do now?"

Rory gave the question some thought. Then he leaned over and tapped on the GPS screen, "Okay, first we get new wheels, just in case this car *is* bugged. Or maybe they spotted us coming out of the hospital and have our license plate. I don't know, I'm just trying to think of everything to keep us safe." He scrolled through some screens and then set the GPS for the nearby John C. Munroe Hamilton International Airport.

"Why the airport?"

"They have a car rental agency there. Quickest way to get new wheels," Rory explained as he accelerated into the passing lane.

Chapter 17

WITHIN AN HOUR they had picked up a BMW 328I from a rental counter. Rory had used cash to pay for a week's rental and bribed the young agent generously to keep his credit card and driver's license info out of the computer system. The young man had been delighted to be part of an undercover operation. After taking the lock box containing his Baby Eagle from the trunk, along with his shoulder holster, he set them in the back seat of the rental, Rory then smashed his cell phone with the heel of his boot, just in case it *had* been compromised. As they drove away from the rental parking lot, he wondered what they should do next. He had an idea and in ten minutes he had taken the BMW westbound again on Highway 403.

"Are we going back to your cabin?" Jane asked. It was the first time she had really spoken since they had left this highway to get the BMW.

"No."

Jane looked at him, "So where...?"

"Just before Dr. Mensen was shot, one of the men asked about the CT scan they had done of your brain," Rory said. "They wanted to know who looked at it. When the doctor didn't answer, that's when they decided to go on a rampage and just eliminate everyone."

Jane began to cry again, "And it's all because of me."

"No," Rory said firmly. "Everything that happened in that hospital is on those men, *not* on you. You didn't shoot anybody. *They* made the choice, understand? I can understand your feeling guilty, but I don't want you blaming yourself. If anyone is to blame, it's me. I took you there. If I hadn't made that choice, Dr. Mensen would still be alive. His students and the other staff would still be alive. But it happened. And I will make them pay," Rory said with hard finality.

Jane nodded, wiping a tear rolling down her cheek, "So what do we do then?"

"We need to find to find answers," Rory said. "At this point, we don't really know *where* you were held. We don't know *why* you were held. We don't know *who* held you and we certainly don't know *who* those men are." Rory held a finger up in emphasis, "*But*...we do know they're very interested in *what* is in your head. It's apparently so important, they were willing to kill every single person they felt just knew about it. It would seem to me at this point that the key to unlocking this whole mystery is to understand *what* is in your head."

Jane's face was a mask of concern as more tears rolled down her cheeks, "But we can't go back to the hospital. They might be waiting. More people could die."

"You're right," Rory agreed. "But Dr. Mensen asked if he could send all your files to a doctor in London. He asked for your permission, remember?"

Jane thought about it for a moment and then nodded her head slightly, "He asked that student to take them."

"Right. She left just before we headed to get something to eat. Do you remember the name of the doctor she was taking those files to?"

Jane cleared a lump in her throat, "Not really. It was a Swedish or a Dutch name. I think it was...Van something or other."

Rory cursed under his breath. He wished he had paid more attention when Dr. Mensen was talking about it. A thought popped into his head. "This Van something or other...he was associated with the University of Western Ontario in London, isn't that what Dr. Mensen said?"

Jane nodded, "I think he had something to do with a hospital and the University, but I'm not sure what. I was too busy feeling sorry for myself."

"It's understandable," Rory said. "You were in shock. We were *all* in shock when we saw that thing."

"But everything happened so fast. And so soon after we left that room," Jane reasoned. "Do you think that student had time to leave and avoided running into those men?"

Rory shrugged, "I'm not one hundred per cent sure. But if I'm right, those gunmen landed on the roof of the hospital and came down to look for you. That would mean she didn't run into them because she took the stairs or elevator down to the lobby and got away."

"Why do you think they came down from the roof? Why not just in the back door or something?"

Rory didn't want to get too deep into the military-style execution on the entrance and exit the men had performed. That could make Jane more paranoid. "It doesn't matter. It's just a theory. All we can do is *hope* the young woman got away. And unless you have another idea, it's the only hope we have right now."

Jane shook her head, "No, I can't think of anything else."

Rory stepped on the gas, "Okay then, let's head to London."

Both Rory and Jane were tense and quiet for the next hour as the Jaguar passed through Brantford and then Woodstock. Highway 403 had merged into Highway 401 and the traffic was heavier but neither really noticed. For his part, Rory was thinking about all those people back at the hospital who had been shot because they had decided to be there on the day *he* had decided to take Jane there. Despite what he had said to Jane, it was hard to cast off the feeling of personal guilt. As they were nearing Ingersoll, a green road sign indicated there were several fast-food places, a restaurant, accommodations and two gas stations off the next exit. That made him glance down at the gas gauge. He cursed under his breath. It was low. Usually rental cars were filled when you took them out. It would figure he would get one that wasn't.

Jane didn't say anything as he took the exit ramp, turned right and then pulled into the gas station. She just continued to stare out the window as he pulled next to a pump.

But as Rory began to fill the rental car, Jane got out and stood beside him. The constant worry was very evident in her eyes as she watched the others cars filling up and the customers going in and out of the gas bar's convenience store. Every time there was the rumble of a heavy vehicle passing by on the highway not far away, she flinched. And when Rory went inside the station to pay with cash, Jane followed closely, almost glued to him.

Getting back in the Jaguar, Rory gave the situation some thought as he glanced at Jane, watching her put the seatbelt on. No doubt it had been a long, stressful day for her. He looked at the clock and then considered the Comfort Inn & Suites building next to the gas station. "It's getting late in the day. How about if we take a couple of rooms and stay here overnight?"

Jane took a deep breath as she looked out the windshield for a moment and then she nodded, "Yeah. That sounds good. I'm tired...and I'm hungry."

Rory nodded and put the Jaguar in drive.

"Can we stay in one room?" she asked quietly. "I'm afraid to stay by myself...."

"Tell you what, we'll get adjoining suites and leave the adjoining door open. Will that work?" Rory asked her.

Jane nodded her okay.

"But only as long as you promise not to peek when I'm in the shower," Rory kidded.

"I promise," Jane said as she held her hand up like she was swearing an oath. "Then again, I do have amnesia...I have a built-in excuse for peeking. Right?"

Chapter 18

AFTER GIVING FAKE NAMES and paying in cash for two adjoining rooms, Rory and Jane headed to a nearby diner to get something to eat. The first thing Rory did was wait for a patron who was parked right outside the front doors to leave, so he could back into the vacated spot, in case they needed to leave quickly. Then he put the Baby Eagle into the shoulder holster and wore it under his denim jacket. He wasn't going to get caught without it again. Going inside, he asked for the booth just inside the entrance. This way they could watch everyone coming and going through the large, front windows. He had done everything he could to make them as safe as possible so Jane could relax and eat.

And yet, despite the mouth-watering smells inside the restaurant and the fact she said she was hungry, Jane never seemed to notice any of it. Her eyes kept glancing from the front door to the parking lot outside and then to the dozen of other diners sitting around them. Over and over again she patrolled her surroundings with her eyes, never relaxing.

Rory ordered for them and when the waitress left, he reached over and gently placed his hand on hers.

Her body jumped and she went on alert at the touch, "What—?"

"It's okay, it's okay," Rory assured her. "I just want you to relax, okay?"

Jane nodded but her shoulders remained tense, "It's just hard...."

"I know. But just let me do the worrying right now," he said. "You'll end up with indigestion or you won't be able to sleep if you don't relax." He patted her hand, "And a tired and grumpy Jane won't do either of us any good."

Jane nodded, giving him a half smile. She rolled her shoulders forward and backward to relieve the tension.

Rory sat back as the waitress returned, "You concentrate on your meal and I'll keep an eye out for the bad guys. Deal?"

Jane nodded as the waitress set her meal down in front of her. She rolled her shoulders again, "I'll try."

And she did. Rory watched in amusement as Jane downed two large hamburgers and two orders of onion rings. Actually, three plates of onion rings, since she also picked most of the ones off Rory's plate. Rory *was* too busy keeping an eye out for the bad guys to actually eat a lot himself.

The waitress returned with two more cups of coffee and a slice of blueberry pie for Rory.

"Haven't had a nice piece of pie in... oh, I don't know how long," Rory said as he picked up his fork and cut into the slice.

Jane nodded as she held the last bit of her hamburger in her fingers, "Pie is nice."

"Do you remember pie?" Rory asked hopefully as he looked at her in anticipation.

Jane shrugged casually without looking up, "Of course."

Rory opened his mouth–"

"Pi=3.141592653589793238462643383279502884197169399375
342117067982148086513282306647093844609550585–"

Rory just sat there with his fork halfway to his lips.

Jane looked at him with a quizzical look on her face, "What?"

Rory just blinked a few times and he lowered his hand, "Where...did *that* come from?"

Jane blinked her eyes a few times as well when she fully realized what she had just done. She set down the last bit of hamburger on her plate, "I... I don't know...."

Rory set his fork down as he considered Jane in silence for a few moments. He watched as she moved the last bit of hamburger back and forth with her fingers and then he asked quickly, "Can you name me the prime numbers in order?"

"Why would I do that?" she asked in a quiet, sad voice without looking up.

"Just wondering–"

"2, 3, 5, 7, 11, 13, 17, 19, 23, 29, 31, 37, 41, 43, 47, 53, 59, 61, 67, 71, 73, 79, 83, 89, 97, 101, 103, 107, 109, 113, 127, 131, 137, 139, 149, 151, 157, 163, 167, 173, 179, 181, 191, 193, 197, 199, 211, 223, 227–" She stopped and looked up at Rory, a mixture of surprise and uncertainty on her face.

"Wow," was all Rory said after a moment of silence.

"Was...was that right?" Jane asked tentatively.

"I have no idea," Rory said with a shrug and an amused look on his face. "But it sure sounded good."

Jane put her hands in her lap and looked down at the table, thinking.

Rory took a sip of his coffee as he contemplated the woman sitting across from him.

Jane looked up at Rory, "Am I...am I some kind of freak?"

Rory shook his head, "No. I wouldn't say that. A lot of people are good at mathematics. You're just good at mathematics, that's all it means."

Jane narrowed her eyes, "Do you think it's that thing in my head?" She glanced around the room and up at the ceiling, "Do you think maybe it's receiving some kind of signals? Maybe it's feeding me that information."

"Remember, the doctors said they didn't detect any signals," Rory said.

"That's going *out* of my head," she said. "But what about coming *in*?"

"I could be wrong, but I would highly doubt they would miss signals going in or out," Rory reasoned.

"You're probably right," she finally agreed after some thought. "But it just worries me...."

"Look at it this way, you've just learned something new about yourself. You're a whiz-bang at mathematics," Rory said.

"Or a circus freak," Jane muttered as she picked up the last bit of hamburger.

"At least you're not the bearded lady."

"How would you know? I've been shaved everywhere, remember?" Jane replied. She stroked her jawline, "Maybe I do have a beard...."

Rory shook his head and had to smile.

Jane grew serious and looked down at the last bit of hamburger in her hand, "I just wish I could remember who I was."

Rory spoke quickly, "In Texas hold 'em poker, with a 52 card deck, what are the probabilities and odds of getting two aces, two kings or two queens of any suit in your two-card starting hand?"

Jane never hesitated and she answered without looking up, "The odds are 72.7 to 1 and the probability is 0.0136." Her own answer caused her to pause for a heartbeat. She looked up at Rory, "Why? Is that important?"

"It is - if we head to the nearest casino before we get that thing removed. We can clean up," he said seriously.

Jane looked at him for a moment. When a grin played on his lips, she smirked and threw what was left of her hamburger at him.

BEFORE THEY TURNED in for the night, Rory and Jane used a public computer in the lobby of the hotel to do a Google search. They put in different search parameters, trying to find a doctor in the London area that might fit the bill for Mensen's contact.

"There!" exclaimed Jane after a twenty-minute search. "Doctor Hans VanOstrand, Head of Neurological Surgery at Victory Hospital in London, Ontario. That sounds familiar. That *has* to be him."

Rory nodded as he scanned the information on the computer monitor, "It also appears that Victory Hospital is a teaching hospital associated with the local university."

"Are we going to phone there? To see if he got the CT scan and all the test results?"

Rory shook his head, "No. It's probably too late. And I don't want to use a phone or try and send an email, just in case. We'll go a little older school."

"What do you mean?"

"Watch and learn," Rory said as he walked over to the front desk.

Jane followed him.

Rory asked for a piece of paper and a pen. A few moments later, he had the clerk send a fax to VanOstrand, asking if he had received the files for Jane Doe from Mensen. If he had, they wanted to meet with him. Rory added his name at the bottom and asked for a return fax of confirmation either way. He then asked the clerk to let him know as soon as there was a reply.

"Now what?" Jane asked.

"Now we get some sleep and we'll see what the morning brings."

Chapter 19

INTELLIMAX INTERNATIONAL Branch Office, Toronto, Canada

"**WITHOUT OUR ASSET**, things are not going well with our entire operation, gentlemen." Maxwell Brecc said. The anger in his voice was unmistakable. He looked down at each man sitting around the long, glass table in the luxurious boardroom.

There was Conrad Blayze to his immediate left, a muscular man with a blond crew cut and a former member of Navy Seal Team Six. He was the leader of Response Tactical Team One for IntelliMax International.

Next was Arlen Frost, a husky man with close-cropped gray hair and a former member of the United Kingdom Special Forces. He was the leader of Response Tactical Team Two.

Next to him was Clevon Sharp, a black man with a shaven head and gold, wire-rimmed glasses. Sharp was the former head of the National Security Agency in the United States until Brecc had lured him away by tripling his salary.

Next was Cyrek Stratis, the former CEO of the Federal Greek Bank, a former managing director of the International Monetary Fund and an expert on the international monetary and financial systems.

The last man around the table was Bartlett Foxen. He tapped a pen on the table as he spoke up, "Having to take the woman alive put restraints on the tactical team, sir."

Blayze nodded his head in agreement, "Taking the woman alive did limit our choices in the operation."

Maxwell Brecc scowled, "Is there *any* possible way we can simply cut the brain from the head of this woman and use it for our purposes?"

Bartlett Foxen smirked at the remark, "No. That's just the stuff of science fiction."

"It seems to me that what we're doing right now is the stuff of science fiction, Mr. Foxen," Brecc countered in a loud voice. He didn't appreciate a subordinate treating him with disdain.

Foxen recognized he was close to stepping over a boundary. He straightened his tie and cleared his throat, "We still need the whole head...and body, sir."

Maxwell Brecc stared at Foxen long enough to reinforce his position of authority. It was also an uncomfortable moment for several of the other the men around the table.

But Frost was not cowed and he was more than happy to let Foxen sit on the hot seat for a moment before he spoke, "And we have to admit there was no way of knowing the amount of resistance the man with her would put up."

"Do we have any idea who this man is?" Brecc asked after a moment of thought.

"Using facial recognition software and the security video feed at the police station where they first were spotted, we were able to identify him. His name is Rory Mack Steele," Foxen answered. "He's a private investigator, licensed in both Canada and the

United States. His family owned company, Highlander Investigative Services, has offices here in Toronto and in New York–"

"Investigative services!" Stratis exclaimed. "Is he looking into our operation?"

Foxen shook his head, "No. I don't believe so–"

"How can *one* private investigator prevent our reacquiring our asset?" Brecc interrupted in a loud, agitated voice.

"I lost four highly trained men in the operation. This man is much more than a simple private investigator," Conrad Blayze countered.

Brecc looked sternly at Blayze.

"I've spent my entire life in this profession. Without a doubt, Steele has Special Forces training. He remained calm, cool and collected under fire. We can't take him lightly," Blayze continued, refusing to wilt under the scrutiny.

"Our technicians and analysts are working to confirm his background and skills, sir," Foxen added.

"Do you want me to take out his office?" Arlen Frost asked. "A few well-placed charges would remove his intel and assistance–"

"Unfortunately, that would also hinder our efforts to track Steele and the woman," Foxen countered. "Once we knew who he was, we dedicated a technician to monitor Highlander Investigative Services. We intercepted Steele's communications with his office as well as the appointment that was set up at the hospital by his office. He doesn't have satellite service or a dashboard navigation system in his vehicle that we can track, so we need to leave his communications with his office intact for now."

"Foxen is right," Clevon Sharp interjected. "We need to allow Steele to lead us right to him and the woman. He has no idea of our capabilities."

"I agree," Brecc said after some thought.

Sharp continued, showing anger as he looked directly at Blayze, "Then again, our capabilities are not what they should be. Because we *don't* have the woman!"

Blayze answered with a sneer, "I'll let you lead the tactical team if you want. You can show us how it's done, Clevon."

A smile lingered around the edges of Brecc's lips. He loved it when his employees bickered. He felt it kept them on edge and alert. He let a few more remarks fly back and forth between the two before he broke in, "Mr. Stratis. How is our special project going?"

Cyrek Stratis shook his head, "Not very well, I'm afraid." He took a deep breath before he continued, "Without the capabilities our asset was providing us, things have slowed to a trickle. We had the Sherbank in Russia, their largest bank, ready to flow to the tune of $71 billion in U.S. currency. The Industrial and Commercial Bank of China, one of the big four over there, was ripe for 12.55 trillion Renminbi. That's $1.9 trillion in U.S. currency. Now...I'm afraid our special project is dead in the water."

Brecc's jaw clenched with anger.

"The Deutsche Bank, the China Construction Bank and the Central Bank of Korea were being probed for their protocols and we were within a day of success. We were *one day* away from cracking them," Stratis emphasized. "But we have been shut out completely since the asset disappeared. I was personally looking forward to dealing with the Central Bank of Korea–"

"We have billions of dollars worth of other equipment in the compound," Sharp said in an incredulous voice. "I find it hard to believe we can't get the information we need."

"Unfortunately it's true," Foxen said. "Cracking the newest Electronic Banking Internet Communication Standards - as well as the internal protocols for each financial institution - was a piece of cake for the asset. Without those capabilities, it would take months. That was our problem *before* we acquired the asset. Every time we would get close, they would change the protocols as a matter of standard procedure. I'm taking a look at intercepted communications right now to see what else we could do...but–"

"We have to get this back on track," Brecc interrupted loudly. "Mr. Foxen, do whatever you need to do to get our special project back on track. Just make sure our operation is not compromised."

"Understood, sir," Foxen replied with a nod of his head.

"What about the incident at the hospital?" Stratis asked as he sat forward in concern. "Will that cause us any problems?"

Foxen shook his head, "No. We have analysts monitoring communications between the authorities and so far all the evidence they have collected, purposefully left behind by the team, points to a terrorist act. Any eyewitnesses were eliminated."

"And we took our fallen comrades home with us, as per our code, No one was left behind for them to identify," Blayze said coldly.

Foxen nodded, "Mr. Blayze and Mr. Frost will continue to ensure any further tactical operations will be sanitized of incriminating evidence and seeded with the appropriate evidence to reinforce the idea these incidents are acts perpetrated by terrorists."

"And our technicians have infiltrated their facilities and can easily manipulate any type of information in their databases, including forensic results, without their knowledge. If something does slip through, we can intervene in real time," Clevon Sharp added.

"Good, good, that makes me feel better," Cyrek Stratis said as he sat back again.

"Of course, we could do a better job if we had the woman," Sharp added.

He and Blayze exchanged angry looks again.

"Mr. Sharp is correct. We *must* get our asset back, gentlemen. That's priority one," Maxwell Brecc concluded. "And Mr. Blayze and Mr. Frost...?"

Blayze and Frost looked up at Brecc.

"When you do locate the asset again...I want this Steele *dead*."

Chapter 20

THE ROOM TELEPHONE rang the next morning at 8:15 AM, just as Rory was coming out of the bathroom and donning the shoulder holster with the Baby Eagle. He jumped for the phone. It was a young lady from the front desk. A fax had just arrived.

"Jane," he yelled.

Jane came bounding through the adjoining door from her suite. "Did we get a return fax?"

"Yes, we did. Let's go see what kind of an answer we got." Rory grabbed his denim jacket and slipped it on as he headed for the door.

Jane was very eager for some good news and she was out in the hallway first, leading the way, bounding down the stairs to the front desk.

The young lady behind the desk handed the fax to Rory.

Jane eagerly read it over his shoulder.

FAX

    To: Mr. Rory Steele

    From: "Doctor H.D. VanOstrand, MD, FRCPSC

Message: I rec'd the complete set of files and look forward to consulting with Jane Doe. My office is Suite 2A, Yellow Zone A.

"HE GOT THEM," JANE said with excitement. She clapped her hands like a little girl.

Rory nodded. He was glad she was excited. It was better than leaving her mind on what had happened back in Hamilton. They grabbed a quick breakfast at the small restaurant and within two hours they reached their destination in London.

VICTORY HOSPITAL, LONDON, Ontario, Canada

Victory Hospital was a six-story, red brick building situated just six blocks north of the highway. Rory could barely keep up with Jane as they walked from the back of the parking lot to the state-of-the-art research and teaching facility. Rory allowed her the opportunity of enthusiasm while he kept a watchful eye on everything around them. He wasn't in the mood for a surprise attack like back in Hamilton.

Jane moved eagerly across the front driveway and through the crowds of people moving in and out of the soaring arched entranceway. The inner glass doors slid open as Jane approached. She looked back over her shoulder at Rory, "Do you think they can do the surgery right here? Take it out, I mean?"

"Don't you get your hopes up too high just yet," Rory cautioned as he followed her into the busy front lobby. "We don't even know if the doctor will know what it is, let alone if he can take it out."

"I think I'm an optimist," stated Jane with a smile. "I'm going to think positively."

Rory didn't want to dampen her upbeat mood and didn't say anything more. But he wished he could feel as upbeat as she was.

Jane slipped eagerly through the crowd of people and across the room to stand below a large sign that illustrated the floor layout of the entire hospital. Jane scanned it quickly and pointed to the outline of a yellow zone on the second floor, "There it is. He's in the neuroscience section." She then spun around in circles with her finger pointing outward, "And the elevator is...over there! Let's go."

Rory had to smile at her enthusiasm. He just hoped she wouldn't be disappointed by whatever the doctor had to say. If Dr. Mensen and all those other doctors couldn't identify what was in her head, the odds were not good that this Doctor VanOstrand could either. But they had to try at least.

Rory led Jane into the next crowded elevator. He moved to the back and she pressed herself up against him for security. He could see her head moving constantly moving back and forth as she watched the passengers around them. The elevator car slowly rose to the second floor. The doors slid open and Rory and Jane exited to find themselves in a purple zone.

Signs on the wall indicated the yellow zone was to the right. Rory kept a constant watch around them as they headed down a long hallway, following the series of direction arrows on the wall. The second floor was as busy as the main floor had been. Doctors, student doctors, nurses, orderlies, and patients moved up and down the hallways with visitors and loved ones mixed in. The heavy smell of bleach hung in the air and mixed with the scents of disinfectant and iodine.

Leaving the purple zone and entering the yellow zone seemed to make Jane happier, if that was possible at this point. No doubt she was anticipating a good outcome the closer she got to meeting Dr. VanOstrand. A few minutes later, as they approached a cross hallway, she pointed ahead, "There's a sign that says we have to go down that way on the left."

Rory nodded but he glanced back. Something in the back of his mind said something wasn't right. His military training and years of experience in the investigative business left him with a nagging feeling but he couldn't put a finger on what was bothering him. He looked back at Jane and put a hand out, "Just hold on for a moment—"

But he was too late. Jane had already sped up, eager to get to the doctor. She turned the corner and disappeared from his sight.

Rory hustled to keep up with her and he was running by the time he turned the corner. Finally reaching her, he put a hand on Jane's arm, slowing her pace, "Just take it slow. Okay?"

Jane looked at him with a puzzled look on her face, "Why?" She pointed ahead to another cross hallway, "The sign says he's right down there on the right."

"I know. It's just...." He looked down the hallway, trying to find what it was that bothered him.

Frustration showing on her face, Jane pulled her arm away, "But we're getting close. He can help me. I know he can."

Rory glanced back behind them and suddenly realized what it was. The last hallway and this one was empty of people, unlike every other part of the hospital they had passed through. Or was he just being paranoid—?

Jane was off again, rushing towards the next hallway and VanOstrand's office. Rory was caught off guard and he had to walk faster again to catch up with her. Jane turned the corner to the right and Rory followed, still trying to catch up.

The light sound of their shoes echoed off the walls of the wide hallway.

But *just* their own shoes. There were no other sounds, no footsteps no voices, no medical machinery running anywhere.

Where was everyone?

At the far end of the hallway, a young woman in a white smock emerged from an open office doorway and turned in their direction. She walked slow and careful for a moment, looking down like she was trying to keep her footsteps light. Then she glanced back towards the doorway. A moment later her pace picked up.

Jane slowed her own pace for the first time and glanced back at Rory, "She looks scared."

Rory nodded, "Yeah, she does–"

The young woman began running towards them. Her high heels clicked heavily on the terrazzo floor, echoing loudly off the white walls. But she was no more than thirty feet down the hallway when a man stepped out of that same doorway behind her.

Rory's blood ran cold.

The man behind the woman was dressed in black from head to toe, including black body armor and the same type of black ski mask they saw back in the Hamilton hospital attack. More importantly, he held a Heckler & Koch UMP submachine gun.

Rory reached ahead decisively and stopped Jane, then stepped ahead of her.

The black-clad man raised the submachine gun and fired.

The young woman's body exploded, blood and pieces of internal organs spraying everywhere, as she was ripped in two by .45 caliber slugs.

Blood spattered the walls and stained the terrazzo floor in front of her as she fell.

Jane screamed.

Rory heard blood-stained bullets zipping past them.

More automatic weapons gunfire sounded and muzzle flashes illuminated the office doorway where the woman had come from.

Rory had no doubts the gunman in the hallway had a partner who had probably just killed VanOstrand. Time to go. He reached forward, grabbing Jane's arm, urging her to move.

Jane stayed frozen in place, still screaming.

The man in black pointed down the hallway towards Rory and Jane and yelled into his tactical mic, "I have them. Converge on me. Now!"

Rory reached out and grabbed Jane, pulling her towards him, "Run."

Jane turned slowly on legs of jelly and stumbled past Rory, her hands up near her head as she continued to scream.

Rory pulled her past him, turned and set his hands on her shoulders, "You need to run, Jane." He glanced back. Fear struck hard when he saw the black-clad gunman raise the submachine gun and aim directly at him.

Chapter 21

JANE DOE STUMBLED and nearly went down. Rory put his hands under her arms and nearly lifted her off her feet. Keeping himself between her and the gunman, he struggled to keep her moving back down the hallway. He hoped the gunman wouldn't fire, fearing the bullets would go through him and kill her. Yeah, trust a gunman out to kill you, Steele. Jane again stumbled in fear but Rory kept her on her feet and moving. He pushed her around the corner and hoped he could move fast enough himself, knowing he was going to be vulnerable for a brief moment.

The machine gun roared and .45 caliber bullets ripped and chewed apart the wall just behind Rory, the sound of the thuds in the plaster coming closer just as he was turning the corner. He felt a tug on the material of his jacket at the edge of his shoulder. The bullet had been that close.

The bullets ripped into the corner of the far wall and Jane screamed again, falling to her knees with her hands over her ears.

Rory ran into her body and stumbled over onto the floor, landing hard. His wrists bent backward when he had tried to break his fall and he cursed hard at the pain. He clenched his jaw in determining and pushed it from his mind. There simply wasn't time. No doubt teams of men would be closing in on their position, just like in Hamilton and the pain they would inflict would be a lot greater. He got to his feet and tried to pull Jane up, "We have to keep going."

But Jane was frozen in fear and her body resisted, refusing to cooperate.

Rory put extra effort into it and finally pulled her to her feet. "Jane. We can't stay here. We have to go," he urged again.

Jane's body was slow to respond, fear paralyzing her muscles but she finally began running woodenly.

Rory followed behind her. He pulled his Baby Eagle and glanced back over his shoulder as they ran down the hallway.

Fifty yards down the hallway, Jane screamed and dropped to the floor.

Rory turned back around and looked passed her as he tried to slide to a stop.

Two men in black body armor and black ski masks and carrying Heckler & Koch UMPs were running from the other end of the hallway towards them.

Rory, still sliding, raised his handgun and fired a shot.

The two gunmen immediately ducked to each side of the hallway as the sound reverberated off the walls.

Rory's feet bumped into Jane's crouched form, stopping his forward momentum as he fired again

The two men thought better of their position and scrambled back down the hall into the safety of a doorway on each side.

That gave Rory an opportunity to find safety themselves and he looked around quickly. There was an exit door to a set of stairs just ahead on the left. He pulled Jane to her feet and pointed with his gun, "Run for that exit."

Jane took off at a low slow run, her body sluggish with fear.

Rory followed just to the right of her, firing alternate shots to each doorway to keep the two men ahead pinned inside the rooms.

Jane reached the exit door and frantically slammed her shoulder into it, pushed her way through.

Rory glanced back quickly. The other gunman or his partner hadn't turned the corner yet in pursuit. But as he looked back in the direction of the other two, the barrel of a machine gun snaked around the door frame. He ducked his head instinctively and made a jump for the door before it closed, landing on his knees on the concrete floor on the other side.

.45 caliber bullets ripped across the door frame and the door and then ripped into the far wall of the stairwell through the crack just before the door closed.

Jane screamed as she fell against the stairs and put her hands on her head to protect herself from the flying splinters and sharp fragments of wood and concrete.

Rory felt a sting on his cheek as a splinter from the door stabbed him. He brushed it from his skin and ignored the pain. As soon as the firing stopped, he got to his feet, took a quick step to the stairwell railing and looked down.

Running footsteps pounded up the stairs from somewhere below. Someone was headed up this way but there was no way of knowing if it was hospital security or the attackers. And they couldn't wait to find out.

Jane slid across the stair to put her back against the concrete wall, fear etched on her face.

"Move up to that first landing," Rory said as he pointed up the stairway.

"What?"

"Go up to the first landing." Rory leaned over the railing again, looking below and listening.

Jane looked up, hesitated for a moment and then got up and climbed the stairs. On the next turn in the stairs, she squatted and placed her back against the concrete wall.

The pounding footsteps from below slowed.

Rory could hear shouting. It reverberated off the concrete walls. He turned his head, trying to hear what was being said. It sounded like someone was issuing instructions. He thought back to the Hamilton attack and how they had coordinated their efforts. That's what they were doing now. That was why their tenuous position in here wasn't being rushed from the hallway yet either.

"Now what?" a scared Jane asked from above.

Rory wasn't sure. He stepped back to the exit door quickly and pulled it open slightly to look in the direction they had come from.

Two men dressed in black ski masks were cautiously moving down the hallway towards them. That meant both ends of the hallway were being cut off in a coordinated effort.

Rory sensed something and he pulled back and ducked–

Bullets ripped through the door as it was closing.

Jane screamed, hands over her head.

Rory looked up at her. He had trapped them both in the stairwell and the gunmen were converging, just like back in Hamilton. As she had so eloquently asked; Now what?

Chapter 22

RORY CLOSED HIS EYES, trying to figure out what to do. He chastised himself for not planning better before they even came inside the hospital. He should have had an escape plan. That was a rule – the words struck him. Escape plan? He opened his eyes as his thoughts went back to the Hamilton attack. Would these attackers use the same entrance and escape route he assumed had been used in that attack; namely, the roof? It made sense. It was unlikely they would have walked in through the front door, dressed head-to-toe in their black, attack garb.

The light echo of boots sounded on the steps below.

Rory knew they would be moving up the stairs now, slow and cautious, while the two groups outside in the hallway kept them pinned in here. He made a decision. It was a gamble, but there was no other choice. He bounded up the stairs, grabbed Jane's hand and urged her upwards.

Jane rose and moved with him but her fear made her movements wooden. Her toe stubbed into the first stair and she stumbled. She kept moving at Rory's urging but it was a difficult climb for her. They reached the third-floor stairwell and she looked to the exit door to the hallway.

But Rory kept them climbing.

At the next turn in the stairs, he paused to look over the railing while urging her to keep going.

Jane was moving better now, taking the stairs two at a time now but her breathing was short and choppy.

Rory saw shadows moving along the outer wall, heading up towards them. They were definitely coming after them. He bounded up the stairs after Jane.

Jane reached the next landing with an exit door and glanced back.

Rory jabbed his thumb upward, encouraging her to keep going.

Jane bounded up the stairs.

Rory jogged through the landing and took the stairs two at a time himself now. When he reached the first turn in the stairs, there was a loud bang from below. Rory whirled around, bringing his weapon to bear down towards the landing.

One of the gunmen had pushed open the stairwell door they had just passed, slamming it back against the wall in the hallway. He appeared in the stairwell, looking down over the railing. He looked up. Realizing his target was above him, the gunman raised his machine gun.

Rory was faster. He skillfully placed a shot through the left eye hole of the black ski mask.

The gunman's body fell backwards, raising the machine gun and spraying bullets up the right wall of the stairwell as his dead finger stayed tight on the trigger.

Jane screamed and threw herself onto the stairs and against the railing on her left.

The gunman's partner, halfway through the doorway, was knocked back by the falling body.

Rory was up and running, pulling Jane to her feet before the dead body below hit the floor.

Bullets smashed into the walls and ricocheted off the railing as the second gunman shot upwards from the stairs below.

Jane screamed and stumbled, banging her shin against the edge of a stair.

Rory realized he had to give her a brief moment to recover. He blindly stuck his hand over the railing and fired two shots into the stairwell below, making sure they ricocheted off the concrete wall to add to the effect. "C'mon, Jane. Keep going."

It worked. The firing from below stopped.

Grimacing in pain, Jane gave him a nod as she rose and began a limping run up the stairs again.

Rory waited a moment, listening.

The sound of dozens of heavy boots pounding upwards began echoing off the walls again.

Jane ran to the next landing where she stopped. She was breathing in short, sharp gasps as she bent over and massaged her sore shin.

Rory took off up the stairs, two at a time. He joined Jane on a twenty-foot long landing and realized they had reached the highest floor. The exit to the roof was at the other end of the landing.

"What now?" asked a scared Jane.

"Hold on," Rory said as he leaned over the top railing and fired two more shots to slow them down.

But Jane wasn't listening. She turned and headed right for the exit door to the roof and possible escape. She ran hard and threw herself against the emergency bar, pushing the door open and she disappeared outside. The exit door banged closed.

"Crap," Rory said as he realized what she had done. He fired two more shots down the stairwell.

The running sounds below stopped.

Rory turned and ran hard, slammed into the emergency bar and pushing the door open, hoping Jane wasn't in trouble. He found her twenty feet away, spinning around in circles, looking in all directions. The rooftop was filled with towers, pipes, duct-work and various mechanical structures. And pieces of open, blue sky was evident in all directions. They had nowhere to go.

"Now what?" Jane cried as she continued to spin around and move across the rough surface of the rooftop, looking for a way out.

Damn good question, thought Rory. There was no sign of how—

"Can we use that?" Jane yelled as she pointed desperately to the other side of the roof.

Rory jogged ten feet and looked in the direction she was pointing. Bingo! Just as he had hoped. There was a helicopter sitting on the far side of the rooftop. A possible way out.

Then again, maybe not. A man in a black ski mask, carrying an H&K UMP submachine gun was running from the front of the helicopter on the left, heading their way.

Rory figured the man had been alerted to the fact that the targets were coming up to the roof. Rory ran for Jane while looking for a place to hide but he couldn't see anything promising. He looked back towards the helicopter.

The gunman spotted them and raised his submachine gun.

Rory reached out pushed Jane's shoulder hard, propelling her behind a huge air conditioning unit for the building.

Jane stumbled and turned, falling on her butt with her back to the air conditioning unit.

Rory dove for a spot behind the air conditioning unit himself.

The gunman opened up and Jane covered her head with her hands, screaming and kicking her feet as bullets ripped through the sheet metal of the air conditioning unit above her head.

The gunfire stopped.

Rory kept his head down and crawled for the edge of the air conditioning unit, hoping to get a shot at the gunman.

The submachine gun exploded again and more bullets ripped into the air conditioning unit, causing Rory to stop and duck his head.

"What do we do now?" Jane cried.

Rory rolled over and sat up with his back to the unit, Baby Eagle at his shoulder. He had no idea. This man was keeping them pinned down, no doubt waiting for the others to reach the roof.

More bullets ripped through the air conditioning unit.

Rory checked his weapon. Crap! He suddenly realized he only had two shots left in a magazine that held 12. He searched his pockets for the extra magazine. More crap! Must've dropped it somewhere.

"What is it? Are you out of bullets?"

Rory shook his head, "No. I've got two left–"

"Two! With all those men chasing us?" she said in a shrill voice.

Rory put a hand out towards her," It's okay. It'll be fine."

"It'll be fine? You have two bullets and–?" Jane said something under her breath and set her head back against the air conditioning unit, closing her eyes tightly.

Rory wanted to say something else to assure her, but he had no idea how they were going to get out of this.

Chapter 23

RORY GLANCED AROUND the corner of the air conditioning unit. The gunman was approaching their position in a crouch. The problem was...there were a number of six-inch pipes between the gunman and the air conditioning unit and Rory doubted he could get a clear shot. And there wasn't much time before the rest of the gunmen came pouring out of the stairs onto the roof. He took a deep breath and let it out slowly as he raised the weapon. He had to try at least – the sound of skin slapping against skin caught his attention. He turned his head and looked at Jane.

Jane was clapping her hands together rapidly in front of her face, "Ohhhhhhhh, I can't believe I'm going to do this."

"What –?"

"Just get ready," Jane instructed him in a high and squeaky voice.

"Ready for what?"

Suddenly Jane rolled to her left towards the far side of the air conditioning unit.

"Jane, no–!"

But it was too late. Jane reached the far edge quickly, stood up and stepped out from the safety of the air conditioning unit with her hands up. Her voice was shaky as she yelled, "Hello? I'm the one you want." She took a few steps to the side, "Here I am. Come and get me. Just let him go."

Rory counted to three and then spun quickly to his right and rolled six times away from the air-conditioning unit into the open.

The man had his eyes and weapon trained on Jane and he was just a tad late in reacting. He swung his weapon and fired, the bullets ripping a line of jagged holes in the elastomeric roof coating, trying to track Rory as he rolled.

Rory stopped rolling, brought the Baby Eagle up...shifted his aim to a risky head shot when he realized the man wore a vest...and fired twice.

Blood and gore exploded through the material of the ski mask.

Rory was up and running over to Jane before the body slumped to the rooftop.

Jane was frozen on the spot, looking across at the bloody head of the gunman.

Rory grabbed her hand, pulling her towards the helicopter. "Don't do that again," he yelled.

"You're welcome," she said in a voice barely above a whisper. "I was just kind of tired of hearing myself scream."

Rory pulled her as fast as he could across the rooftop. The smell of gunpowder hung heavy in the air as they skirted the dead body and ran for the helicopter He yelled at Jane as he ran for the pilot's door, "Go around to the passenger side and get in."

Jane skidded sideways as she stopped her momentum, changed directions and ran around the helicopter for the other side.

Rory climbed into the pilot seat, placing the empty Baby Eagle back into the shoulder holster.

Jane fought with the door on her side before she could get it open.

Rory was already flipping switches when she got herself seated.

"Can you fly this thing?" she asked.

"Maybe," Rory said as he glanced over towards the area of the roof door.

"Maybe? What do you mean maybe!" Jane yelled.

The two Pratt & Whitney PT6C turboshaft engines of the AgustaWestland AW139 started. Slowly the five-blade main rotor began to turn.

"Hurry, hurry, hurry," Jane yelled above the increasing sounds of the whining engine. She looked anxiously across the roof.

The blades began to speed up.

Rory watched the instruments and glanced up at the blades, mentally urging them to go faster.

"They're here," Jane yelled as she pointed in the direction of the roof door.

Rory looked over and saw half a dozen gunmen moving across the roof. He reached for his Baby Eagle and then cursed when he remembered it was empty. He looked at the automatic weapon over beside the dead body. Too late now dumbo, he thought.

The gunmen began running towards the helicopter.

Rory twisted the throttle and worked the anti-torque pedals. A moment later, the Pratt & Whitney helicopter lifted a foot off the roof.

The gunmen lifted their Heckler & Koch UMPs when they realized he was about to take off.

Now two feet off the roof, Rory turned the helicopter around to put the tail towards the gunmen, then he banked hard right, tilting the helicopter as he headed for the edge of the roof.

Automatic weapon fire exploded behind them.

Jane screamed and her body slid to her right, banging on the door.

It flew open.

Rory realized in horror that Jane had forgotten to close the door on her side. He lunged and grabbed her wrist at the last minute with his right.

Jane's feet and lower body slipped outside the open door. She grabbed desperately for the seat with her other hand, screaming with all her might.

Feeling himself losing his grip on her wrist, Rory unconsciously removed his left hand from the control stick, intending to reach across and secure her. Quickly the helicopter began spinning out of control, rising higher in tight spirals.

Jane screamed as the world turned in a blur.

Rory grabbed for the control stick with his left hand.

The AW139 straightened out.

Rory's body was now tilted hard to the right as he held Jane with one hand and the stick with the other. He desperately worked the throttle and the anti-torque pedals, trying to get away from the sound of the gunfire...and he misjudged.

They were headed straight down into the roof!

Rory desperately tried to orient himself, pulling back on the stick. The helicopter wasn't responding. He pulled with all his might.

A dozen black-garbed gunmen dropped as Rory skimmed the top of the roof over their heads.

Rory now pushed on the stick and slanted the helicopter to the right.

The helicopter barely missed the large air conditioning unit and several stainless steel pipes sticking up from the rooftop.

Jane was screaming as she clawed at the seat, desperate to get herself back inside the helicopter.

Rory pulled on her wrist with all his might.

Jane finally caught the edge of the seat and pulled hard, slowly pulling her legs back into the helicopter, enough at least to get her feet anchored on the edge of the open door. She managed to get herself back in between the seat and the instrument panel.

"Close the door," Rory yelled as he held her wrist tightly.

Jane struggled to get herself around and pulled the door shut.

Rory let go of her hand and pulled himself upright. He heard the roar of automatic gunfire and he dropped the helicopter over the edge of the roof.

Jane screamed as they headed downward at a 45° angle, heading directly for a meeting with the cars in the parking lot.

Rory smoothly leveled the helicopter out and zoomed a few feet over the tops of the vehicles. He circled to the left and climbed back towards the hospital. Just past the edge of the building, he dropped down again and held his altitude just over the rooftops of the surrounding homes. Rory could see startled people looking up in the streets. Once they were beyond the range of the gunman's weapons, Rory began to gain altitude and turned to the right, heading to the south of London.

"How did they find us?" Jane cried. She was still shaking as she sat there. Her voice sounded hoarse from all the screaming she had done.

Rory shook his head. He had no idea.

"What...what about the doctor?"

Rory shook his head again, "I'm not sure. But I think that was his office where the young woman came from...."

In their hearts, both he and Jane knew that Doctor VanOstrand was probably dead. Just like Doctor Mensen. And no doubt the CT scans were also gone, probably destroyed.

Jane licked her lips, "What do we do now?"

Rory didn't answer her as he turned the AgustaWestland AW139 medical helicopter to the left and followed high over Highway 401, heading east. The truth was, he didn't have an answer.

After a few moments of silence, Jane asked, "Presuming those men are with the ones who held me...if they want me back...why were they shooting at me?"

Rory watched the scenery below and then shook his head, "I don't think they weren't shooting at you, Jane. Every shot they took was aimed directly at me. Although...I have to admit they would've killed us both if they had killed me while I was at the controls of this helicopter...."

"So...they want me...and what's in my head?"

Rory didn't say anything.

"Well they can't have it," she yelled.

Fear struck in Rory's heart as he realized she was opening the door to the helicopter.

Jane was jumping!

Rory lunged for her and jammed his fingers into the waistband of her blue slacks at the back.

The helicopter veered and plummeted as Rory's fought to regain control with his left while holding her inside the helicopter with his right hand again. But this time, she wasn't helping him. She was fighting him.

"Let me go," she yelled, struggling to jump. "I don't want any more people to die because of me. I don't want you to die because of me. Let me go. Please."

Rory pulled with all his strength and slowly got her back over the seat. "Closed the door or you'll kill us both," he yelled above the sound of the wind whipping into the cabin.

They were skimming just over the trees now, the AW139 swinging back and forth as Rory struggled to maintain control while fighting to keep Jane in the helicopter.

Jane fought to break free and Rory fought to keep his grip on her slacks. He pulled hard, sliding her across the seat towards himself.

Jane struggled for a few more minutes and then collapsed on her left side against his shoulder. Heavy sobs shook her body as she broke down. "I can't take this. I want to know who I am. Why can't I remember? Why, why, why," she kept asking as she cried.

Rory took the AgustaWestland AW139 medical helicopter higher over the highway. He wrapped his right arm tightly around Jane's shoulders as she cried. He couldn't blame her. He had been in a lot of cases where people couldn't understand why bad things were happening to them. That was often normal for innocent people. But when you couldn't even remember a single thing about yourself, about your background, about your friends or about your family, that added enormously to the nightmare.

RORY HUGGED JANE TIGHTER and applied full power to the throttle, thinking as he watched the cars zipping back and forth on the highway far below them. Rory had absolutely no idea what to do next. How *had* those men found them? And so quickly? He had dumped the car and his cell phone and covered his tracks well, that he was positive of. He knew Jane hadn't made any calls because they were together all the time. If she had made any calls in the night back at the hotel, it would've shown up on the bill in the morning. And there wasn't a single charge for a telephone call. The only charge was for the fax messages, sent and received. Then again, who would she call anyway? Had Doctor VanOstrand called someone and they had picked that up somehow? That *had* to be the answer. But something in the back of Rory's mind told him it wasn't. There was another answer. He just couldn't put his finger on it yet.

Chapter 24

THE PRATT & WHITNEY PT6C turboshaft engines purred as Rory continued flying the AgustaWestland AW139 to the south. Moving at 193 mph, it didn't take them long before the shoreline of Lake Erie appeared ahead. Rory glanced at Jane. She was slumped in her seat and hadn't said a single word since his struggle to keep her from jumping from the helicopter. Once she had stopped crying, she had merely sat there, staring out the side window. But she looked calm enough now that Rory decided to do a little reconnaissance near his cottage while he had the helicopter. He angled the nose of the helicopter east, to follow over the shoreline and then looked over at Jane, hopeful she would respond. "You feel up to helping me with something?" he asked gently.

It took a few minutes before she did respond. She turned her head slightly but her focus was off somewhere in the distance. Her voice was a hoarse whisper, "Pardon?"

Rory wondered if she was really up to this, but he had to try something. Right now they had no direction. No way to help her. "I thought it might be a good idea to take a bird's eye view of the area around my cottage while we have this helicopter. Maybe we can figure out where you were being held."

Jane just stared off into the distance, not answering right away. Then she looked down at her hands clasped in her lap, "I told you, I really can't remember much."

"I know. I'm not expecting much. The area around my cottage has a number of streams and a lot of open fields and farms for miles. One looks pretty much like the other. Even more so at night, I would guess."

Jane looked out the front of the helicopter and nodded, "Especially when you're running scared."

Rory nodded, wishing he could do more to ease her pain than just listen.

Jane wrung her hands together.

Rory saw the mounting anxiety and tried to lessen the pressure on her, "Tell you what, don't sweat it. Just keep an eye on the ground below. Maybe something will look familiar. That's all we can do, right?"

She nodded slightly in answer as she turned her head and looked down over the terrain.

Rory started surveying the terrain below as well, not really expecting to find anything. On the left were miles of lush green fields, stands of trees and the open fields of farm after farm. On the right were the blue waters of Lake Erie, dotted with a number of lake freighters, a few fishing boats, some sailboats and a number of powerboats marking their way with white capped wakes. Across the lake, they could see the distant shoreline where the State of Pennsylvania met New York State.

It wasn't long before they were flying over the 200-year-old fishing village of Port Dover. Boats of all sizes were moving back and forth from the marina on the eastern side of the town. The Lynn River split the village in two and provided a natural harbor where commercial fishing tugs were built and berthed. Swimmers and bathers played on the beach to the left. Rory angled the helicopter north-east to take them a little further inland, then turned directly east towards Peacock Point.

After a few minutes, Jane leaned a little forward, looking down through the bubble of the cabin, "What's that down there?"

Rory stretched in his seat to look at what she was pointing at, "That's the industrial area of Nanticoke. That large complex you're looking at is a steel company."

"It's big."

Rory pointed to the northeast, "And that's an oil refinery." Rory gave her a few moments to look at the large facility and then he turned the helicopter to the southeast. "And that down there is the Nanticoke Generating Station. That long pier jutting out into the lake is where they off-loaded coal to be burned to generate electricity. The government phased it out because of all the greenhouse gases it was creating."

"It still looks pretty busy, though. There are a lot of cars in the parking lot," Jane said.

Rory had to agree. "They must've started up again," Rory surmised as he eased the throttle and did a little sightseeing around the site. He thought back to that 1,000 foot long Great Lakes freighter he had watched from his front porch. Maybe they *were* delivering coal. He shrugged it off, "I only spend a couple of weeks a year at my cottage so I don't keep up on the local happenings."

Jane turned to look at him, "I assumed that's where you lived."

Rory shook his head no, "No, I live in the Toronto area where I have my office."

"That's where Mandy is?" Jane asked.

"Yes," Rory said as he applied the throttle and headed east-ward at a faster clip, "Let's head over to my cottage and take a lit-tle look around that area before we dump this thing."

"I hope you mean *land* this thing," Jane said.

Rory looked over at her, "Okay, we can do that instead." Rory felt good when Jane smiled.

The terrain over to his cottage wasn't much different than what they had flown over since they had left the hospital behind in London. Trees, fields, lakes, streams, and farms...nothing stood out beyond the ordinary. After flying back and forth a few times in the area without really seeing anything that triggered a com-ment from Jane, Rory angled the nose of the helicopter towards the northwest. But nothing caught his eye or Jane's attention af-ter another ten minutes of flying over this terrain either. Just more farms, fields and trees. He decided enough was enough. He swung the helicopter to the northeast, "Okay, let's head back up to that airport where we left the Jaguar. We might as well try and find another—"

"What's that?" Jane asked. "Another part of the industrial area?"

Rory took a look at where she was pointing. That was a very good question. Rory turned back west, increased his speed and quickly gained some altitude. In a few moments, a massive site that covered one thousand acres stretched out below them. The right side of the site was filled with tall masts, massive satellite dishes and large structures that looked like large white golf balls. Over on the left side of the compound was a central cluster of buildings, surrounded by a number of other buildings, some large and some smaller structures. Rory recognized three of the outer buildings as backup generators and several as underground bunker fuel tanks. Whoever these people were, they were concerned with having absolutely zero downtime for whatever they were doing.

"Do you know what that place is?" Jane asked again.

Rory didn't answer. He simply stared as they circled the massive site below. One building in the cluster had caught his attention in particular. He dropped lower to take a closer look. It was a large, three-story black glass building. Rory had seen something similar before in intelligence operations. They would be pumping white noise between the walls of that building to ensure no signal or voices leaked out. That was to prevent anyone from spying on them. Which is what Rory and Jane were doing right now. That made him feel a little uneasy. What kind of response would these people take if they felt he and Jane were too close?

"What are those big white golf balls?"

"Radomes," he answered in a quiet, distracted voice.

"What do they do?"

Rory didn't answer her. Something else on the perimeter of the compound caught his attention. Rory dropped the helicopter down to one hundred feet over an open field on the eastern side and angled the nose towards the compound. It wasn't long before they were hovering, staring at a huge fence that was surrounding the entire site. Several hundred yards of open grass or gravel circled the outside and the inside of the fence all around the compound.

"What's wrong?" Jane asked as she looked at Rory and then at the fence.

Rory didn't say anything. He brought the helicopter up above the trees and moved the helicopter slowly northward along the fence line. He hovered when he spotted a small stream in the trees below.

A loud roar ripped through the air over top of them and the helicopter was suddenly rocked by a blast of air turbulence.

Rory fought to gain control as the helicopter bucked and jerked.

"What was that?" Jane cried as she held onto her seat.

Getting the craft settled, Rory applied the throttle and lifted the helicopter higher before he turned the nose to the north. His eyes scanned the horizon until he spotted a CF-188 Hornet off to their left. The world-class fighter jet was banking right and circling back towards them. Rory turned eastward and applied full throttle. He knew he couldn't outrun a supersonic aircraft, but at least he could show he was complying.

Within moments the CF-188 Hornet shot low with a roar over top of the helicopter again, rocking it back and forth.

"Answer me?" What's happening? Why is that jet doing that?"

"It's a Canadian Air Force jet," Rory yelled over top of the jet noise. "He was warning us off. That compound back there must be a military installation."

Rory watched as the fighter jet quickly gained altitude, "He'll leave us alone now that were leaving."

"Why would he do that? Is he crazy? He could've killed us," Jane yelled.

Rory nodded in agreement but he was bothered more by something else. "Did you recognize anything about that place?" he asked her after a few moments.

"No, why?"

Rory didn't say anything as he gained more altitude.

"Tell me what you're thinking, please," Jane pleaded. "You're scaring me. The military...fighter jets...."

"The top of that fence had razor wire," he said finally.

"Which means what? Come on Rory, talk to me. Tell me what's going on. Things are bad enough...."

"Those cuts you had on your body are consistent with razor wire. And considering how close that place is to my cottage...."

Tears filled Jane Doe's eyes and she swore a blue streak.

Chapter 25

RORY SPOTTED THE John C. Munroe Hamilton International Airport in the distance ahead. An Antonov An-24 cargo airplane was circling in the distance while a Boeing 747 was on its final approach.

"Do we land on a landing strip like that big plane is doing or is there a special place for helicopters?" Jane asked as she leaned and pointed at the 747 smoothly dropping closer to landing.

But Rory didn't answer. He had no intention of landing at the airport. Instead, he was scanning the terrain ahead for a possible landing spot.

Jane fidgeted in her seat as they cut the distance to the landing strips in half. A low roar filled the cabin as the 747 was just touching down.

Rory spotted a farmer's field just to the left. A stand of trees between it and the airport meant they wouldn't be seen by the control tower once they were down. That would work nicely. He turned the helicopter to the left and began dropping lower. In seconds the helicopter was passing low over a highway.

A car zipped by below them and Jane was immediately alert and concerned, "What are we doing?"

Rory didn't say anything. He was concentrating on the terrain below as the helicopter moved low over a stand of trees.

Jane gripped the edges of her seat as the helicopter stood still in the air, hovering over the tree-tops. She watched the trees tops whip back and forth under the harsh downward draft of the blades, "Rory, please tell me what we're doing."

"We're going to land here," Rory answered as he continued to survey the green field just to the west of the trees.

"On the trees?" Jane almost choked in panic.

"No, no. Don't worry," Rory said as he slowly began to hover away from the trees and towards the field.

"I'm sorry, but it's too late to tell me not to worry," Jane squeaked as she strained her neck to look at the terrain below.

Rory realized the field was filled with tomato plants. But the plants were low enough that Rory surmised they wouldn't be hiding a nasty surprise...like a hole that would tip them over. He picked out the flattest spot and began a slow descent to the ground–

"Are you crazy?"

"Probably."

"But the airport is right there," Jane said as she pointed back over the trees. "Why are you landing here–?" Her head swiveled around, "Did you spot something at the airport. What was it?" Fear was rising in her voice.

"No, it's fine," Rory assured her. "We just can't take a chance setting down at the airport. That military jet back at the compound may have alerted the local police to look for us at a nearby airport to check us out–"

"The police? Like the one you said called someone?"

"I doubt that officer would be all the way up here. But there could be another one on someone's payroll. But even if they turned out to be okay, it would take time for us to explain things. Which only gives someone nasty the opportunity to catch up with us–"

"Why don't we just set it down at the airport and run–?"

"If we don't alert the tower that we're setting down over there, we'd have security guards all over us, which also delays our getting away," Rory said as he slowly maneuvered the helicopter downward.

Jane scared voice could barely be heard over the engine noise, "Do...do you think those same men who were at the two hospitals...could be waiting for us?"

Rory was going tell her it would be okay, but he wasn't sure himself. He concentrated as he set the helicopter down.

The craft jerked as the wheels set down and then tilted a little to the left before it settled firmly on the ground in the tomato field.

Rory cut the engines and opened his door, "Let's go. Keep low to avoid the blades when you get out."

Jane jumped out her side, keeping low as the rotor slowly lost momentum. The rich smell of damp earth filled the air and Jane stumbled a couple of times as the heels on her shoes sank in the soft soil. Making it around to the front of the helicopter where Rory was waiting, she hunched her shoulders, grasped his hand for assurance and glanced around, "Now what?"

"We left the Jaguar in the parking lot in front of the airport, remember?"

Jane nodded, "Yeah."

"Then let's go. If someone saw us landing here, we should be able to get there before airport security comes out here to investigate," Rory said as he headed for the trees, pulling her by the hand. Moving across the soft ground and the tomato plants, they made their way into the stand of trees. In a few moments, they emerged on the other side between two large pine trees. A highway was just ahead. Then there was a stretch of open farmland and then Airport Road running along the airport in the distance. A road off to the left connected the two.

Rory hesitated for a minute, they would be out in the open but they had little choice.

Two cars passed by as they stood there. Neither slowed.

Jane pressed herself against him as she watched the cars fade into the distance, "Are we going or...?"

Finally nodding, Rory said, "Yeah, we're going. But we'll have to run. Is that okay?"

"Are you willing to carry me?"

Rory raised an eyebrow.

Jane squeezed his hand, her voice shaky, "I'm just kidding. Let's go."

Rory squeezed her hand back and then he guided her out to the edge of the highway. With no cars in sight, they ran across to the other side and headed left. They were out in the open now, the sun beating down on them as they ran along the side of the highway. Within a few minutes, they reached the connecting road. Their feet crunching hard on the gravel shoulder, they ran for Airport Road.

Jane stumbled a few times as she tried to look behind her, watching for any signs of trouble.

Within ten minutes, their breath raspy and heavy they crossed Airport Road and were running up the front entrance road to the airport parking lot.

Jane stumbled a couple more times as fear tensed her muscles but Rory kept her upright and moving.

Finally reaching the concrete parking lot, they ran hard for the parked Jaguar sitting in the middle.

Rory pulled the keys out of his pocket and clicked open the doors as they approached it. Both of them had little breath and energy left as Rory was put the Jaguar in gear headed for the exit. He crossed Airport Road without stopping and heading for the road that would take them back to Highway 403.

"What are we going to do now?" Jane asked. Her breathing was still heavy.

Rory didn't answer. He really didn't have an answer.

"Do you really think that place we saw back there, where the jet buzzed us, was where I escaped from?"

Rory preferred not to answer because he was still trying to figure it out himself.

"What do they do there? Do you know? And *why* would they hold me there?"

Rory remained silent, thinking as he leaned over and worked the GPS, looking for the closest gas stations.

"Rory?"

"I really don't have any answers. But I'm going to try and get you some."

"How?"

"Just sit tight."

The GPS found several gas stations that would be just off the next exit. Jane stayed quiet as Rory checked each one out. The first three didn't have what Rory needed. The fourth gas station did; an outside pay phone booth.

"Who are you calling?" Jane asked as they parked beside the phone booth.

"A friend," Rory said as he got out. "I'll explain more later."

Five minutes later he was back in the car. "My friend will meet us at the Sheraton Hamilton Hotel in downtown Hamilton. We can take a room there and rest. It's also attached to a large mall and we can pick up some items. And hopefully, we both can get some answers for you as well."

Chapter 26

SHERATON HAMILTON HOTEL, Hamilton, Ontario, Canada

"**RORY YOU NEED** to see what's on television," Jane yelled from the living room.

Rory finished buttoning his shirt as he walked out of the bathroom after a hot shower. He had hoped it would relax him but it wasn't working very well. "What is it?"

Jane was standing up in the living room and simply pointed to the television, "A news report is coming up."

"What is it –?"

CBC NEWS FLASH

"Canadians were shaken today with the report of a second violent terrorist attack on Canadian soil. Victory Hospital in London, Ontario was attacked earlier today by submachine gun-wielding terrorist who killed 37 people and wounded 83 others. Four of the wounded are in critical condition. Eyewitness accounts report the terrorists wore body armor and black ski masks and used weapons identified by police sources as .45 caliber weapons, possibly Heckler & Koch UMP45 submachine guns.

This is reportedly the same weapon that was used in yesterday's terrorist attack at Hamilton University Hospital on the campus of Hamilton University. Forty-four people were killed in that attack and sixty-eight others were wounded, many severely. The word Jihad was spray painted on several walls in both hospitals. Authorities are not saying much but they do say the attack was designed to maximize the severity and length of the psychological impact on the everyday population–"

RORY PICKED UP THE television remote control and turned the television off.

"Why would they talk about it being a terrorist attack? Is that who was really after me, terrorists?"

Rory put the remote down and shook his head, "No. I don't think so. I saw them putting that word on the wall at the first attack but that was just a ruse. The news report didn't mention anything about you. Either because the authorities don't know about you and why the attack took place...or it's a cover-up."

Tears formed in her eyes, "Even I know a cover-up is not good–"

"It doesn't change a thing," Rory said calmly. "We're going to be meeting someone shortly who can give us some information and maybe help us out. We just have to be more cautious from now on. We *are* going to figure this thing out, all right?"

Jane nodded but she didn't look too convinced.

Actually, Rory wasn't really convinced himself. It definitely did look like a cover-up. And with the military aspect surrounding that compound, the cover-up may just involve the highest authorities in the military. Maybe even the government. But if that was the case, the question was why?

Rory realized Jane was looking at him. He had been spaced out in his thoughts and that had scared her. He took one of her hands and squeezed it as he led her across the room, "Don't worry about any of it right now. I want you to go into the bathroom and get ready. I want to see this new outfit and the cute shoes you told me that you got in the mall."

Jane blinked her eyes a few times, looking directly into his silver-blue ones. Then she gave him a half smile, trying to be brave and then headed into the bathroom.

Rory sat heavily in a chair and let out his breath, shaking his head.

RORY ESCORTED JANE Doe into Chagall's Restaurant in the Sheraton Hamilton Hotel. Glasses clinked and the smell of burgers, fries, salads, and desserts greeted them. Several of the men did a double-take when they saw her. Dressed in her new yellow outfit, the cute yellow shoes, and a new blonde wig - Jane had also used a stencil to paint a set of eyebrows to go along with the makeup she had picked up - and she looked stunning.

Rory watched the men for a moment, concerned it was another attack team who had been waiting for them to show up. After the other attacks, there was no way of knowing if they had tracked them here as well. It was a tense few moments. But when it appeared to be just men looking at a beautiful woman, he turned his attention to the rest of the people in the restaurant, looking for the man they had come to meet. Rory finally saw him.

The man had chosen a secluded table at the far end of the restaurant, near the back exit. Roy led Jane to the table and greeted the man as they approached, "Hey, Kal."

Kal.looked up and smiled, then pushed his chair back, stood up and embraced Rory, slapping him on the back several times. "Rory! It's been a long time bro, good to see you again."

When Kal man released him, Rory turned and made the introductions, "Kal, this is Jane, the one I told you about. Jane, this is Kal Maza. We served together in the military a long time ago."

Kal Maza had a military-style buzz cut, a two-day growth of black stubble and flashed an easy, lop-sided grin as he reached over and shook Jane's hand, "How could someone so beautiful have such bad taste in men?"

Jane looked at Rory for a moment, her eyebrows knitting together.

Rory just smiled.

Then Jane looked back at Kal, a playful grin caressing in her lips, "Actually, Mr. Maza, I have amnesia. I really have no idea what a good man looks like."

"Call me Kal," he said as he laughed. "And that explains it."

Rory shook his head in amusement, especially with the fact Jane looked so pleased with her ability to joke. "Did you bring the things I needed?" he asked Kal.

Kal nodded and he pointed to a duffel bag sitting on the floor beside his chair, "Yeah. Everything you asked for."

Rory lowered his voice, "I didn't say this on the phone but I also need some information. Sensitive information, I'm afraid."

Kal nodded as he pursed his lips and then gestured for Rory and Jane to sit across from him, "Why don't we have lunch and we can talk."

As they sat down, a young server appeared and took their order for drinks.

When the server left, Kal looked directly at Rory, "So, what do you need bro?"

Rory hesitated for a moment. He looked at Jane and then started to talk in a low voice, "There's a compound down in the Nanticoke area that I need to know about Kal. It looks military–"

"It's not," Kal replied quickly.

Rory was surprised. He hadn't expected that answer...and especially so fast.

Kal looked intensely at Rory for a moment, "Why do you need to know about that compound?"

Rory considered his friend for a moment. "Look. If it's a problem Kal, I can walk away right now–"

"I just need to know why bro," Kal said. "The things going on down there are highly classified and–"

"I'm pretty sure she was being held prisoner there," Rory said.

"Held prisoner? Are you sure?"

"Like I said, *pretty sure*. It looks like she escaped by climbing over the razor wire around the compound. If you saw the blood...."

Jane put her hands between her knees, her eyelashes fluttering at the memory of it but she sat there quietly

Kal just looked at Jane for a few moments. Nothing on his features indicated what he was thinking.

The server came back with their drinks and set them down around the silent table. "Are you ready to order??

Rory glanced at Jane and then Kal before saying, "Could you give us a few more minutes?"

"Of course. I'll come back in a few minutes."

Kal was still deep in thought as the server left. He looked at Jane one more time and then addressed Rory, his low voice, "Why would they keep her prisoner there? That doesn't make any sense."

Rory decided to open up a little more, "You heard the news reports about the shootings at the two hospitals?"

Kal nodded, "Here and in London. Attributed to terrorist cells acting out their jihad idiocies–"

"It was set up by the attackers to make it *look* like a Jihadi terrorist act," Rory stated firmly. "They *deliberately* left behind misleading evidence."

"Are you sure?" Kal asked, a little skeptical.

Rory nodded his head firmly in confirmation, "We were there, Kal."

"You were?"

Rory nodded, "I saw the attackers myself. I saw one of them paint jihad on the wall in Hamilton."

Confusion registered on Kal's face, "But how do you know it was fake?"

"They were actually after Jane," Rory stated.

Kal looked at Jane in surprise and then back at Rory, "Are you sure?"

"I actually heard them say they had eyes on her, Kal. They had Liberator III Secure Dual-com tactical headsets. Those are high-grade systems used by law enforcement, personal security teams and...."

Nodding, Kal added, "And by the military and for-hire mercenaries."

"Exactly."

Kal took a breath and let it out slowly, considering the information. Then he glanced at Jane, "But why would they...?"

"We went to Hamilton University Hospital to try and get some answers on the reasons for her amnesia. The doctor helping us there did tests, including a CAT scan. It showed something implanted inside her head," Rory explained. "The doctors had no concrete idea on what it was."

Kal looked at Jane, his eyes scanning her blonde hair, thinking.

A self-conscious smile flickered on Jane's lips as she sat there, the object of their discussion.

"I saw the attackers asking *specifically* about that scan, Kal," Rory added. "Whatever is in her head, it's important enough that the attackers killed everyone involved with the examination and the scan itself. And I have good reason to believe that the attackers are associated with that compound somehow. And they want Jane back for some unknown reason. I'm hoping we can find out why and how to help her recover her memory."

Kal sat back, considering what Rory had said. He looked down at the table, drumming his fingers and thinking.

Rory glanced at Jane and gave her an assuring nod.

Jane glanced at Kal, not looking too confident that they would get any help here. She squeezed her hands tighter between her knees.

The server came back and each ordered a sandwich, coleslaw, and fries.

They ate in silence for a few moments until Kal spoke, "Have you heard about Echelon?"

Chapter 27

"**ECHELON?**" Rory shook his head slowly and then looked at Jane.

"Don't look at me, I can't remember a damn thing," Jane said as she shrugged.

Kal smiled at her pluckiness despite her situation, "Echelon is a SIGINT program, foreign signals intelligence."

"Sig-nit? What does that mean exactly?" Jane asked him.

"SIG...INT," Rory said. "It's the first three letters of each word...*signals intelligence.* It refers to intelligence gathering through the interception of signals, the communications between two or more parties."

Kal nodded affirmation, "In this case, it involves intercepting all types of electronic communications. Echelon is a global program, supposedly started way back in the 60s when the Cold War was still going on between the United States and the United Kingdom on our side and the Soviet Union and their allies on the other side. These days it's also referred to as Five Eyes –"

"Did you say Five Eyes?" Jane asked as she leaned in. "That's a strange name."

Kal nodded, "Spooks love their weird names–"

"Spooks?" Jane shook her head softly.

"That's what they call anyone in the government involved in spying or espionage, that sort of thing," Rory explained.

Jane nodded her head in understanding, "Oh. Okay."

"Five Eyes is an alliance of intelligence operations that includes five nations," Kal continued. He held up a hand and ticked a name off each finger, "The United States, the United Kingdom, Australia, Canada and New Zealand. Other countries such as West Germany, the Philippines, and several Scandinavian countries are involved as third parties but those are the five main players. They share their information, their top secrets, through a network operated by the United States' Defense Intelligence Agency called Stone Ghost."

"That's one I'm familiar with from my military days," Rory said with a nod.

"Echelon is their worldwide intelligence gathering system and analysis network. The capabilities they have today are far beyond the cold war days. They can now intercept and examine the content of satellite signals, telephone calls, Internet traffic, faxes, and e-mails –"

"Faxes?" Jane asked as her eyes opened wide. She looked at Rory. "Maybe that's how they knew where to find us?"

Rory nodded and cursed, "I thought I was being so smart going old school with a fax message. I never even thought about them having that capability."

Kal didn't say anything.

"So how does that compound down in the Nanticoke area fit in?" Rory asked him after a few minutes of reflection.

Kal took a discrete look around before he continued talking, "In very simple terms, Echelon consists of monitoring stations around the world. The older compounds had equipment that could intercept signals from geostationary communication satellites and the like. They were upgraded as we created more advanced systems. But these days most communications are through fiber-optic cables. 90% of all worldwide communications are not in the air where we can snag them, like the old days. So the newer compounds are being set up in places where they can intercept all kinds of signals. The compound down in Nanticoke is the newest setup. A central hub for fiber-optic cables and Internet traffic has been secretly created underground down there. With the combination of equipment they have installed, the Nanticoke compound can handle the older style of communications as well as the new. It's actually the main hub for Stellar Wind."

"Stellar Wind? I've really been out of the loop," Rory said as he shook his head.

"The National Security Agency in the United States started the operation after 9/11," Kal explained. "Bush put it into operation under the Patriot Act. It's all about collecting mountains of information through the data mining of every type of communication we engage in around the world today. A lot of people talk about the biggest spy center being down in Utah. But nobody talks about the one in Nanticoke. It's bigger and more powerful."

"But you say it's not military?"

"Oh, they're behind it. Make no mistake about that," Kal said with assurance. "But the National Security Agency jackasses in the U.S. decided to outsource intelligence gathering to supplement its own pool of supercomputers that they use to do the job."

"They're outsourcing intelligence gathering!" Rory said in amazement.

"The claim it's more cost-effective," Kal said with disdain. "Of course, a lot of members of Congress are in the deep pockets of some businesses in the data mining and intelligence fields that saw a real opportunity. Billions of dollars worth of opportunity. The military oversees the outsourced operations, make no mistake about that. In this case, it's a joint Canadian and U.S. cooperation, but private enterprise runs it."

"But why in Canada?"

"It's all part of a much larger plan set in place by the Five Eyes countries," Kal stated. "With all the terrorism problems happening around the world, there was a need to upgrade the whole Echelon network. Canada began their part of the plan by establishing CSEC."

"CSEC? What's that?" Jane asked.

"The Communications Security Establishment Canada," Kal explained. "They are the Canadian SIGINT force and work closely with their counterparts in other countries, like the U.K. Government Communications Headquarters and the U.S. National Security Agency. We had a small operational signal intelligence collection station at Canadian Forces Station Leitrim. But we needed to get bigger and better like the Americans did with their new National Cybersecurity Initiative Data Center in Utah. The United Kingdom is working on their new site as well. Australia and New Zealand have older systems but new ones are in the planning stages."

"And that's where this Nanticoke compound comes in," Rory reasoned.

"Exactly," Kal confirmed. "And consider this. The way Echelon is set up now, the government of each member country can state categorically that they do *not* monitor their own citizens.

They only monitor foreigners. It keeps the journalistic watchdogs appeased when the issue of privacy arises. And the truth is, under this arrangement, the United States, which is the biggest user of the Intel, doesn't have to monitor American citizens. They can let their partners do that."

Rory nodded his head in understanding, "Sweet. Canada doesn't monitor Canadian citizens. We only monitor foreign citizens...which just happens to include Americans, Australians...."

"You got it, bro. Between every member of Five Eyes, they can monitor every single person on the globe and share the data."

"Okay. But why not just expand CFS Leitrim? It's close to Ottawa and Parliament Hill and the usual government oversight. Why put up a new one all the way down in the Nanticoke area?"

That made Kal smile and shake his head, "C'mon bro, think about it. Along with political oversight, which they don't really want, it would also be closer to public scrutiny through the constant media attention focusing on everything governmental up there. Some reporter would always be nosing around. This way, the Nanticoke compound is out of the way in the middle of farm and tourist country."

Rory nodded his head, acknowledging his brief naïveté.

Now Kal leaned a little closer, "But there are other reasons for placing it down there. The old electrical generating station, mothballed by the provincial government to reduce greenhouse gasses, it's actually part of the overall compound structure. The company behind this whole thing leased the station for a pretty penny. They're supposed to turn it into a biomass generating station eventually but right now they've installed expensive coal-scrubbing technology to eliminate 97% of a coal-fired power plant's sulfur dioxide emissions to appease the environmentalists."

Rory nodded, "I saw a freighter delivering coal like the old days. Buy why would they need all that power?"

"The generating station supplies the massive amount of electricity needed to run the super computers in the compound. And they're able to pull water directly out of Lake Erie through an underground piping system to cool those same computers that run 24 hours a day, seven days a week sifting through the world's communications. It's a unique, self-contained operation."

Rory shook his head as he did some thinking, "The whole thing would require a massive amount of money to set up and run. Who's the private company running the compound?"

"A company call IntelliMax International," Kal told him. "They originally provided business intelligence to private enterprises and corporations. But they saw where the real money was and moved into the private intelligence field. The CEO is a man by the name of Maxwell Brecc."

Chapter 28

RORY WHEELED THE JAGUAR in and out of the heavy traffic, in a hurry to get to their next destination.

Jane sat quietly in her seat for a long time before asking a question, the concern in her voice very evident, "But...how do we know those men won't find us at this hospital too?"

Rory opened his mouth and then closed it. A moment later he spoke, honestly, "We don't. But we can't sit in a hotel room, hiding forever." A moment later he glanced at Jane, "Or would you prefer that? It's really your decision and I guess I should have asked that before...."

Jane took a deep breath and shook her head, "No. I can't just sit around. All I do is wonder who I am, if I have children, a family...." He voice faded away and she stared out the side window.

Twenty minutes, later Rory pulled the Jaguar to the curb beside Hamilton East General Hospital. He put the car in park and turned the engine off, then looked at Jane, "There's still time to change your mind. Kal set up this appointment through secure channels with a military doctor he says we can trust. We just have to trust the secure channel *is* secure from these guys."

Jane nodded, "I understand." She glanced at the brick building, "So he works here?"

No. But the doctor does have contacts here that will let him do a CT scan off the books. He's done medical work before for undercover operations so this isn't new for him. We're coming here as Mr. and Mrs. Cooper. We'll pay cash to him and he'll reimburse the hospital. If the military is involved with that compound as Kal says, I'm hoping a military doctor can figure out what's in your head and cure your amnesia. But if you still don't feel safe...."

Jane looked nervously at the people walking by on the sidewalk. She was obviously having an internal struggle. "I don't know what's worse...being afraid every time I have to walk into a hospital now... or staying like this and not knowing who I am." She looked at Rory with tears in her eyes, "I guess...there are worse things than dying. Although it's easier saying it than doing it." She opened her door and got out.

Rory got out and joined her on the sidewalk, looking both ways for any potential trouble. People were walking back and forth and nothing caught his attention.

Jane reached out and took his hand for comfort.

Rory could feel her trembling. He squeezed her hand in assurance and they walked down the street to the front entrance and went inside. The lady at the information desk directed them down the hallway to the far end of the hospital. Rory was constantly on alert. There weren't as many people here as at the last hospital but Rory cautiously watched every person they passed. Anyone could be a potential threat. Every doorway they passed could hold men in ski masks with submachine guns, ready to jump out. They finally reached their destination without incident. Over top of a door on the right was a sign that read 'MRI - CT Scans - PET Scans'.

Jane squeezed his hand harder as they stepped inside.

It was a small, light green waiting room with a receptionist behind a sliding glass window on the right.

"Yes, can I help you?" asked the young lady as she slid open the glass.

"Yes, I'd like to see–" Rory almost asked for Colonel Tomlinson but caught himself, "Dr. Sparks."

"Your name?"

"Mr. and Mrs. Cooper."

"One moment. Have a seat please." She slid the window closed and turned in her chair to a phone.

Rory and Jane sat side-by-side in a couple of old wooden chairs. Jane refused to let his hand go. A few minutes later a door opened on the left-hand side and a tall man with a gray buzz cut entered the waiting room, "Mr. Cooper and Mrs. Cooper?"

Rory and Jane stood up, Jane still holding his left hand tightly.

"This way please," Tomlinson said as he disappeared back through the door.

Rory let Jane go through the open doorway, still on guard. He pulled the door shut behind them.

Tomlinson was already down a hallway, waiting for them outside another open doorway. As they approached, he motioned with his hand for them to go inside.

Rory and Jane walked into a room filled with medical equipment, including a large CT scanner.

Tomlinson pulled the door shut behind them. "Kal told me this was a sensitive matter so I didn't want to say anything out there. I'm Dr. Marvin Tomlinson," he said as he held out his hand to Rory.

Rory shook his hand, "My name is Rory Mack Steele. And this is Jane."

"Nice to meet you," the doctor said as he shook her hand. "Now, why don't you fill me in on what is happening. All Kal said was that you needed a CT scan as soon as possible."

Rory looked at Jane, then addressed the doctor, "Before we start, I think it's a good idea to let you know how dangerous this is. Those terrorist shootings at the two hospitals that were on the news were actually attempts to kidnap Jane here."

Tomlinson's eyebrows raised in surprise.

"And the last two doctors who tried to help us were killed in the attacks. The attackers seem to be able to find us and they could be here at any minute—"

"I'm in the Army. I've been shot at before," Tomlinson said.

"I understand that. But one of the shooters at the hospital was very interested in her CT scan, so if we do another one here—"

"I appreciate your candor but it doesn't change anything. I have an oath to help the sick, no matter what. Now why would they want to kidnap her? And what does this have to do with the CT scans that were done?"

"Unfortunately, those are questions, I can't answer. I have no idea," Rory said. He looked at Jane, "What I can tell you is, when she showed up at my place, she had already been held as a prisoner."

"Where?"

"My best guess is the new SIGINT compound set up down in Nanticoke," Rory added.

Tomlinson raised an eyebrow.

"But it's only a guess because...she has amnesia...and...the strange thing is...she's had every hair on her body shaved off."

Jane Doe reached up and removed her blonde wig.

Tomlinson blinked in surprise.

Jane stepped up to him, turned around and ran her fingers along the general area of the scars at the back of her head, "Apparently, I also have scars back there from some operation or...I can't really feel them but...."

Looking closely, Tomlinson ran his own fingers along the scar lines. "Yes, I see them. Why don't you sit in this chair, so I can take a closer look?"

Jane placed the blonde wig on a counter and sat down.

Tomlinson pulled over a stool and sat down behind her, running his fingers over the fine lines on the back of her head.

Rory took a step and indicated how the scars went up over her head.

His eyebrows knitting together, Tomlinson sat up straighter, examining everything in detail.

Taking a step back, Rory said, "She can't answer the question why she has the scars. She can't remember an operation or an accident. And she has no idea why her entire body is shaved either."

Tomlinson nodded. After a few moments of examination, he turned and walked over to the CT scanner and flipped a switch, "Okay, why don't we get started. I presume you know how this works, Jane?"

Jane nodded and walked over to the motorized table and lay down on her back, folding her hands nervously over her tummy. Tomlinson pushed buttons and she slowly moved through the circular opening into the huge CT imaging system.

Rory and Dr. Tomlinson went into the side room to work the CT imaging system. They both watched the large LCD screen in front of them as the image data began to build.

Rory knew what to expect.

Tomlinson did not. He sat up straighter as the 3D image slowly revealed the black, nearly transparent, fabric-like material that flowed across the top of Jane's brain.

Rory leaned forward, still fascinated at how the material conformed itself perfectly to the convolutions of Jane's brain. "I heard the doctors using the term graphene when they looked at that thing," Rory said in hushed tones to the doctor.

Nodding, Tomlinson stared at the image, "I've heard of it. You know the military, they'll experiment with anything."

Both men watched as the countless numbers of thin, silvery nano-wires appeared on the image.

"They go right down into her brain matter," Tomlinson whispered to himself.

Rory nodded, "The doctors referred to it as a possible BCI–"

"A brain-computer interface?"

"Yeah."

Tomlinson nodded after a moment, "Yeah, that makes sense."

"But you looked at her head, doc. There are no physical means of connection. And they said they couldn't detect any signals–"

"Doesn't mean they're not there."

Rory looked at the 3D scan, rubbing his chin with his hand, "A wireless connection would make sense."

Tomlinson nodded, "Everything is going wireless these days."

"So they could communicate with that thing through satellite?"

"It's possible," Tomlinson agreed. "Maybe even through the Internet."

"But like I said, the doctors didn't detect any signals."

"And like I said, that doesn't mean they're not there. Wi-Fi networks operate on two standard frequencies, 2.4 and 5 GHz. This thing might use something else. And it's possible it's just lying dormant, waiting for the right frequency to trigger it and make it active."

Rory looked at the 3D image, wondering what Jane had gotten herself into. And whether they were about to be under attack again at any moment.

Chapter 29

TOMLINSON DID A COMPLETE battery of tests on Jane and then asked for some time to go over everything. Four hours later, he joined Rory and Jane in the hospital cafeteria at an out-of-the-way table. He was carrying a thick folder containing the printouts from all the tests he had done beyond the CT scan. He asked Jane to sit next to Rory and then he sat down across from them.

"So what do you think, Doc?" Rory asked him.

Tomlinson stayed silent as he moved a few plates away from the center of the table and set the thick folder down.

Jane exchanged a nervous glance with Rory.

Flipping open the thick folder, Tomlinson pulled out a few sheets of paper and laid them out on the table for the three of them to look at. He handed another sheet of paper over to Rory and Jane.

Rory took the paper and looked at it while Jane leaned against him, looking over the paper herself.

"This looks like a toxicology screen," Rory said.

"Correct," Tomlinson said. "I'll cut right to the chase. I found evidence of some type of benzodiazepine in your system, Jane."

Jane looked scared at the mention of a drug.

"What exactly is that?" Rory asked.

"A benzodiazepine is a psychoactive drug with a core chemical structure of a benzene ring and a diazepam ring. That basic structure can be further manipulated to enhance specific properties."

"What's it used for," Rory asked.

"Doctors can use this family of drugs in treating anxiety, insomnia, alcohol withdrawal–"

Jane interrupted anxiously, "Insomnia? So it can make someone drowsy or put them to sleep?"

Tomlinson's eyebrows knit together and he nodded, "Yes. In those cases it's used as a hypnotic, a sleep-inducing drug to help insomniacs There are other types used as a surgical anesthesia, but you don't wake up feeling refreshed with those–"

"That's probably why I felt like crap," Jane said to herself.

Cocking his head, Tomlinson looked at Jane for a moment and then added, "However it was used on you, it was done a high number of times–"

Jane looked up at Tomlinson, "How would you know that?"

"Because it appears to me that your body has developed a tolerance to the drug."

Rory looked at Jane, "That must be how you were able to escape. They weren't giving you enough of the drug."

Jane nodded as her eyes shifted back and forth, thinking over what she was hearing.

Rory turned his attention back to the papers on the table and picked up a long printout.

"That's her brain-wave readout," Tomlinson said.

"Do you see anything significant?" Rory asked.

Tomlinson shook his head, "No. Nothing that stands out. Everything is within normal parameters. And I couldn't detect any signals coming from that device in your head, Jane. I tried different methods to detect something, but appears to be dormant–"

"But what is it?" Jane interrupted roughly as she shot forward in her chair.

Rory patted her hand gently to calm her down.

Jane sat back, "I'm sorry. I'm just so frustrated. I can't remember anything and I need to know what's going on."

Dr. Tomlinson nodded his head sympathetically, "I can understand your frustration. I wish I could give you a better answer. All I can say is the device in your head *appears* to be what the other doctors surmised, a brain-computer interface–"

Jane interrupted angrily, sitting higher in her seat, "Appears? So, after all this, you really *don't* know anything more than the other doctors did–"

Rory put his hand on hers again.

Jane gave Rory a sharp look. Then she visibly sank a little lower in her chair, trying to calm herself as she closed her eyes and rolled her shoulders to relieve the tension. "Sorry," she said to Tomlinson,

Tomlinson nodded, "I understand perfectly."

Rory addressed Tomlinson, "Okay, let's go with a brain-computer interface theory. What would they be trying to do with that type of device?"

Tomlinson shook his head slightly, "I really have no idea. A device like that could cover a wide range of applications. I've been in the military long enough to have seen all types of experiments attempted to create better soldiers or spies. And I've been privy to see paperwork on past experiments that made me shudder at some of the experiments set up and attempted over the years. But truthfully, I've never really seen anything that looks like what you have."

"Fair enough," Rory said. "Any guesses?"

Tomlinson stared at the table for a few seconds before he continued, "The latest applications I've seen tried had to do with trying to use a brain-computer interface to run something external to the brain. It's actually termed MMI for a mind-machine interface. In one case the doctors had a fifty-eight-year-old woman, who was a quadriplegic, hooked to a computer through her skull. Using the power of her mind through the computer connection, she was able to guide a mechanical hand to grab a container of coffee with a lid and straw and to lift it to her lips."

Rory nodded as he ran a hand through his black hair, "Yeah, I've seen reports on television about that. In the case I saw, they were using a test subject to put a letter on the computer screen. Or to control the mouse–"

"Is that what I am? A test subject?" Jane complained.

Rory grimaced, "Sorry about that."

Tomlinson pushed on, "There haven't been many successes beyond the one I mentioned. But doctors have also tried to use a device like this in the brain for medical reasons. There have been successful experiments where a blind person was helped to see in a limited capacity. The way it works is the light bypasses the damaged eye and is fed directly into the part of the brain that allows a person to see. In either case, it opens up the possibility of controlling artificial limbs or–"

"But I don't have any medical problem like that," Jane said. "Do I?" She looked to Rory for confirmation.

"Nothing that I could see," answered Rory. "And I could see everything."

Jane blushed.

"The only other thing I've seen in cases like this - is mind control."

"Mind control?" Jane pointed to her skull. "Like someone is trying to control me with this thing in my head!"

"It's a possibility. There have been attempts at mind control by the military since the 50s. But I don't know of any attempts that were ever successful," Tomlinson said. "The other possibility would be to use it as a tracker. They could keep a record of every place you go. There have been thoughts about doing that to captured terrorists. Then they let them escape and follow them to find any cell they work with or to thwart future plots. But that thing you have in your head seems to be awfully big for that."

"Is that thing the cause of her amnesia?" Rory asked pointedly.

"Hard to say, but it could be caused by the device or by trauma from implanting the device," Tomlinson explained. "There is some glial scarring. That's scar tissue buildup from the body's reaction to the material inserted in the brain tissue. I also noticed some neuronal cell death—"

"Cell death?" Jane's blue eyes blinked several times rapidly at the word death

Tomlinson grimaced, "Sorry to be so clinical. It's not...."

Rory changed the subject, "How about this, doc? Any idea why they would shave all the hair off her body? Would that be in conjunction with this thing in her head?"

Tomlinson shook his head slowly, "Nothing that I know of."

Jane sat forward, again "Whatever it is, can you take it out?"

Tomlinson made a face, "It would be extremely risky."

"I can't live like this," Jane said in a loud voice as she threw her hands around. "I don't know who I am. I don't know who my loved ones are. I don't know where I come from. Now we're talking about brain scarring and dead cells."

The other people in the cafeteria went quiet and looked over in their direction. Rory put his hand on hers to calm her down, "You're drawing attention to us."

Jane pulled her hand away roughly, "I don't care!" Tears filled her eyes as she crossed her arms over her chest.

Both Rory and Tomlinson stayed quiet, sympathetic to her plight but unable to do anything about it. Rory clenched his jaw in frustration.

Tomlinson spoke up after a few minutes of awkward silence, "The surgical team who did the implant probably had notes on the device and the procedures they had to follow to put it in. If you had those notes, then there is a possibility I could take it out. No promises, Jane. But...."

Rory sat back in his chair, feeling a little defeated, "The problem is, doc, we have no idea *who* did it...or *where* it was done."

After a few moments of awkward silence, Tomlinson gathered up the papers from the center of the table and returned them to the folder. "I'll leave this with you," he said as he placed the folder in the middle of the table. "Without anything to go on, there's not much else I can do. If you can find *any* information on the device, I'd be more than willing to perform an operation. But until then...." Tomlinson stood up.

Rory stood up, shook his hand and thanked him.

Jane just sat there, rocking a little back-and-forth in her chair and looking extremely depressed.

Tomlinson just nodded at Rory. He could understand her anger and frustration.

Rory sat back down as Tomlinson left the cafeteria.

Jane's voice was quiet and far away, "Maybe I'll just walk in front of the car. That should solve everything."

Chapter 30

JANE DOE SAT depressed and silent as Rory drove away from Hamilton East General Hospital. The traffic was heavy and it took nearly a half hour to get through the downtown area.

As they were stopped at a red light, Jane said, "Where are we going now?"

"Oh, so you're going to talk t me now, are you?" Rory asked.

"Sorry. I guess I was just feeling sorry for myself," she said glumly.

Rory glanced over at her. He couldn't do much to cheer her up and his heart went out to her, "I can understand it. I just don't want you to give up, okay? We'll figure it out yet."

Jane gave a couple of half-hearted nods but crossed her arms defensively as if she was afraid to let any more of the world in to hurt her.

Rory cranked the wheel of his Jaguar to the right and stopped at the curb beside a parking meter. "And to answer your question...*this* is where we're going."

Jane looked out the window on her side at a large, four-story, two-tone gray building. The main floor consisted of a wide expanse of glass that ran the entire city block. She read the sign that was displayed on the central pillar, high over the entrance, "The Hamilton Public Library? What are we doing here?"

"What do you think you use the library for?" Rory asked as he opened the door on his side.

"We're going to borrow a book?"

Rory shook his head as he got out, "No. C'mon." Closing the car door, he walked around the back of the vehicle to the trunk.

Jane got out on in her side and walked back to join Rory.

Rory pressed a button on his key fob to open the trunk and reached into the duffel bag Kal had given him back at Chagall's Restaurant in the Sheraton Hamilton Hotel. "Libraries are for more than just borrowing books, young lady," he said as he un-zipped the bag.

Jane crossed her arms, "So what are we here for then?"

Rory pulled out a USB thumb drive, slipped it into his pock-et, zipped the bag back up, closed the trunk and locked the car. "I want to find out what I can on IntelliMax International," Rory explained as he took Jane's elbow.

"That's the company your friend mentioned."

"Exactly."

"Why them?"

"That's the private company running the compound. Re-member?"

Jane nodded as he led her to the front door of the library, "Okay. But...?"

"If we find out about them, maybe we find out about the compound."

"Okay. Makes sense. I guess."

Rory pulled the door open and Jane moved in ahead of him. The place was well lit and had a light, airy feeling to go along with the heady bouquet of old books with an undercurrent of hand sanitizer.

Rory let Jane's elbow go as they approached the young man sitting behind the central reception desk, "Excuse me. Is it possible to use one of the public computers here? I'll pay if –"

"No need for that sir," the young man said. "We have 50 public computers here. Just give me a minute." The young man reached over for a clipboard and flipped through the papers attached to it.

Jane leaned closer to Rory and whispered, "But–"

Rory put a finger to his lips.

Jane held her tongue but didn't look too happy about what he was planning to do.

"Yes, I have a few free," the young man said finally as he stood up. "Just follow me." The young man led them across a wide open area filled with people.

Rory's head was on a swivel as they followed the young man, watching for anyone that might look suspicious. No one seemed to pay the slightest attention to him in return.

Jane's arms were crossed over her chest as they walked. She glanced suspiciously at everyone around them as well but nothing looked out of place.

The young man led them to a dedicated space for one of the public computers. He tapped the keyboard to make sure it was on and the monitor sprang to life. "You can use this," he said. "There's no one scheduled on this location for the next two hours."

Rory thanked him and then sat down behind the keyboard as the young man left.

Jane pulled a chair over quickly and sat next to him. She whispered urgently, "But Rory, are you sure we should be doing this? If those people can spy on the Internet and everything else as your friend said, won't they find us as soon as you enter the company name you're searching for? Those guys found us through a Fax. Isn't that what you said probably happened...?"

Rory pulled the USB thumb drive out of his pocket and held it up to Jane, "Right. But this thumb drive runs TAILS, The Amnesiac Incognito Live System–"

Jane reacted visibly when she heard the name Amnesiac.

Rory passed over the situation without commenting, "It's open-source software that allows anonymous browsing. It will hide the IP address of this computer so they can't monitor or track us. And we won't leave any trace of us on this machine after we're done."

Jane considered the thumb drive for a moment and then looked at Rory, "You're sure?"

"As sure as I can be. We have to take a chance and try something, right?"

Jane chewed on her lower lip for a moment and then nodded reluctantly.

"All the same," Rory added as he looked around at the crowd of people, "keep your eyes open. We can't afford to let our guard down."

That last comment obviously increased Jane's nervousness. She glanced around as Rory plugged the USB drive into one of the ports in the front of the computer tower. A small light flashed on the thumb drive and a moment later the computer began to reboot. The next forty-seven seconds passed like an eternity as Rory and Jane watched their surroundings and then a rudimentary screen appeared as TAILS went to work. Rory used the built-in browser to call up several search engines and began searching the Internet for information on IntelliMax International.

"So what exactly are we looking for?" Jane asked in a quiet voice as she glanced at the computer screen.

"I'm not really sure, to be honest," Rory admitted. He scrolled through the search pages, looking for any single piece of information on the company behind the compound.

Jane continued to nervously watch the people around them while glancing back at each screen of information Rory brought up from time to time.

At one point Rory leaned forward and ran a finger across the computer screen.

"What did you find?" Jane asked as she leaned in closer to Rory

"It looks like the head office for IntelliMax International is in New York...but they have a branch office in Toronto."

"But how does that help us?" Jane asked as she glanced nervously at a young couple walking by.

"Dr. Tomlinson said he might be able to help you if we found any information on that device," Rory explained. "Again, the only possible lead we have is that SIGINT compound in Nanticoke...and that's *if* you were held there...."

"You seem convinced I was," Jane said.

"It's the only place down there near the cottage that seems to fit," Rory answered as he continued searching. "But it's heavily guarded. Breaking in there will be difficult to say the least. And probably extremely dangerous. But...since this IntelliMax International appears to be the company running the compound...."

"Maybe they have the information we need in one of their company offices," Jane said as she finished his thought. She nervously watched two young men walk by and then gave a slight nod, "Okay, that makes sense. But...."

"I know. It's really a long shot. But it's the only lead we have...." His voice trailed off as he read something on the monitor.

"What's wrong?" Jane asked him. Her right knee began to bounce as her nervousness went another notch higher, "Rory?"

"Kal said the place was run by a chief executive officer by the name of Maxwell Brecc. The problem is Mr. Brecc doesn't really seem to exist beyond a few references to his company."

Jane considered that thought for a minute and then she shrugged, "Maybe the guy who knows how to spy on everyone, knows how to hide better than the rest of us."

"Possibly," Rory conceded. "But with the constant outcry about government spying and the invasion of privacy, it's highly unusual for someone like this Brecc to be flying under the radar. There are a lot of activists dedicated to exposing people like Brecc and his type of company. And in an Internet search like this, you would normally find conspiracy theories, comments, blog postings and even Wikipedia pages set up to spread the information about these people. But in this case, there's nothing beyond that one screen of information I found. If they're in business, you would think they would be advertising and letting people know what they can do. But...it's like these people have cleaned up behind themselves...and they're keeping it clean. And that's not an easy thing to do."

Jane's foot began tapping out a rhythm on the floor and her breathing increased.

Rory noticed it. He reached out and gave her hand a squeeze, "Don't worry. Everything will be fine."

Tears formed in Jane's eyes, "I'm scared Rory. And hearing about these people makes me even more scared."

"Everything will be fine."

"But they sound so powerful. If they can do things like you're saying...."

Rory gave her hand another squeeze. There wasn't much he could say to lessen her concern because he felt some of it himself, "Why don't you go to the reception area and see if you can get a pen or a pencil to mark down the address for the office in Toronto."

Jane's voice was shaky as she stood up, "Are...are we going there?"

"I'm not sure what we're going to do yet," Rory said truthfully. "But unless we can come up with something else...."

As Jane went to the reception area, Rory began searching Google maps for views on both the IntelliMax International branch office in Toronto and the compound in Nanticoke. Other than walking away and leaving Jane with amnesia for the rest of her life, these two locations were their only two options. He found something on both but was very surprised to find the aerial view of the compound. Considering its strategic importance to the military, he had to assume they would eventually clean up this vital piece of information. He immediately saved copies of what he had found to the USB drive. He also went back and saved a copy of the page with the small piece of information he had found earlier. That done, he returned to studying both the branch office in Toronto and the compound in Nanticoke. The branch office was the safer choice, he reasoned, but the odds were low that they would find something there to help Jane. The SIG-INT compound in Nanticoke was the more dangerous choice and would have to serve as their last resort. And the irony was not lost on him. Because if they went there, it could very well be the last thing they ever did.

Chapter 31

INTELLIMAX INTERNATIONAL Branch Office, Toronto

RORY AND JANE sat quietly in the Jaguar, looking at the twelve-story, post-modern building across the street. Rory shook his head softly. He had expected to find a single-suite branch office. Instead, a sign across the front indicated the whole thing was the IntelliMax International Building. These people had some serious money behind them. It was 6:30 PM and most of the staff had left. Only a single security guard was left sitting at the security desk in the middle of the lobby. But Rory still had the problem of getting inside.

Jane looked over at him, "Is that security guard going to leave too? He just seems to be sitting there."

"Yeah. And I doubt he'll leave," Rory answered. "This is a pretty secure building. I wasn't expecting it, but I guess it makes sense for a company involved in the spy business to have night security. Even if it's only one man, he'll have an array of cameras and sensors he can watch at that desk. And he'll have quick access to police if he needs backup."

Chewing on her lower lip for a moment as she looked back at the guard and the building, Jane then asked, "So how do we get in then?"

Rory looked over at her, "*We* is not going in, *me* is going in."

Jane raised her painted eyebrows, "First, that is not grammatically correct. And I'm not even sure how I know that. But secondly, I am not staying alone out here. When you go inside, I *will* be glued to your butt."

"It's going to be too dangerous–"

"And how safe do you think I'll be out here alone?" she said strongly. She waved her arms around in anger, "I don't remember who my friends are and I don't remember who the bad guys are. Every time someone walks by the car I have no idea if they're a threat to me or not. Are they a good guy? Are they a bad guy? I have no idea. None."

Rory looked at her, watching the flood of anger and anguish pouring from her.

Jane looked into Rory's silver-blue eyes, "You're the only person I can trust. You're my only friend."

"And I have seen you naked," Rory said after a moment.

"Why do I suddenly wish you were the one with amnesia," Jane complained as she crossed her arms across her chest.

Rory winked.

Jane smiled and hit him on the shoulder with the back of her left hand.

Rory pretended it hurt, rubbing his shoulder. But inside he felt sorry for her. Fighting for your life was one thing. Many of his clients had gone through the traumatic event of running for their life and had survived. But they usually had something to hold onto. They usually had loved ones or friends to live for and to turn to for comfort. Jane had nothing like that. He looked back at the building, "Well, it's all academic anyway. That place is sewn up tighter than a drum. I have no idea how–"

"Can you break into a vehicle?"

Rory was confused by her question. "I'm trying to break into a *building*. Why ask me about a vehicle?"

Jane pointed across the street, to the front of the building next to the one they were casing, "I just saw some men wearing coveralls come out of that building over there. They went to the side door of that van, took off the coveralls and put them inside. Then they disappeared down the street. They're probably going to get something to eat or get a beer or...I don't know but...."

Rory was still confused as he squinted at the gold van she was pointing at. A sign on the side said 'Bert's Bug-A-Boo Fumigators'. He looked back at her like she was crazy. "How does that help–?"

"We could wear their coveralls and bluff our way inside. Unless you have a better idea," she said as she shrugged.

Rory thought she was crazy. Then again.... After a few moments of thinking, he pressed the button to open the trunk for the Jaguar, stepped out into the warm night air, closed his door and walked to the back of the vehicle.

Jane got out and quickly walked to the back of the Jaguar.

The trunk lid was open and Rory was bent over, looking for something in the duffel bag Kal had given him.

Jane leaned over to see what he was doing, "What are you looking for?"

Rory didn't say anything as he slipped a small item into his pocket. Then he straightened up, putting an item into the waistband of his pants under his light jacket.

"What's that –?"

Rory put a finger to his lips as he closed the trunk lid.

A few minutes later Rory and Jane sidled up to the driver's side door of the gold van. "Keep an eye peeled for anyone coming," Rory whispered as he took the item from his waistband.

"What's that?" Jane whispered as she stretched her neck to look.

Rory held it towards her in the palm of his hand, "It's a Jackknife lock picking set. Just keep an eye out for anyone, especially those workers."

Jane nodded as Rory went to work but she was obviously nervous as she looked up and down the street.

Rory slipped the tension tool into the lock and then started working the pick. In less than a minute they heard the van's door lock click open. Rory opened the door and whispered to Jane, "Go around to the other side."

Jane hurried around the front of the vehicle as Rory slipped into the van and pulled the door closed. She pulled on the door handle for the driver side and was surprised when it was still locked. She peered into the van and whispered, "Rory–"

The long side door of the van slid open.

"Oh!" whispered Jane in surprise.

Rory stepped out onto the sidewalk, holding something in his right hand.

Jane stepped beside Rory and peered into the dark van, "You have to teach me that some time."

"As long as you promise not to forget it," Rory said as he handed her a pair of coveralls.

"Very funny," she said as she grabbed the coveralls. "I forgot to laugh."

Rory picked up a second pair of coveralls as he watched Jane put on her pair. She had spunk. Which was good. He didn't want her giving up in despair. Rory slipped his pair of coveralls on and then helped Jane roll up her pant legs and the sleeves a couple of times.

Jane spotted something on the floor of the van. She reached in and pulled out a couple of ball caps with a bug logo. She slipped one on and handed the other to Rory.

Rory reached in and pulled out a red fumigator's kit, handing it to Jane. He picked one out of the van for himself, then slid the side door closed. "Ready?" he asked Jane.

Jane took a deep breath to prepare herself and then nodded her head yes.

Chapter 32

SIDE BY SIDE, Rory and Jane approached the IntelliMax International building. Reaching the large glass doors of the entranceway, Rory pulled on the long handle. It was locked as expected. He pulled and rattled the door a few times to act as if he had expected it to be open. Peering through the glass, Rory saw the guard sitting at the central security desk, watching them. Rory pounded on the glass doors, then waved at the guard to come to the door. It took him three tries before the guard stood up and shook his head like he was being put out.

"He's doing it. He's coming to the door," Jane whispered.

The guard walked to the door like it was a huge chore. He reached up and turned the lock, then opened the door a crack, "What?"

"We've been sent to check out the 2nd floor," Rory said as he tried to pull the door open.

The security guard firmly held his grip and pulled back on the door, "No, no, no, no, no. I don't know nothing about it. And no one comes in here without security clearance and an official pass."

"Didn't our supervisor call you?" Rory asked him.

The security guard shook his head firmly no.

"Are you sure? Maybe you could check your paperwork again," Rory suggested.

"Don't need to," the security guard said firmly.

"Come on man. We're just trying to do our jobs," Rory muttered.

"I told you," the guard said firmly, "*No one* comes in here without security clearance and a pass–"

"Aw please, Conrad," Jane pleaded.

At first, Rory thought she knew the man. Which could be either good or bad. Then he realized she had picked up his name from the guard's name badge on his chest pocket. Clever.

Jane flashed a smile and coyly batted her blonde eyelashes a couple of times. "We've been sent over here at the last minute, Conrad. I'd much rather get it done quickly and be with my girl friends at the local watering hole than here with this big lug."

Rory's eyebrows rose as he watched her work the man.

"You from around here? Me too," Conrad said, now interested in letting them in. He pushed open the door.

"Where do you hang out?" Jane asked as she slipped inside.

Rory slipped in behind her.

"The Little Whistle Pub," Conrad said, He put his thumbs in his belt and puffed his chest out.

"Really? We've been there once but–"

"Look, why don't you two kids continue your date once we finish our work," Rory said grumpily. He stepped past the security guard and turned around. He jerked a thumb over his shoulder as he walked backward, "Okay if we use the elevators, Connie?"

Conrad nodded, a scowl on his face at the use of Connie.

Jane took some quick steps towards the elevator, then turned and walked backward as well for a few steps, wiggling her fingers at Conrad, "I'll see you after."

Conrad nodded once and smiled.

Jane turned and hurried after Rory. She glanced back over her shoulder once.

The guard was walking back to the security desk but he was looking over his shoulder as he did, very obviously checking out Jane's body.

Rolling her eyes, Jane hurried to the elevator. The elevator doors opened as she reached them and she stepped inside and settled at the back of the car.

Rory stepped inside, turned and pressed a floor button, a wry smile on his face, "I guess there are some things you never forget."

"I guess not," Jane said. She wiggled her fingers at the guard again as the elevator doors closed. "But why did you say we had to go to the 2nd floor?"

Rory shrugged as the elevator rose smoothly and quietly, "It seemed like a good idea at the time. I saw people at the windows earlier on the 2nd while we watched the building, so I knew there were offices there. Plus it gets us away from your boyfriend on the 1st."

"Why Mr. Steele, I do believe you're jealous," Jane teased.

"Of old Connie? Fat chance. Hey! And you called me a big lug," Rory complained as the elevator came to a stop.

Jane shrugged, "I just call them as I see them."

The elevator doors slid opened, Rory pressed the button to keep the doors open and he stepped out onto the 2nd floor.

Jane stepped out beside him, "Now what?"

"I have no idea," Rory said. "I was hoping there would be a directory downstairs as we came in, maybe showing us the way to Research and Development or maybe an IT department where we could search the computer files. But there was nothing." He looked up and down the hallway.

Jane looked up and down the hallway as well. Then she looked up at the ceiling, down at the floor and then up and down the hallway again. A moment later she said, "The prototypical office building is a 12 story structure like this one, which looked to have a footprint of 160 feet by 240 feet. Counting the standard basement, you get an average of 500,000 square feet of office space." She pointed to an office door, "With an average office space being 150 square feet, the amount of time it would take to–"

Rory was staring at her.

"What?"

"Where does that come from?" Rory asked as he shook his head slowly in wonder.

Jane thought about it for a moment, then shook her head as well, "I have no idea. I'm not even sure why I said it. But...."

"But what you're trying to tell me is...we have quite a butt load of offices to go through. And no plan on how to do it."

"Yeah, I guess so," Jane agreed.

Chapter 33

RORY SET HIS fumigator kit on the floor, put his hands on his hips and looked down the hallway again, thinking. They had an entire office building to go through and no plan. Then again, even if they had a plan on how to go from office to office–

"Would this Brecc himself have an office here?" Jane asked.

Rory turned and looked at her. He gave a slight shrug, "I have no idea. I imagine he would have a branch manager or someone in charge to run this office."

"So how do we find the office of the person in charge?"

Rory jerked a thumb upwards, "The big-wig guys usually take the penthouse suite." He realized what Jane was suggesting and he nodded his head in agreement, "That's a great idea."

"It is?"

Yeah. You're obviously more than a pretty face."

Jane beamed.

Rory jerked his thumb upwards again, "I would say we head for the top floor."

Jane turned on her heels to head back toward the elevator.

"No. We better take the stairs," Rory countered as he picked up his fumigator kit. "Your boyfriend might see the elevator going up and decide to investigate."

Jane turned back around and followed Rory towards the end of the hallway. "He's not my boyfriend," she complained.

"But you're working on it," Rory said as he stopped in front of the door leading to the stairs.

"Maybe," Jane said as she stopped behind Rory.

Rory unzipped his coveralls, reached inside and pulled something out.

"What's that?" Jane asked as she leaned over to see what Rory had in his hand as he zipped his coveralls back up.

It was a small plastic gun. The handle and main part of the gun were a gray color. The barrel was yellow and there was a long green tube on top of the barrel.

"You're expecting to use a child's toy if someone confronts us?"

Rory grinned proudly and held the toy gun up to show her, "It's one of the things I asked Kal to put in the duffel bag. It's a Super Soaker Xtra Power. I was really good with these when I was a kid."

Jane shook her head, "You're expecting them to laugh themselves to death?"

"Watch o' skeptical one. Kal and I used these on a number of missions." Rory opened the door. Leaning against the door jam, he looked inside the stairwell, scanning high up the wall. He spotted a security camera just above the first turn of stairs. He lifted the toy gun and took careful aim. He pulled the plastic trigger. A stream of black liquid shot upward and coated the camera lens. He looked back at Jane, "Neat, eh?"

Jane shook her head, "You're such a big kid. But I do remember one more thing...only Canadians use 'eh.'"

Rory nodded, "You don't."

Blinking, Jane gave him a half-smile, "Does that mean I'm not Canadian?"

"I'm not sure, but you're making progress." Rory held the super soaker up, "Now let's go." He turned and led her up the stairs.

As she bypassed spots of black paint splattered on the floor, Jane shook her head, "You're taking out the cameras but you're also making a mess."

"We've also discovered you're a clean freak," Rory complained as he climbed the stairs.

"Oh, right. Good," Jane remarked with some delight.

Rory took out each camera as they made their way up the stairwell. They were both breathing hard with the long climb by the time they reached the 12th floor. On the landing, Rory cautiously cracked the door and peered out into the hallway. He placed one foot outside the doorway and looked up. To the left, high on the wall, was a surveillance camera looking down the hallway. Rory leaned out and took care of it with the Super Soaker.

"What if the guard notices all those cameras blacked out?" Jane asked him.

"Since they're all going up the one set of stairs, it should look like the circuit breaker for the stairway tripped," Rory answered. "Hopefully, he'll have to head down to the basement to reset it. But you're right. We don't have much time." He motioned for Jane to follow him and he headed down the hallway for a fancy oak door he had spotted. It was flanked by opaque, etched glass on either side. Reaching it, Rory tried the knob. The door was locked as expected. Rory slipped the Super Soaker into his fumigator bag, then pulled out his lock picking Jackknife.

Jane kept watch, nervously looking up and down the hallway, expecting someone to appear at any moment.

The door lock clicked. Rory stood up, opening the door slowly. There was no one on the other side.

Jane quickly moved past him into the office and Rory followed behind. They found themselves in a fancy reception area. A number of plush chairs lined the walls on both sides. Hanging on the walls were expensive looking pieces of art. A shiny wooden desk with a computer on top was on the far side of the room.

Jane walked quickly across the floor to an impressive oak door just past the desk. She reached for the doorknob.

Rory hustled across the reception area, "Be careful–"

Jane looked back at Rory, "It's locked."

Rory nodded. "Try not to be a bull in a China shop," he said as he knelt and pulled out his lock picking Jackknife again.

"I just want to find something," Jane said in frustration.

The door lock clicked. "I know. But we just got in here, Have patience." Rory stood up and slipped the Jackknife into his pocket, "Let me go first in case –"

"We don't have time," Jane said as she quickly opened the door and went inside.

Rory shook his head and blew out a frustrated breath.

"Wow, this guy must be rich," Jane muttered as she flipped the light on.

Rory stepped into the office behind her, "You do realize someone could see the light on?"

But Jane wasn't listening as she walked around the room, looking at everything.

Rory shook his head in frustration. But as he looked around, he had the same thought as Jane, this was definitely a plush office.

A large, fancy desk on the far side dominated the room. Two high-back chairs were on this side of the desk and a plush, high-back chair was on the far side. More expensive looking art lined the rich redwood paneling of the walls.

Jane was already searching, checking out the bookshelves on either side of the room.

"The spy business must be lucrative," Rory said as he walked over to the desk. He went on the far side, pushed back the chair and sat down. Opening up the middle drawer, he began rifling through the papers he found inside. Finding nothing of importance, he put the papers back in the drawer and pushed it closed. Then he started with the top drawer on the left-hand side of the desk, pulling it open and examining its contents. He closed it and moved his attention down to the second and the third drawers. Still nothing.

Jane finished going through all the books on the shelf to his right and let out a low growl of frustration, obviously angry at not finding a thing. She moved across the room to the bookshelves to Rory's left.

Rory heard her slam a few books back into place after she looked through them. He considered asking her to tone it down but he was afraid it might only get her angrier. And he couldn't blame her. He refocused on his own task and painstakingly went through the drawers on the right side of the desk. But there was little inside them as well. So far, there was nothing that pertained to Jane or the Nanticoke compound. "Now that we're in the building, I'm beginning to think this was a fool's errand. Why I thought some clue would simply be sitting around...." He shook his head as he slowly closed the last drawer, "We may have no choice but to head to the Nanticoke compound for answers. And that's assuming *if* you were held there–"

Jane exploded, "That's all you keep saying. If, if, if, if, if, if, if, if, if! I can't take it anymore." She threw one of the larger books across the room. It landed hard on the floor, breaking apart at the spine. She put her hands to her face and began crying.

Rory calmly walked around the desk and picked the book up, setting it down on the desk. Then he walked over to Jane and put his hands on her shoulders.

"Don't touch me!" she yelled and pulled herself away, standing with her back to Rory.

Rory was left standing there in shock. He didn't know what to say. Or do. After a few moments, he turned back to the desk, pick up the broken book and walked back to the bookshelf. The silence was awkward.

"Do we have any idea how we can get inside the compound?" Jane asked in a low voice. She was wiping her eyes, still standing with her back to Rory.

"Not a clue," was all Rory said in reply as he set the book back into its place.

"Then I guess we better figure out a plan," Jane said. She turned around and looked at Rory as she wiped tears from her cheeks, "If that's okay with you?"

Chapter 34

INTELLIMAX INTERNATIONAL Branch Office, Toronto

BARTLETT FOXEN stood next to the long glass table in the luxurious boardroom. Conrad Blayze and Arlen Frost sat next to each other on one side of the table, looking up at a bank of three television monitors high on the wall on the other side of the room. The monitor on the left flickered to life and the image of Clevon Sharp appeared. A few seconds later, the monitor on the right flickered and the image of Cyrek Stratis appeared.

"Why are we doing a conference call unprepared?" Sharp complained. "Who called this?"

"I did," Foxen said.

Sharp became more irritated, "I have things to do. I don't have time for this—"

"Be quiet," Foxen said sternly.

Sharp straightened his gold, wire-rimmed glasses as he glared through the screen at the Englishman. He had always considered the man beneath him, mere muscle while he and the others were the brains and should be afforded more respect for their contributions to the project.

The center monitor flickered to life and Maxwell Brecc appeared. He looked concerned, "Why the urgency, Mr. Foxen?"

"We've had a breach at the office here, sir," Foxen explained swiftly.

"How is that possible?" Brecc asked, obviously disturbed.

"A security guard allowed two exterminators into the building without security clearance or a proper pass," Foxen explained.

"How in the world did that happen?" Stratis asked angrily. "All the security guards are well-trained and highly paid to ensure loyalty and obedience—"

"One of the exterminators was a woman. The guard obviously let the wrong head do the thinking," Blayze said sarcastically.

"Fire the man!" Stratis said loudly. "There's no place in the organization for incompetence—"

"No need for that," Blayze interjected coldly. "He didn't have a family. And he won't be missed by friends since there is evidence he's taken a job across the country and moved away."

Stratis raised his eyebrows when he realized what Blayze meant. Then he smiled and nodded smugly.

"But that's not the problem," Foxen said as he picked up a small remote control from the table. "Under normal circumstances, we would simply take care of the situation. But I wanted everyone to take a look at the surveillance footage of the two exterminators. It will appear on the left side of your screen." Foxen watched as the three men looked at the left side of their screens and then pressed play on the remote control.

Sharp could be seen squinting as he watched, "Is that...?"

"The woman," Brecc stated firmly.

"Yes sir," Foxen confirmed.

"Is that the same man who has been helping her?" Stratis asked as he watched the footage play.

"I had our analysts go through every piece of the footage using facial recognition software to be sure," Foxen said. "But it *is* the same man with her. Rory Mack Steele."

"What in the world were they doing in our building?" Clevon Sharp asked.

"We're not exactly sure yet," Foxen admitted as he stopped the video feed.

Frost spoke up, "We do know they went up the north stairs, blacking out each surveillance camera with black paint."

"Which means this Steele has military training as we suspected," Blayze said.

Foxen nodded, "After our last meeting I had the technicians do a deep background check on him. It shows Steele served ten years in the Black Watch, a Canadian Army military regiment. The last seven years indicates he was attached to the Canadian Special Forces Operations regiment."

"As I said," Blayze added smugly.

"We acknowledge your brilliance," Clevon Sharp interjected. He ignored Blayze's glare back at him and turned his attention elsewhere. "Mr. Foxen, at our last meeting you said that this man with the woman is a private investigator. So I ask again...*what* were they doing in our building?"

Foxen took a deep breath and looked to Frost.

"It looks like they searched the executive office on the 12th floor," Frost said.

"We found one of the books with a broken spine," Foxen continued as he put his hands behind his back. "It would appear they searched the desk in the interior office and each book in the room."

"How did they know where to go? And what were they looking for?" Stratis asked in a panicky voice.

"We have no idea," Foxen admitted. "But–"

"But the very fact they were there, tells us they're digging deeper," Brecc interjected.

"It appears they're starting to figure things out," Sharp said with alarm.

"And they're *not* running and hiding, as we would expect," Frost added.

Everyone went silent as they considered what the information meant for their operation. Obviously, things were not going as they had planned. It was Maxwell Brecc who broke the silence.

"Steele is trying to help the woman," Brecc said slowly as he nodded his head slightly. "Very chivalrous of Mr. Steele."

"But they seem to know things. What if they start talking?" Sharp asked.

"We'll know if they do," Foxen stated.

"But you didn't know they would be at the building did you?" said a flustered Sharp.

"They wouldn't be the first ones to come forward with this type of story, Mr. Sharp," Brecc said.

Sharp sputtered a few more words in anxiety.

"We'll manipulate things and plant stories so they'll simply look like another couple of conspiracy nuts," Brecc assured him. "But Mr. Sharp is right. They are figuring things out and becoming more cautious in their communications. But the fact that they're not running should help us. Steele is the type of man who won't give up until he figures things out. Until he rescues the damsel in distress. That means he and the woman will come to us eventually, one way or another."

"That's the way we see it," Frost said.

Foxen and Blayze both nodded their heads in agreement.

"But I had another reason to set up this emergency conference call," Foxen said as he took a couple of steps forward. "In my conversations with Mr. Stratis, it has become apparent our special project has become impacted to a dangerous degree."

"Protocols are being changed as we speak," Stratis said quickly. "It could be just the normal changes that take place from time to time. Or it could be that our probing through more conventional methods has been detected. Either way, things are changing faster than we expected. Everything is grinding to a halt. We won't be able to finish anything that was close to completion in time. And the fact is, without our asset, from this point on we can't operate with the same quickness and efficiency as we previously did."

Brecc cursed.

"And we are still having problems delivering the quality material our military and government friends have come to expect," Foxen added.

Stratis leaned forward, "If the military and government agencies decide to work with someone else, we can't cover our special project—"

Maxwell Brecc slammed a fist down on the desk in front of him. "We can't let this continue on. We can't. There is too much at stake."

"I agree," Foxen stated. "Which is why we needed to talk immediately. We need to go with the proverbial plan B."

Brecc looked at Foxen for a brief moment, thinking. Then he nodded, "I agree. Do we have up-to-date dossiers on candidates?"

"We've kept everything up to date," Blayze stated. "We're ready to go."

"Good," Brecc said. "Do it. And make sure every loved one is cleaned up properly behind the operation. And since Steele and the woman should be coming to us, get ready. We need to get out asset back as soon as possible. But if plan B is fully successful, Mr. Foxen, I want you to take both Steele *and* the woman out. Permanently."

Chapter 35

NANTICOKE, ONTARIO

RORY SAT IN the pickup truck he had rented, scanning the compound with the Steiner Military 10x50 LRF laser range finder binoculars Kal had put in the duffel bag for him. He had used the range finder to map out the precise distances between structures and buildings as well as the distances from the perimeter fence to each structure. There was so much open ground cover he doubted he could infiltrate the compound that way very easily. Now he was watching the front entrance, trying to discern a pattern or some way to get past the guards at the gates instead. So far, nothing stood out. Nothing looked promising.

"Do you see a way in yet?" Jane asked. She had been sitting beside Rory in the truck for the last two hours, wringing her hands and fidgeting.

Rory set the binoculars down on the steering wheel and shook his head, "No, not yet. Breaking into an installation like this, run on military discipline and precision, is extremely difficult. It takes a *lot* of patience and planning."

"I'm afraid patience isn't something I have a lot of. Or time," Jane said. "If they catch me again...." It sounded like she was about to cry.

"I know," Rory said in a sympathetic voice.

Jane crossed her arms over her chest to keep herself from fidgeting any further. She clenched her jaw hard in an effort to keep the tears from flowing.

Rory mentally considered what they were up against. The massive one thousand acre compound was built on completely flat ground. In fact, the outside terrain was also flat for miles around. All the trees and shrubs had been stripped away to create a two-hundred-yard perimeter around the outside of the compound. There was no way they could approach the compound unseen, even at night. Rory decided to take a break and see if his brain could come up with a plan. Or maybe simply come up with an idea on what to do next, because a workable plan didn't seem feasible right now. He passed the binoculars over to Jane, "Why don't you put these away and we'll take a break."

Jane hesitated before taking the binoculars. Then she took them and placed them in the case at her feet without a word. But her face showed disappointment.

"Don't worry, we're not giving up. We're just taking a break and we'll be back," Rory said as he put the vehicle in drive.

"I know," replied Jane. But she still looked less than convinced.

Rory did a u-turn on the sparsely traveled roadway and headed away from the compound.

TWENTY-FIVE MINUTES later, Rory and Jane sat across from each other in a side booth inside a small country restaurant.

There was light chatter from the other patrons and the deep rich smell of coffee, burgers, fries, and apple pie floated in the air.

The waitress returned with two plates of fish and chips and set them down, the stoneware plates clinking on the black Formica table top.

Jane picked up a hot French fry from her plate and crunched into it, "Mmmm, it's been a long time since I had a good French fry."

That comment surprised Rory, "Really? You can remember that?"

Jane considered the thought as she put the rest of the fry into her mouth. "Yes and no," she said.

"Yes and no," repeated Rory in amusement.

Their waitress returned to the booth with a bottle of Heinz ketchup and set it down with a clink.

Jane picked up the ketchup bottle and unscrewed the cap, "I don't really remember the last time I had French fries. But I get the feeling it's been a long time. But I remember the taste...and liking the taste and...I don't know. It's just....*there*."

Rory shook his head as he opened a small packet of tartar sauce and poured the contents onto his battered fish, "This amnesia stuff is strange isn't it?"

Jane nodded but she seemed to deflate a little at the actual word, a definite reminder of her mental state.

Rory chastised himself for not thinking. He wasn't really sure what was harder, living with amnesia or being around someone who had it and making the mistake of repeatedly bringing it up thoughtlessly. They sat quietly eating, Rory not really sure what to say. The only good thing seemed to be that Jane was enjoying her meal and she worked away at her plate without a word. His thoughts turned to the compound again as the waitress refilled their coffees after clearing their plates.

"So how do we find a way into the compound?" Jane asked as she sipped her coffee and watched the traffic pass by on the road across the gravel parking lot.

"There's that *we* again," Rory said.

"You're my comfort blanket right now," Jane said with a smile.

Rory didn't say anything.

The smile left Jane's lips, "Look. I know it's dangerous–"

"It isn't just dangerous, it's impossible," Rory said firmly.

"But can't we sneak in together, maybe inside a laundry truck or something?"

Rory couldn't help but smile and shook his head, "No. That's how convicts *escape* a prison in the movies, not how you break *into* a secure facility."

"How about a delivery van?" she countered.

"No. It wouldn't work–"

"How do you know? You haven't tried it," Jane countered in anger.

"Look. No one can get inside without the proper credentials," Rory said firmly. "Any delivery van is going to be on a list. The driver will have to show photo identification. Or maybe they even have to pass an iris scan, which is like a fingerprint, only using your eye–"

"I know what an iris scan is. I can't remember specific things, but I'm not totally dumb. I'm not a dumb blonde," Jane countered defensively.

Rory ignored her comment and pushed on, piling on the evidence for avoiding the compound, "They have guards and surveillance equipment up the wazoo. They probably use facial recognition software on anyone nearing the compound and we would be identified in a heartbeat. The only way we can get in...is if someone lets us in." Rory realized his voice was getting louder and he shut his mouth, sat back and stared out the window.

Jane sat back hard in her chair, looking defeated.

Rory felt sorry for her. But he also realized the impossibility of what she wanted to do. Breaking into the SIGINT facility would take a trained professional. Rory might just be able to do it, but not with her tagging along. But he also knew she wouldn't simply give in and wait it out somewhere.

The bell over the front door to the restaurant jingled and a moment later Jane's eyes take on a startled look. She was looking at something over Rory's shoulder.

"What's wrong?" he asked in a quiet, calm voice without turning. But he didn't feel calm inside.

Jane continued looking over his shoulder as she replied in a low voice, "A bunch of men just came into the restaurant. They're...dressed in black...like we saw in those attacks at the hospitals...."

Chapter 36

RORY SLOWLY SAT FORWARD, slipping his hands onto the table towards a butter knife. As his fingers closed around it, he spoke in a low, calm voice, "Are the men looking this way? Are they coming this way?"

Jane shook her head slightly, "They're...they're just standing there by the front door...looking around...."

"Can you stop looking at them? We don't want to attract their attention," Rory instructed her quietly.

But Jane couldn't look away. "Do you think they're looking for us?" she asked in a low voice as she stared over Rory's shoulder.

Rory reached out and put his left hand on hers to break the spell, "Jane?"

The contact worked. Jane blinked and then lowered her eyes. But her hands were shaking as they lay on top of the table.

Rory got up slightly and bent across to an adjoining table to grab the sugar. As he did, he glanced discreetly to the left.

Six somber-looking men were standing just inside the front door. They were definitely dressed in black garb, similar to their attackers, and they had the presence and demeanor of trained military personnel. The only thing missing were the ski masks and the weapons.

One of the men turned and looked directly at Rory.

Rory didn't see a flash of recognition from the man's eyes.

But the man's gaze was hard as he studied the man reaching for the sugar.

Rory slowly slipped back into his seat. "Is he still looking this way?" he asked as he added a little sugar to his coffee.

Jane glanced up discreetly. "Yes," she whispered. Then her voice got high and squeaky, "Now one of the other men is looking right at *me*-"

"That's okay," Rory said. "Just stay calm. They're just looking at a beautiful woman. And they're envious of me...."

"Yeah, sure. Isn't that called b.s.?" Jane whispered as she continued looking at the men. Her hands were shaking a little harder.

A slight smile crept across Rory's lips, "Yes. Now can you look away?"

But Jane was frozen again as she sat there, shaking and staring over Rory's shoulder.

A waitress passed their table, heading for the front door. "Hi guys," she said cheerfully as she greeted the men. "Are you just going to stand there all day or you going to take a seat?"

"Just looking for you, sweetheart," a deep voice said in reply.

"Yeah, right," the waitress replied with a smirk. "Follow me and I'll give you the best table in the house."

Jane's body sagged with relief as they looked away from her. Her hands are still shaking and she licked her lips, "Oh god, I was so sure...."

Rory reached across and placed a hand on hers again to calm her, "It's okay. Just try to relax." He listened as heavy boot steps moved across the restaurant behind him and towards his left.

The men flirted with the waitress who did the same in return. They were led to a table two rows over from Rory and Jane, where they were seated.

Jane looked nervously in their direction.

Rory put his elbows on the table and held his coffee cup up near his lips. "Try not to look them," instructed Rory again in a quiet voice. He took a sip of coffee.

But Jane continued to have a hard time taking her eyes off the men.

"Jane?"

She swallowed as she finally complied and looked across at Rory. She tried to pick up her coffee cup but her hands were shaking too badly. She set it back on the table.

"It's okay. They haven't recognized us," Rory said gently. "Just try to act normal. We're just hiding in plain sight, right?"

"But what if they *do* recognize us?" Jane asked in a shaky voice. She wrung her hands together, trying to keep them from shaking.

"Just stay calm as best you can," Rory urged her as he took another sip.

Jane reached for her coffee cup again. Her hands shook but she slowly placed her elbows on the table and held the coffee cup near her lips, copying Rory. "I'm so scared," she whispered.

"I know." Rory set his coffee cup down. Then he reached over and took several napkins from the holder. He made a show of setting them on the table in front of him. "Your hands are shaking a lot, Jane. If you spill coffee on your chest, I'll just reach over and wipe it off, okay?"

Jane looked at him for a moment and then a smile played on her lips, "Why, Mr. Steele, are you hoping to cop a feel?"

Rory winked at her.

The small joke definitely was calming her down.

The two of them sat there for a few more minutes, sipping their coffee.

Rory took a glance to his left. The six men were looking at the items on the menu. But Rory noted they still kept an eye on their surroundings as they browsed the menu. They were definitely professionals and well trained. He slowly set his coffee cup down and pulled money out of his pocket. He left more than enough to pay the check. "Let's go," he said.

Jane closed her eyes and steeled herself to move.

Rory rose from his chair and stepped to the side of the table, holding his arm out towards Jane.

Jane rose shakily from her chair and stepped over to Rory, taking his arm.

Rory guiding her towards the door, "You're doing good. Just take it slow and normal. We're just a couple out on a date."

Jane couldn't help herself as they approached the front entrance and she glanced at the men.

"Try not to look at them," Rory whispered urgently as he pulled the front door open for her. The bell overhead jingled.

"Sorry, I can't help it. I think one of them is checking out my butt," she whispered as she passed Rory.

"That's good. I doubt they'll recognize you that way," Rory said as he let the door close behind him.

Neither of them said another word until they got back into the truck.

"Oh, wow," Jane muttered as relief spilled out of her. Her body was shaking again.

Rory knew exactly how she felt. He gripped the steering wheel and looked towards the restaurant.

"Do you think they were with the men who attacked us?" Jane asked him. "Or is the way they were dressed just a coincidence?"

"They had the bearing of men with military or mercenary training," Rory said. "Considering how close we are to that compound, if they weren't part of the attack at either of the two hospitals, I'm sure they're part of the same group that was."

"So what do we do now?" Jane asked quietly. Her right knee was bouncing with anxiety.

Rory didn't answer her but he wondered the same thing. Considering the resources available to the group that was after Jane, they weren't going to be able to stay free much longer. Even if they hid out, the odds were great they would be found fairly quickly. If the compound was monitoring all communications as Kal had said, they would be limited to smoke signals to reach out for help. And that meant they probably had access to the wide range of surveillance cameras in use around the country as well. That made hiding even more difficult since he and Jane would have to eventually use an ATM or a convenience store. And once these men found them again, Rory couldn't keep winning against every military assault designed to recapture Jane. The only answer still seemed to be the same; head to the compound where they would least expect them to be. He made a decision.

Chapter 37

RORY PUT THE TRUCK in gear and pulled back onto the road. But instead of heading towards the compound, he headed in the opposite direction.

Jane crossed her arms and appeared to be holding herself together in the silence of the truck cab. She had noticed they were driving away from the compound and she wasn't happy with the idea.

Rory drove for fifteen minutes before he slowed down and pulled off the road into a large, gravel parking lot. He parked in front of a large building with a sign that read Town & Country Equipment over the entrance. The building and parking lot were surrounded by acres of farm tractors, cultivators, chisel plows, disc harrows, cultipackers, air seeders and manure spreaders along with a lot of other strange farm equipment.

Jane sat up straighter and looked at where they were, "What are we doing here? I thought we would be going back to the compound?"

Rory didn't answer. Turning off the pickup truck, he opened the driver side door.

Jane reached for the handle on her side.

"You stay here," Rory instructed her as he got out. "We can't take any more chances that a local working at the compound could recognize you."

Jane didn't look too happy at being left behind. She crossed her arms over her chest and sat back in a sulk.

Rory closed the driver side door and disappeared inside the building.

As Jane sat there, her sulk turned to fidgeting, apprehension and watching every vehicle coming and going. Every slight noise made her jump. Whenever she heard a vehicle passing by on the highway behind the truck, she was sure those men back at the diner would be coming after. Or maybe it would be another set of men. Dressed in black. Coming for her.

Fifteen minutes later Rory came back out of the store with an older gentleman.

Two teenage boys came hustling out behind them and headed over to the right side of the building, where they disappeared around the corner.

Rory and the older gentleman walked around to the back of the pickup truck and lowered the back tailgate for the rear cargo area.

The gentleman was carrying some type of long straps with aluminum S hooks on each end.

Jane couldn't sit still any longer without knowing what was going on. She got out of the pickup truck and moved towards the back where Rory and the older gentlemen were still talking. Her nose wrinkled at the smell of pig manure coming from an adjacent farm and she put the back of her hand to her nostrils.

The older gentleman laughed lightly, "We call that the smell of money around here, ma'am."

Just then, one of the teenagers came back around the corner, carrying two long pieces of perforated aluminum, one under each arm.

The older gentleman took one of the aluminum pieces from the teenager and leaned one side of the metal against the tailgate. He placed the other end on the ground about six feet away from the pickup bed. The teenager did the same thing with the other piece.

"What are those?" Jane asked as she stepped back a few feet, her feet crunching on the gravel.

"Heavy-duty gauge, portable, aluminum truck ramps," Rory explained as he stepped away from the truck to stand beside Jane.

"What are they for–?" Jane was interrupted as a loud noise came roaring around the side of the building.

The other teenager was grinning like a fiend as he drove a four-wheeled vehicle in a wide circle around the back of everyone. The vehicle looked like a large, open golf cart but there was only one long seat - where the passenger sat behind - instead of two seats side-by-side. As Rory and Jane moved to the side at the urging of the older man, the teenager drove the vehicle to the bottom of the ramps and slowed to a crawl as he gauged where the wheels were.

"What's that?" Jane teenager as she backed up further, a little afraid of the noise.

"A quad bike," Rory explained in a louder voice to be heard over the noise.

"A...quad bike?" Jane said loudly. She was confused at what was happening, "What are we doing with–?"

Rory just put his hands to his lips to quiet her as the teenager rode the quad bike up the ramps and onto the bed of the truck.

The other teenager and the older gentleman quickly picked up the two ramps and slid them in on either side of the quad bike. The teenager turned off the quad bike and tossed the keys down to Rory.

The older gentleman tossed the long straps with the aluminum S hooks up to the teenager who then secured the bike to the side panels on the truck bed. Then he turned and shook hands with Rory, "There you go. You're all set, sir. Thank you for the business."

"You're welcome. Thank you for your service." Rory shook the hand of each teenager who then followed the older gentleman back inside the store. Rory got back into the truck and motioned for Jane to do the same.

Jane got back into her side quickly pulling her door shut. She looked through the back window at the quad bike, "What are we doing with that?"

"Quad bikes like that are used by a lot of farmers around here to run around their fields," Rory explained as he started the pick-up truck. "I thought we could go back to the compound with it. We can use the quad bike to take a look around the back and side perimeters that we can't see from the front road. Since it appears you found some way out, maybe we can find it to get back inside-"

"Really!" Jane was excited and leaned over and gave Rory a big kiss on the cheek.

"Wow. What do I get if we *do* get us inside the compound," Rory said with a big smile.

"If we do get inside and get this thing out of my head, you won't be able to walk for a week!"

Rory looked at Jane in surprise, "Where did *that* come from?"

Jane immediately blushed a deep red.

"I hope you remember that," Rory said as he put the truck into reverse gear.

Jane looked at him with an innocent look on her red face, "Remember what?"

Chapter 38

THE HOT SUN BEAT down as Rory carefully backed the four-wheel quad bike towards the lowered tailgate of the pickup truck. They were parked on the edge of a secluded back road, not far from the compound.

Jane was walking backward, rolling her hand, "Keep it coming. Keep it coming."

The back wheels bumped onto the top of the aluminum ramps with a metal ring.

Taking a quick look at where each wheel was, Jane then yelled over the sound of the bike's motor, "You're okay. You can back up."

Rory drove backward down the aluminum ramps, hit the ground and skidded to a gravel-crunching backward stop on the shoulder of the road.

Jane quickly picked up each aluminum ramp and eagerly tossed them onto the bed of the truck where they landed with a bang. Slamming the tailgate shut, she then ran back to jump on the quad bike and sit behind Rory. As she slipped her hands around his waist, Rory turned the vehicle right and drove down the slight incline, across the shallow ditch and up the other side where he slowly drove into a grassy field.

"Keep your eyes open," Rory yelled over the noise. "And just make sure your hands don't wander."

"I'll try to remember that, but no promises," Jane said loudly in his ear.

"That's all I can ask," Rory said as they began driving towards the trees in the distance.

"Ask what?" Jane yelled as her hands slipped a little slower down his waist.

Rory only shook his head and grinned as he tromped down on the gas.

Jane let out a quick scream and held on tighter.

Laughing, Rory applied more power and in a moment, they were accelerated across the open grass field, grasshoppers jumping out of the way of the hissing wheels. There was no doubt she was happy right now, but Rory had to wonder - what happened if they couldn't find a way in? It wouldn't take much to put her into another deep depression. And he doubted they *would* find a way in.

For her part, Jane hung on tight and she watched the area around them as Rory had asked her. But every so often, she set her eyes in the direction of the compound, determined to get inside and find her memories.

Reaching the tree line, Rory slowed and maneuvered his way in between white pine, ash and elm trees. Dry leaves crumbled under the four wheels of the quad bike as he threaded his way. Birds twittered overhead, offsetting the seriousness of what Rory and Jane were attempting; penetrating a secure facility. After ten minutes of slow, careful driving they reached the far edge of the trees. Rory stopped the quad bike just inside the tree line and idled the engine. Dead ahead was the two hundred yards of open space, separating them from the tall security fence surrounding the compound.

"I haven't seen anyone so far," Jane said.

"No, but keep your eyes open for any movement inside or outside the fence," Rory instructed her. "I'm sure there are surveillance cameras somewhere as well."

Jane tightened her grip around Rory's waist, "I never thought of that. And you didn't bring your squirt gun."

Rory didn't say anything in reply as he surveyed the perimeter along the fence line. After a few moments, Rory slowly drove into the open and turned right, following the tree line on the right and the security fence far on the left. The same open space went on for acres. At one point, the trees on the right disappeared, to be replaced by an open grass field with scrubby bushes dotting the landscape. Rory drove on for another few minutes, then turned the quad bike to the left, towards the fence. Taking them a hundred yards closer to the fence, he stopped and idled the quad bike. He reached down and picked up the binoculars, peering through them. He checked back and forth along the fence line.

"Why did you drive closer? Do you see a way in?" Jane sounded excited.

Rory didn't say anything for a minute, then he lowered the binoculars. "Unfortunately, no." He hated to disappoint her but he didn't want to raise any false hopes either. Rory pointed high up on the fence, "Do you see that wire running horizontally, just a few feet below the top of the razor wire?"

Jane shaded her eyes against the sun as she looked ahead over Rory's shoulder and nodded.

"And then another one running a few feet lower? And then another down lower?" he added.

Jane nodded as she looked at where Rory was pointing, "What are they?"

"That's part of an intrusion detection system. It sends a signal to a monitoring center when someone comes close to the fence, let alone try to climb it," Rory explained. "And do you see those square boxes on top of the vertical posts? See there and there," he said as he pointed at various locations.

Jane nodded, "Okay...?"

"Those are CCTV."

"CCTV?"

"That stands for closed-circuit television cameras," Rory explained. "They'll send a picture of anyone getting close as well."

Jane pulled her arms tighter around Rory, "D-do you think they can see us now?"

Rory thought about it for a moment and then nodded, "Probably." He found himself looking up and down the length of the fence, half expecting to see someone coming for them. He put the binoculars down. Turning the quad bike to the right, he accelerated smoothly, moving further along the perimeter. Reaching the far end, Rory slowed and drove around the corner of the fence line. He stopped the quad bike and picked up the binoculars again, peering up at the corner. After a few minutes, he passed the binoculars back to Jane and pointed up to the top corner of the perimeter fence, "See that small square metal box at the top?"

Jane fiddled with the focus, "The one that looks like a square horn?"

"Correct," Rory said. "That's a microwave transmitter. It's probably sending a signal to a receiver three hundred yards further down the fence. It's another part of their intrusion detection system."

Jane lowered the binoculars, "Razor wire, fences, cameras...I get the feeling you're telling me we can't get in. But I got out of there, Rory? I don't understand...?"

"This place was designed to keep people out, not for keeping people in," Rory reasoned. "If you reached the fence from the inside and climbed to get *out*, like I think you did, that would set off alarms. But by the time they get here, you would be on this side and you can run away. Trying to climb the fence and get *in*...means we climb the fence to get inside...we set the alarm off...they come out to see and we meet them as we head for the buildings inside. It's a totally different scenario."

Jane nodded her head, "Okay. I guess I can see that. But...is there any way at all...?"

Rory scratched the stubble on his beard, There are some possibilities but–" The conversation was interrupted by a deep growl in the distance.

It was a large, black Humvee, heading straight for their position along the fence line.

But as he watched it, Rory realized this wasn't just the commercial type of Humvee most people saw. This was the real deal, an HMMWV, a full blow military vehicle and definitely *not* the local welcome wagon.

Chapter 39

JANE DOE POINTED in the direction of the massive vehicle, her voice filled with alarm, "Who's that?"

"I'm not sure," Rory said as he looked in the other direction and then looked up, his eyes scanning the bright blue sky for another military jet closing on them as well.

Jane lifted the binoculars to her eyes, "The windows are too dark and I can't see inside."

"Let's not wait around to find out who they are," Rory said as he turned the handlebars. "Hang on."

Jane dropped the binoculars in his lap and slipped her arms around his waist again. She held on tightly as Rory accelerated and turned the quad bike in a tight circle to the right and back around the corner of the fence.

Rory accelerated along the fence and a moment later, looked back over his shoulder to see if the Humvee was coming around the corner after them.

Jane raised her right arm and pointed ahead of the quad bike, yelling in Rory's ear, "Look."

A second black Humvee was at the far end of the clearing around the compound and closing in on them from that side.

Rory veered left to find someplace to hide. But he cursed under his breath when he realized there was only an open field in that direction. No trees. No foliage. No cover,

The second Humvee veered to the right to cut them off.

Jane shouted in Rory's ear, her voice filled with fear, "They're just not trying to scare us away, are they?"

Rory didn't reply, even though he knew the answer. There was no doubt to him that they were *not* just trying to shoo away some locals. One Humvee would accomplish that. He gauged the distance to the open field and determined the second Humvee would catch them easily and they wouldn't be able to make a run for it. Rory steered hard left and the quad bike skidded sideways.

Jane squeezed her arms around his chest and screamed as she fought to stay on the bike.

The quad bike straightened out and Rory accelerated back towards the corner of the security fence. He was gambling that the first Humvee coming this way would have to swing a little wide to turn the corner. And he was right. Barely.

The first black Humvee shot around the corner, not far from the fence.

The quad bike scraped against the back end of the black Humvee as it passed. The glancing blow caused the quad bike to veer and Rory had to fight to maintain control.

Jane squeezed the breath from his chest.

Rory straightened the quad bike out, accelerated and looked back after a few moments.

The second Humvee had swerved out wider to avoid the first one coming around the corner.

Rory realized he had gained some distance but it wouldn't last long. He scanned the flat terrain up ahead.

"Trees! We can hide," Jane yelled as she pointed at an angle off to the right.

Rory looked at where she was pointing. A thick spread of trees in that direction offered escape, provided they could reach them in time. He angled the bike that way and then glanced back. He cursed under his breath. He had the quad bike at full speed and one of the black vehicles was already gaining ground on them.

After a few moments, the harder ground gave way to a softer sand. That gave Rory some hope. The smaller quad bike should have better traction than the two larger vehicles in pursuit. Rory leaned forward, willing the quad bike to go faster. He caught movement high on the left in his peripheral vision. He turned his head and expected to see another Humvee.

Instead, he saw a figure in black walking forward on the top of a tall maintenance platform on the other side of the fence.

Why would they need a spotter?

The figure stopped walking and lowered a long, pipe-like object to his shoulder, aiming it towards the quad bike.

Rory realized what the figure had on his shoulder. He recognized the outline of an M203 grenade launcher! He began a zig-zag – too late.

There was a loud, sharp bang and then a puff of smoke shot from the end of the grenade launcher.

Rory felt more than heard the 40×46mm round bury itself in the sand underneath the quad bike.

A ground burst tossed them into the air, along with a ton of sand.

The world tumbled before Rory felt his body hit the ground hard. He rolled over twice, watching the body of Jane Doe bounce like a rag doll just ahead of him before darkness fell and he lost consciousness.

Chapter 40

RORY SLOWLY REGAINED consciousness. His first sensations; his ears felt blocked and there was a slight ringing in the background. A vague recollection of an explosion came to him. That would make sense. It was probably the reason why he had a headache as well. The smell of concrete mingled with an undercurrent of urine and he wondered where he was. His eyelids felt heavy and he struggled to lift them. As his eyes opened, a searing light hurt his eyes and he squeezed them shut. He slowly opened them again. Why was that bright light there? He felt a kink in his neck. He turned his neck to stretch the muscles and then tried to lift his head. What the–? His arms were straight over his head. Rory tried to pull his arms down. He heard the slight rattle of chains. He struggled to lift his head and he shook his hands again. He realized he was chained to the ceiling. And he was pulled high enough that he was standing on his tip toes. His calves hurt. Chained to the ceiling...a bright light in his eyes...what was going on? He tried to look around but the blinding light straight ahead made it impossible to see anything outside its glare.

He closed his eyes and tried to remember what had happened...the four-wheel quad bike...the compound...the explosion...then another thought struck him. Jane! Where was she? He was supposed to protect her. Failure was not an option. Rory desperately pulled down on the chain, then shook his arms hard to see if he could dislodge himself. No good. He could feel hand shackles around his wrists, Rory concentrated on flexing his hands and fingers, trying to feel how the shackles were attached. Maybe he could find a way out...no good...they were welded to a heavy link chain. Impossible to break. These people weren't playing around. He heard a door open somewhere ahead of him.

Boot steps echoed off the walls.

Rory squinted against the harsh light, listening. He estimated three - no - make that four hazy shadows on the other side of the bright light.

He heard a door close with a bang.

A voice sounded somewhere beyond the harsh glare, "Light in your eyes?"

The voice reminded Rory of a drill sergeant or a squad leader in the army.

The light turned off, to be replaced by the softer light from a large, single light bulb in the ceiling above. There were actually five men in the room. They were all dressed in black. They had to be the same men who had attacked them at the hospitals.

"Better?" The man who was speaking had a gray crew-cut. His black T-shirt was tight from the muscles underneath. He had a military bearing and looked straight at Rory with a cool detachment. The others carried themselves in the same manner and had close-cropped, military-style haircuts.

Rory took a quick survey of his surroundings. He was in a large room with concrete walls and completely bare of any furniture. Dead ahead was a heavy metal door, the kind that was meant to make sure anyone kept inside this room, stayed here.

One of the men walked over to Rory's left and disappeared from view.

Rory turned his head, trying to see where the man went. The metal sound of a chain rattling in that direction reached his ears.

Rory's arms were jerked higher as he heard the chain over his head grind harshly through a chain sheave. Now higher on his toes, the pain in his lower legs and feet intensified.

"Legs hurting a bit, Steele?" asked the man with the gray crew-cut.

Rory grit his teeth and didn't answer. But he was surprised. They knew who he was.

"Can you tell me who you and the woman talked to over the last few days?" gray crew-cut asked.

Rory clenched his jaw. No way he was going to say anything about Kal or–

His body exploded in pain as someone punched him in the kidneys from behind.

Rory's mouth opened in a silent, agonizing scream. It took a few moments before the pain retreated enough for him to hear someone was talking to him.

"We can do this all night, if you want, Steele. Make it easy on yourself," gray crew-cut said.

Rory ignored the man and prepared for what he felt was coming again. Sure enough, his body exploded in pain as another blow was delivered to his kidney area from behind.

As the pain subsided, Rory lifted his head and looked towards the leader of the group again. He wanted to remember his face. Then he realized gray crew-cut wasn't looking at him now.

He was looking down at something in his hand. It looked like a black and yellow plastic gun.

The man concentrating on turning something on the side of it with his fingers as he spoke to Rory again, "We've modified a few of these. It's our latest persuader. Let's see how it works." He pointed the gun directly at Rory, pulled the plastic trigger and two darts on a wire shot out and buried themselves in Rory's chest.

Rory's body convulsed as an electrical charge coursed through his body. His body shook and danced. It felt like everything inside his body was on fire. As the pain slowly subsided, Rory felt the tiny darts being pulled from his chest.

"These Tasers don't deliver the full charge to incapacitate the subject, Steele," gray crew-cut said calmly. "Just enough to let you know we mean business. Just tell us every individual you talked to and all this will be over."

Rory looked up just in time to see another Taser aimed in his direction.

Two darts shot out, burying themselves in Rory's chest again.

Rory could hear the chains rattling overhead as his body jumped and twisted from the electrical charge. It felt like his heart would explode from his chest. As the pain slowly drained away, Rory's hands were jerked hard upward by the chain again, nearly pulling his arms out of the shoulder sockets, adding a different agony to his body. Someone kicked his feet out from under his body and Rory felt a groan rip through his throat. He struggled to get his body back on his toes to relieve the strain. But as he did, a punch to his kidneys sent another crash of agony through his body. Rory's shoulder sockets screamed in pain as he fought desperately to get his feet back under him.

"Who did you talk to, Steele?" gray crew-cut asked firmly again.

Rory ignored the question as he finally got himself back on his tiptoes. But it offered little relief. Every socket, joint, and muscle in his body screamed in agony.

"Keep in mind, Steele, that we don't have any compunction about using advanced interrogation techniques. There is no government or civilian oversight regarding the use of hypothermia or waterboarding here."

"Why am I not surprised," Rory whispered sarcastically.

Gray crew-cut considered Rory for a moment.

Rory tried to prepare for the next blow from behind. Or the next Taser–

"You do realize the woman won't stand up to these interrogation techniques like you can, Steele? Once we get started on her in a few moments...." His voice trailed off, the full meaning of his threat left hanging in the air.

Fear and concern for Jane ripped through Rory's heart. He pulled on the chains and tried to shake free, ignoring the pain in his body, "You leave her alone. You leave her alone, you hear me?" Rory tried desperately to pull free from the chains. "If you hurt her, you're a dead man," he growled. "You're all dead–"

Rory's words were cut off and his body shook hard as another Taser shot sent electricity coursing through his veins. His vocal cords tightened so hard no sound came out, despite his involuntary scream of pain. After a few moments, he fought again to get back onto his tip toes, trying to offer his body some kind of temporary relief. He could hear several of the men talking in low voices and he wondered what they had planned for him next.

"Hey, Steele?"

Rory lifted his head just in time to see two men grinning, each aiming a black and yellow Taser at him. A moment later, they each pulled the trigger. Two sets of darts shot out and buried themselves in his chest. Rory's body danced and jerked on the end of the chain with the double jolt of electricity coursing through him.

Rory heard himself scream before he blacked out.

Chapter 41

THE DARKNESS SLOWLY dissipated as Rory's eyelids fluttered open. His head was hanging down and it hurt. He tried to lift his hands to his forehead but he couldn't. Why couldn't he move his hands? He vaguely remembered the Tasers and wondered if he was paralyzed. His eyes slowly focused and he realized he wasn't hanging from the ceiling anymore. Instead, he was sitting in a chair with his arms strapped to the armrests. Wide metal cuffs encircled his wrists and they were shackled together by a sturdy padlock joining two heavy chains. He tried to move his legs but they wouldn't budge an inch. He tried to shake them free and he heard a rattle. Leaning forward a bit, Rory realized his legs were strapped to the chair legs. And his ankles were shackled together like his wrists. The chain from ankle to ankle went through a U-bolt in the concrete floor. These guys weren't taking any chances with him. Rory looked around. He was alone again. But he was sure that wouldn't last for a long period. Those men would be back.

Then he remembered the comments about Jane and interrogating her. Was that where they had gone? Rory shook his body with anger, trying to break free from his restraints, but it was useless. Everything was strong and tight. Rory calmed himself, trying to figure out some other way out of this. But it was useless and time passed. Rory found himself dozing off when his attention was caught by a noise at the door.

It swung open and the man with the gray crew-cut walked back into the room.

Rory's jaw tightened with anger as he wondered if the man was returning from an interrogation session with Jane.

The man was silent as he stepped aside. The other four men entered the room and fanned out a bit as they approached Rory.

Was this round two? He looked for Tasers in their hands.

One of the men carried a short, heavy set of chains. He stood beside Rory as another one of the men bent down and undid the cuff on Rory's right ankle. He slid the chain out from the U-bolt, then re-cuffed the ankle. The heavy length of chain was passed to him and he connected it to the chain connecting Rory's feet. The other end was placed around Rory's wrist chain. A heavy padlock looped the whole unit together, effectively chaining the hands to the feet. Once the heavy padlock clicked shut, two of the men began to undo the straps on his arms and legs, while the others watched. Despite their outnumbering him, they were taking every precaution.

Once all the straps were undone and the chains all linked together, Mr. gray crew-cut barked once, "Up, Steele."

But Rory wasn't going to cooperate. He wanted to see how these men worked together. Mr. gray crew-cut appeared to be the leader, at least for this interrogation. He wanted to see if there was a pecking order among the others. Maybe he could find a weak spot, something he could use against them and escape. Or kill them all.

When Rory didn't budge a man stepped in on each side of him and hauled him to his feet, the chains and shackles rattling heavily.

"Let's go," was the next instruction as the leader waved Rory towards the door.

Rory tried to walk but all he could do was shuffle his feet. He began shuffling towards the door, eying the leader directly in the eyes. Rory swore to himself he would take him out first.

The leader coolly returned Rory's gaze for a moment. Then he turned around, stepped through the door into the hallway and turned right.

Rory shuffled through the doorway and turned right as well.

The other four men followed closely behind.

The leader was paused partway down the hall, looking back at Rory, waiting.

Rory shuffled towards him. Their eyes met again as he approached. Rory's gaze was hard.

The leader gave him a dismissive look and then turned and slowly began walking again, leading the way down the hallway.

As he moved down the hallway, Rory considered his situation. The chains and shackles were heavy and they limited his movement and ability to fight back. And he was outnumbered. He would fight to the death, if necessary. But ideally, he really needed to find some way to survive, escape and find Jane. He studied his surroundings as they moved down the hallway. They passed several heavy, closed doors. There was no indication any of them was an exit. And there wasn't a single window that Rory could use for an escape even if he did manage to shed these chains.

The leader continued to walk down the hallway, never looking back at him.

Rory continued to shuffle and clank his way down the hallway. The leader was staying just far enough ahead to prevent an attack. Rory glanced back over his shoulder, trying to gauge the distance to the four men behind him. They were a little closer. He might be able to catch them by surprise and if one of them had a weapon, he could easily dispatch the rest. Then again, if they killed him, what would happen to Jane? He had to stay alive and find Jane, presuming she was here as well. The odds were still too much against him right now.

The leader stopped walking and pulled open a door on the left. He glanced at Rory and then stepped through the doorway.

Rory shuffled to the open doorway and stopped, looking through, wondering if he should go inside or take the opportunity now to attack the men behind him.

But one of the men behind him lost patience and shoved Rory hard from behind.

Rory nearly fell on his face as he was knocked forward through the doorway. He caught his balance on the other side. He was about to turn and attack the man who pushed him when he saw a familiar figure.

Jane Doe was lying on a large hospital gurney in the middle of the room. Her head was tilted his way but her eyes were closed. She appeared to be unconscious.

Chapter 42

RORY BEGAN TO MOVE towards Jane but he was restrained by two of the men. He tried to pull away but they held him firmly. Then a booming, confident voice sounded out and caught his attention.

"Mr. Steele, welcome to the preparation room. We meet at last."

Rory turned his attention to a tall, imperious-looking man on the other side of the room. His hair and mustache were snow white, his face tanned, and he stood with his hands half inside the side pockets of his immaculate gray suit jacket. What did he mean by preparation room?

Brecc waved a hand toward the heavy chains and shackles, "Sorry to inconvenience you like this, Mr. Steele. But I recognize a competent opponent when I see one."

"I'm flattered," Rory said as he gave the man a hard look.

"I told Mr. Foxen...as well as Mr. Blayze here...that you would prove to be a problem. And I was right."

Rory looked to his right at the leader. So, his name was Blayze. Appropriate name. Rory pictured him going up in a blaze of glory when he got hold of him.

The man returned Rory's gaze without flinching.

"We still haven't been able to persuade Mr. Steele to tell us who he has been talking to," Foxen said. "I'm sure if we give Mr. Blayze more time–"

"Yes, I'm sure he would," the tall man said with a dismissive wave of his hand. "But I'm not going to worry about that. We have to get everything back on track immediately to supply our customers and get back on track with our special project." He took a step towards Rory, "This non-entity has wasted enough of our time already."

Rory coolly stared the man in the eyes. He wasn't sure if you wanted to kill him or Blayze first.

"But I just thought, since you were so diligent in protecting our asset here, I would let you see her one last time, Mr. Steele," the tall man said as he nodded towards Jane.

Rory looked at Jane and then looked back at the man, raising his eyebrow, "If you–"

"Oh, we won't hurt her, Mr. Steele," the man said. "She has to live. She's a true VIP to us. A *very* important person. Unfortunately, you aren't. You, on the other hand, have to die. Despite the fact I appreciate your protecting our asset, you are expendable. And I have to tell you that you've held everything up immeasurably and I can't simply forgive that–"

"You keep calling her an asset," Rory interrupted. "Does she have a name?"

The man obviously did not like being interrupted. He glared at Rory, taking a deep breath before he spoke again. "Her name doesn't matter–"

"Okay. What's *your* name then?" Rory asked.

The man paused, looked at Rory and then laughed, "Why? So you can track me down and kill me at some point?"

Rory nodded solemnly, "Something like that."

The man narrowed his eyes and considered Rory for a moment, "I have no doubts that you would indeed track us all down...which is why will make sure you never get that opportunity. However...just so you know who killed you...my name is Maxwell Brecc."

Rory nodded, "The big cheese of IntelliMax International."

Brecc seemed genuinely surprised. His eyebrows rose, "I'm impressed. You do your homework. And you obviously have sources I wasn't aware of."

Rory glanced over at Blayze and saw he didn't like the fact Rory knew a little too much about their affairs. Or the fact Brecc was even talking to Rory.

"Just a lucky guess," Rory said, not wanting to reveal anything.

"I highly doubt that Mr. Steele," Brecc countered. "We are aware you infiltrated our Toronto offices."

Rory did everything he could to hide his surprise. Then again, he shouldn't be surprised. From what Kal had said, these guys had eyes and ears everywhere.

"I won't even charge you for the book you broke before you die," Brecc said with some amusement.

Rory realized he had really underestimated these people, even though he'd sworn to himself he wouldn't do it again. The problem was, he may not get another chance to correct his mistake.

Just then another door to the room opened up and two men stepped inside. One was a tall man with jet black hair, an immaculate suit, and polished Gucci shoes. His movement was tight and efficient, reminding Rory of men he had seen in military intelligence units. The other wore a white lab coat, gray shirt, darker gray slacks and cheap loafers.

"Ah, Mr. Foxen, glad you could join us," Brecc said. "We need to get things back on track as soon as possible. Mr. Steele here was about to depart our company."

"We will get her ready immediately, Sir," Foxen said in his clipped British accent.

Rory immediately pegged Mr. Gucci loafers as former British intelligence.

Foxen nodded at the man in the white lab coat, "Get her ready, Pollard."

Pollard approached Jane on the hospital gurney and picked up a pair of scissors. He started with her right pant leg and began to cut away her slacks.

Alarm bells went off and Rory immediately started shuffling over to the table, the heavy chains jangling as he moved. Someone punched him in the kidneys from behind and he collapsed to his knees. The pain was immense and his voice was strained, "If you touch her, I'll kill you–" Another blow in the middle of his back knocked the wind from him.

"Taken him away," Foxen yelled.

"No. Put him in a chair," Brecc said with a counter order.

Rory was hauled roughly to his feet, pulled back a number of feet and slammed down onto a chair. He had a hard time getting the breath back into his lungs.

Brecc walked up to Rory, "Very chivalrous of you, Mr. Steele. But I can assure you, we are not going to hurt her."

"I have a hard time believing that," Rory croaked as he looked up at Brecc with a menacing look.

Brecc acknowledged the threatening look with a nod of his head, "Mr. Blayze and Mr. Frost were quite right in their assessment of you. You won't give up easily. In fact, I imagine you will *never* give up. And I'm quite impressed with your concern for our asset."

"She's not an asset, she's a human being," Rory said in a strained voice.

"You were in the military, Mr. Steele," Brecc countered. "You know quite well how humans are used as assets every day–"

"On a voluntary basis," Rory said with a hiss of anger.

Brecc spoke with a shake of his head and a condescending tone of voice, "Mr. Steele. Despite what you think of us, together with this young lady, we are providing a *very* valuable service to the free world."

"I have a hard time believing that."

Brecc pursed his lips as he looked at Rory for a moment, thinking. Then he turned and spoke to Foxen, "Bring her into the control area when she is ready. And bring Mr. Steele as well." He looked back at Rory, "I think you should have the opportunity to see our valuable work before you leave this world–"

"Why delay getting rid of him?" Blayze interrupted. "I think–"

"Just do it!" Brecc demanded as he glared at Blayze. Brecc then turned sharply and walked out the door Foxen and Pollard had used, leaving it wide open.

Blayze grumbled as Brecc disappeared from sight.

Foxen then walked past Pollard over to a table on the far side of the room.

Rory realized Pollard had continued working during the argument. He had removed Jane's slacks and blouse and she was left in her white panties and brassiere.

Rory's jaw clenched with anger. He would gladly plunge those scissors into Pollard's heart.

Foxen walked back towards the hospital gurney with a needle in his hand.

Pollard continued to work, cutting away Jane's brassiere.

Foxen placed the needle in Jane's neck.

Rory went to move but a gun was pressed against his right temple. He had no choice but to watch.

Pollard stripped away Jane's brassiere. He tossed it behind him and then moved the scissors down to her panties.

Rory saw Jane's eyes slowly open.

Jane was in a fog as she turned her head to look over towards Foxen.

Pollard lifted the lower edge of her panties at her hip to slip the scissors underneath.

Jane's hand slowly moved to try and stop him.

Pollard laughed as he worked the open scissors through the flimsy material. He grinned wickedly as he cut her panties away, pulling the material from between her legs to leave her totally nude. He tossed the cut panties on the floor, then worked with Foxen to strap Jane's arms to the side of the cot.

Jane tried to fight back but her efforts were weak.

Rory tried to move to Jane again but the gun was pressed harder against his temple. And hard enough to make him wince in pain. They were delivering a message. Stay still or else. All he could do right now was grit his teeth and watch.

Foxen moved to the top of the hospital gurney, shaking a can of shaving cream. He applied it liberally to Jane's head.

Pollard positioned Jane's legs with her knees up and spread them wide apart.

Rory growled in anger and tried to get up again. A blow to the back of his head filled his vision with stars.

The gun barrel was pressed against his temple again and Blayze hissed into Rory's ear, "Just watch. You move again and I shoot."

Rory thought the barrel of the gun would be pushed through the bone of his skull. He was helpless as he watched the shaving cream passed over to Pollard, who aimed it down between Jane's open legs. The hiss from the can filled the air as the shaving cream coated her genitals.

"This is the part I love," Pollard said as he looked over at Rory and made a show of setting the can of shaving cream down. Pollard then looked between Jane's open legs...slowly lowered his hand down and began to massage between her legs.

"No please," Jane said weakly as she tried to free her hands.

Rory wanted to get up but the gun pressed hard against his temple.

Foxen was now shaving her head. He looked at Pollard, "Stop being a pig and get to it. Mr. Brecc is waiting."

Pollard grinned at Rory as he massaged between her legs for another moment. Then he picked up a razor, bent between her open legs and began to shave her. Rory watched helplessly as the two men shaved her body completely, from top to bottom and under her arms as well. Once they were finished, they unstrapped Jane and lifted her to her feet.

Jane was totally naked and offered weak resistance as the two men walked her towards the open door.

"Bring Steele," Foxen commanded Blayze and his men.

Chapter 43

RORY WAS HAULED ROUGHLY to his feet by two of the men. Another one of the men shoved him in the back. "Move," he ordered.

They didn't have to force him. He wanted to stay as close to Jane as possible, in case he could figure some way out of this. He shuffled as quickly as he could across the room and clanked his way through the open doorway. Rory entered a very large room on the other side of the door. But to his amazement, it wasn't a standard room. It was actually a dome. A huge, black colored dome that rose two stories high. Everything seemed to shimmer, including the black colored floor. As he shuffled forward, Rory realized the sound of the rattling chains was slightly muted, not echoing as he would have expected in a large, open space like this. He stopped in his tracks.

Dead ahead on the floor, right in the middle of the domed room, was a large circle of silver. And in the middle of that silver circle was a large, black chair, sitting on a silver pedestal. Two men were working on the chair, No, not working on it, they were cleaning it. They had large, blue spray bottles in their hands. They would spray and rub hard.

The chair itself was sleek and looked like a space-age dentist's chair. The entire chair was dotted with dozens of inserts that looked like shiny silver dollars, running in rows from top to bottom. Far above the chair, at the very top of the dome, was another large circle of silver, exactly matching the one on the floor below the chair. Rory gaze fell back to the circle on the floor as one of the men dropped to his hands and knees and worked away on the circle's surface. He realized both circles weren't just silver in color. It was actual silver paint. He could see the overlapping flecks as the spray highlighted the surface. He looked again at the pedestal and realized it was also real silver, as were the silver buttons.

Rory's attention was diverted to several other figures in the room. A number of men, wearing white lab coats, were working at an elaborate computer workstation behind the head of the black chair. The place was a hub of activity but their footsteps on the floor were muted as well. Rory wondered what this whole room was all about – he realized there was something he *couldn't* see that really worried him. He couldn't see the large hospital gurney or any sign of Jane. Where had they taken her?

"Welcome to the Light Dome, Mr. Steele."

Rory turned and saw Brecc standing next to a ten-foot-high glass window that covered thirty feet of the curved right wall of the black dome.

Brecc gestured, "Bring Mr. Steele closer so he can see the operations control center."

One of the men pushed Rory in the back and he jerked forward a step, nearly falling over. He turned his head and gave the man a hard glare but was pushed again and had to comply, clanking his way over towards the glass wall. He turned his attention to getting closer to Brecc and finding some way to get the chains around the man's neck but the men pushed him towards a spot some ten feet away from him. He was trying to figure out some way to still get to Brecc and overcoming his men when his attention was caught by the room beyond the glass wall and he momentarily forgot them.

The domed room was overlooking a massive room that rose three stories and was filled with frenetic activity. Spread across the floor of the room was a vast array of desks and computer workstations, each one occupied by a man or a woman in a lab coat, intently engaged in a variety of actives. Dozens of other men and women in white coats moved back and forth between the desks and workstations, most of them carrying computer tablets and wearing wireless headsets and microphones.

Rory noticed that, from time to time, the men and women would all look up at the walls around them and gesture to something. Looking up, he realized that high over the activity of the floor, all three walls were filled with several rows of massive video screens. Some of them were set in 3x3 grids that showed a single image. His eyes focused in on the images and he saw flashing, rolling streams of data, real-time graphs that changed by the second, stock market symbols and other information that Rory couldn't identify. The room below reminded him of television footage he saw of NASA during space flights, but this one was far more impressive.

"An amazing sight, isn't?" Brecc asked as he looked intently at Rory.

Rory pushed back his feelings, not wanting to give Brecc any type of satisfaction, "If you say so–"

"She's ready, sir."

Brecc turned and smiled, "Very good."

Rory's chains clanked as he turned to see what Brecc was looking and he suddenly felt a heavy feeling in the pit of his stomach.

There she was. A naked Jane was being led by Pollard and another man to the middle of the domed room. In fact, she was being led directly to the strange black chair that dominated the entire room.

The two men cleaning the chair grinned as they stepped back, their eyes roaming over Jane's nakedness. Rory felt anger and then his eyes fell on the spray bottles the men had. It was window cleaner. He could smell the light scent of ammonia. Why would they–? He realized they had been removing the tarnish from the silver and that reminded him of one of the uses for silver. It was the single best conductor for electricity, so much better than copper. But it was so expensive it was rarely used for that purpose. Were they running electricity through that chair? Now fear struck at his heart and he yelled as Jane was taken beside the chair, "What are you doing to her?" He attempted to shuffle across to help her but someone grabbed him by the back of the collar and held him in place.

"She won't be harmed Mr. Steele, I can assure you that," Brecc said dismissively.

"You're all heart, bozo," Rory snapped. He was slapped in the back of the head.

Jane was trying to resist feebly but was obviously drugged enough to be pliable. She was turned and seated in the chair before being made to lay back and held in place as silvery, cloth-like straps were placed around her arms and legs. Straps went around her breasts and her stomach to completely secure her to the chair.

"This room is also impressive, isn't it, Mr. Steele?"

Rory turned to see Brecc walk up to him and he gave him a hard look, "If you say so."

"Ah, but I do," Brecc said with a self-satisfied smile.

"I take it this is part of Echelon," Rory said. "Your little part in the collection and analysis network–"

Brecc puffed his chest out, indignant, "It cost the free world billions to build this room. But the return is worth much more than that. This *is* Echelon. The rest are just pretenders to the throne, I assure you."

Rory was about to ask what he meant when he heard Foxen issue an order.

"Get the interface set up."

A white coated man nodded and went to the other side of the chair.

"Prepare the link," Foxen said to another.

Pollard went to a large workstation behind the black chair and began working away at the keyboard.

The man on the other side of the chair lifted his hands up and Rory saw that he had a black object that looked very much like a football helmet. The top of the helmet was studded with silver nails and each nail had a dot of light at the end. The entire rainbow of color was represented in the array of lights. The man placed the helmet gently over Jane's head. It fit perfectly and Rory had the feeling it had been made specifically for her.

"Initializing," Pollard said at the workstation behind the black chair. The colored lights on the black helmet increased in intensity and then began to flick off and on in quick, random patterns. The colored lights increased in intensity and they blinked faster and faster.

A soft, whirling sound echoed from the ceiling.

Rory was startled when millions of tiny, intense lights of every color imaginable sprang to life in the upper half of the black dome. The lights blinked in random patterns and became more intense and blinked off and on faster and faster.

"Powering up," Pollard said as his hands flew over the keyboard at the workstation.

A low hum started in the vicinity of the chair and then a beam of light shot upward from the lower silver circle - penetrated through the black chair and Jane's body - and then shot up to the silver circle at the top of the dome.

Jane groaned and her naked body stiffened, her fingers curled into tight fists and her arms and legs trembled uncontrollably.

Chapter 44

RORY IMMEDIATELY FELT the concern and anger rage through his body. He struggled against his restraints, trying to go to her. "Leave her alone," he yelled. "What are you doing to her? She's in pain."

"It's only momentary, Mr. Steele," Brecc said. "I assure you she is not being hurt."

Rory fought hard against his bonds.

A moment later, Jane's body did relax and her limbs stopped trembling. She seemed to sink gently into the chair, oblivious of anything that was happening.

His chest heaving from his efforts, Rory looked from Jane to at Brecc, his voice low and hard, "If I get these chains around your neck, I'll make sure the pain you feel is more than momentary."

Brecc gave him a dismissive look, calmly turned around and walked back to the window, looking out over the room below.

Rory watched as colored threads of light from Jane's helmet began stretching out to touch the colored lights on the upper half of the dome. Within seconds, millions of colored threads of light flashed like brilliant lightning around the upper half of the room. A soft crackling sound reached his ears, mesmerizing him.

"We're back in business, sir," Foxen said after a few more moments.

"Thank you," Brecc said. He turned, "Mr. Steele?"

Rory's attention turned to Brecc.

Brecc gestured for Rory to look through the window, "Behold the effects of our asset."

His voice was hard as Rory shook his head, "I told you. She's not an–" His attention was caught by the video screens in the other room. All the information he had watched scrolling across them before was now a blur, moving faster than his eyes could even follow. It was astonishing.

Brecc watched the rolling data for a few moments and then turned his attention back to Rory, "What you're seeing Mr. Steele, is just a fraction of the communications going on around the world. E-mails, cell phone calls, faxes, Internet chats, text messages. Even stock market data and–"

"So you're spying on the world to save it? Is that it?" Rory said.

"Precisely," Brecc said. "I'm not one of those who apologizes or tries to use fancy words to justify what needs to be done. We - and I refer to everyone working in this room - *we* do what is necessary to maintain our freedoms. There are those who think they can reason with everyone. And history has shown many of them get run over in a war they refused to believe could happen. There are those who believe that, without maintaining our ethical standards, we will become like those we abhor. Meanwhile, those on the other side have no ethics and dig into our secrets, undermining our society and our freedoms."

"What about the woman in the chair? What about her freedoms?" Rory asked in anger.

"The woman you know as Jane Doe is simply one of those necessities," Brecc said. His attention turned back to the room on the other side of the glass, "It's simply for the greater good–"

"And that justifies putting a brain-computer interface into her head and running all those computers," Rory said loudly.

Brecc laughed as he turned and looked at Rory again, "You still don't understand it at all, do you? You think that device you saw is a simple BCI, a brain-computer interface?"

Rory was confused. He looked around the room and then at Brecc.

Brecc stretched out his arm, pointing at Jane, "The woman in the chair is the greatest mind in the world when it comes to pure mathematics. A Bachelor of Science Degree in Pure Mathematics, an MBA in Applied Mathematics and a Ph.D. in Pure Mathematics. And that was just the start."

Rory looked over at Jane. He now understood how she'd been able to handle those numbers.

"Ah. I see you have experienced her brilliance, Mr. Steele. Let me tell you. No one...and I mean no one...has *ever* been able to understand fields of study like the abstract phenomenon of relativity or the esoteric thoughts surrounding quantum mechanics like this woman. She has the ability to imagine theories that make my brain hurt to even think about them." Brecc then became dismissive, "She could have been an Albert Einstein, a Stephen Hawking. Instead, it was all going to waste, being used for nonessential purposes–"

"According to who?"

"According to me!" Brecc yelled. "According to those of us who are more interested in the future of the world. We knew *exactly* how her abilities should be used."

"That wasn't your call?" Rory yelled back. "It's her life."

Brecc sneered at Rory, almost laughing as he firmly said, "No, it's not. It belongs to the world." A moment later, he turned and sauntered over to Jane's nude form, "You're not capable of understanding the importance of what we're doing. Of *how* we are doing it."

Rory could barely contain his anger, "I'm sure a narcissistic ass like you really believes everything you're saying."

Brecc looked down at Jane's nude form, running his finger along one of the silver straps holding her in the chair, "Such a brilliant mind contained within such a beautiful form."

Rory wanted to rip Brecc's hand off, "Don't you dare touch her."

"Don't worry, Mr. Steele. She is far too valuable for any of that." Shaking his head softly, Brecc looked at Rory, "You still don't understand, do you?"

"Understand what? What the hell are you talking about—?"

"She is *not* running the computers...she *is* the computer, Mr. Steele. Those men and women in the data center are filtering the raw communications input of our entire globe millions of times faster than any computer in any other so-called Echelon compound could even hope to do. And all *through her brain*. They are actually using her brain, Mr. Steele. Can you imagine that?"

Rory looked at Jane for a moment, the full horror at how they were using her slamming home.

Brecc pointed at the nude woman, "Your Jane Doe *is* the Echelon Mind."

Chapter 45

"**WHAT YOU SEE** around you Mr. Steele," Brecc said proudly as he swept a hand around the room, "is an operation that is beyond the understanding of most people today. We have used a little-known discovery around telluric currents made by the genius Nikola Tesla to power this chair."

Rory looked at the chair and the millions of threads of light moving between Jane's helmet and the millions of tiny, intense lights in the upper half of the dome. He only had a vague idea of what Brecc was talking about. But he had to understand what was going on if he was going to free Jane. And men like Brecc usually wanted to show how smart they were. He turned to Brecc and shook his head, "I've never heard of these...these tele-currents...?"

"Telluric currents, Mr. Steele," Brecc corrected. "Telluric currents run through the earth and the sea, they are basically created by the Earth's magnetic field. Three hundred years ago, Alexander Bain created earth magnets by burying plates of zinc and copper in the ground a meter apart and created enough voltage through these telluric currents to run a clock. But beyond inventor Nikola Tesla's plan for a global power grid using electricity intermingled with natural telluric currents, scientists have ignored this avenue of research. It died with Tesla in 1943. But we saw the possibilities, Mr. Steele. We saw a way to help mankind. Our researchers have actually created a secret design that uses this voltage in conjunction with the human electrical system that allows us to use and power the human mind itself."

"If you're using her mind, why are you shaving her?" Rory said in anger.

"Ah, yes. The problem is these currents are very delicate and easily disrupted, which is why our subject has to be shaved completely." Brecc turned and looked at Pollard and the other man standing behind the chair, "But solving that minor problem seems to be the one job that is enjoyed by the members of the team more than any other."

Pollard laughed, looking right at Rory.

Rory glared back at him.

"But there *is* serious work being performed here," Brecc intoned as he gestured around the room. "We have spent a lot of time and money to ensure that the free world stays free–"

"You're just another nut job that needs to be stopped," Rory snapped. As soon as the words were out of his mouth, Rory realized he had let his anger get the better of him. It had overwhelmed his better senses.

Brecc slowly turned and looked at Rory with a cold look on his face. "Drop Mr. Steele into the lake. I've had enough of him." He then turned away dismissively to watch the scrolling data on the screens in the other room.

Two men quickly grabbed Rory's arms and turned him around, moving him towards the exit of the communications room.

As Rory was forced to shuffle back towards the door, he cursed himself for the mistake. Instead, he should have gotten

Brecc to talk more, to give him more information to work with. Now he was going to have to leave Jane behind and try to find some way back to her.

"C'mon, buddy. Move it," one of the men said and he pushed Rory hard.

Rory caught his balance and then found himself being pushed from behind. He had no choice but to shuffle to the door, the chains connecting his arms and legs clanking a tune of defeat. He yelled back over his shoulder as the exit was opened in front of him, "I'll be back, Brecc. Do you hear me? I'll be back!"

"I won't sit up and wait," Brecc said snidely without turning.

Rory was shuffled through the open doorway, taken back through the preparation room and then he clanked his way into the long hallway where he had been interrogated. But they didn't turn him right and back to his cell.

The man in the lead went straight ahead through an exit door.

Rory followed, finding himself outside the building.

Four men, all dressed in black, were standing behind a long, white service van used to transport prisoners. The back doors were wide open, waiting for him.

"Frost here wants the honor," Blayze said.

Another man with a dark crew cut motioned for the three men with him to fetch Rory, "You killed a couple of members of my team, son. That has to be avenged. It's our code."

"And it's my code to kill scum," Rory said.

Someone punched him in the side of the head, nearly knocking him into unconsciousness and he fell to his knees.

He was hauled roughly to his feet and moved towards the van.

Rory did his best to look around, trying to stay conscious, trying to find something that would identify the building that Jane was in. He planned on coming back.

As the men dragged him forward, he looked beyond the white van. Since Brecc had said something about dropping him into a lake, Rory assumed they were still in the compound in Nanticoke, not far from Lake Erie. But he had to be sure. He cursed under his breath. The view was cut off by a number of large vehicles not far ahead of the van and he couldn't see anything.

"Use the old boatyard," Blayze yelled from behind him. "You can use one of the fishing tugs."

Rory took a deep breath to calm himself. He had to keep his wits about him, he planned on coming back. There was just one problem he had to overcome. These men planned on drowning him in the middle of the 210-foot deep Lake Erie.

Chapter 46

A FEW MOMENTS LATER, Rory felt the van pull away. He slowly rolled over, the chains clanking, and he looked through the small back windows, looking for some clue as to where they were. The van turned and he could feel the wheels purring over pavement. He saw the upper edge of the building he had been in. It was a black, glass building and he was sure it was the same building he saw when they were in the helicopter. The van turned in the other direction and he now saw open blue sky. A few moments later, he could see the radomes and towers of a SIG-INT operation in the distance. Which meant they *were* inside the compound Jane had escaped from. That was good. He was determined to return here to get her out again. It was *his* fault she was back inside and he felt the pain of that decision immensely.

A moment later, the van slowed to a stop and he heard voices. He kept an eye on those back windows. He wanted to see some kind of landmarks as they drove, so he could keep himself oriented as to where along the lake they were taking him. He heard the clanking sound of a metal gate opening up. They had to be going through one of the guarded gates. Sure enough, as the van began moving again, he could see a tall fence with razor wire on top–

"Secure him you fools. Don't take any chances with him."

Someone behind him booted him in the head and Rory blacked out.

THE BLACKNESS SLOWLY dissipated and Rory opened his eyes. His head hurt and he felt a groan escape from his lips as he looked around in confusion. He was on the floor in the back of a long van – everything came flooding back to him and he cursed himself. How long had he been out? He had planned to watch for landmarks and to feel and determine every movement of the prisoner van, so he could find his way back, and he had failed.

Lifting his head, he saw blue sky and wispy clouds through the small back windows. He tried to sit up - the clinking sounds of chains made him stop. Looking left and right, he realized he was now chained to bench seats on either side of the van. He pulled hard on the chains, trying to break free, but it was useless. He heard the sound of light laughter at his futile attempts and he felt anger rage through him. A few minutes later, he felt the van turn and come to a stop. Then it backed up, the sky disappeared in the windows to be replaced by a roof of old battered boards, and then the van came to a stop again.

Two men, who must have been sitting on the bench seats towards the front of the van, appeared over top of him, bent over and unchained him from the bench seats. Rory prepared to attack when the back doors of the van opened up.

A gruff voice said, "Haul his ass out there."

Two more men grabbed his ankles and pulled him roughly out of the van, setting him on his feet.

Rory looked around quickly as the men worked to shackle his hands to his legs again, looking for a way to escape. He was inside a rickety, wooden building that smelled of motor oil and fish. This must be the boatyard Blayze had talked about. But as he surveyed his surroundings, he realized there was now a total of eight men guarding him. Eight men that Rory would have to fight through. Now obviously wasn't the time to try and escape.

As the men stood up from their shackling job, hands pushed him from behind, propelling him forward.

Rory began to shuffle across the old concrete floor and away from the van. The chains clanked as he moved past pieces of diesel engines, rusted parts, and thick, heavy rope. He was stopped by the two men beside him when they reached two large doors. Two other men swung them open and Rory was pushed through them and onto a dock. Twenty feet away at the end of the dock, he saw the back of an old 71-foot Great Lakes fishing tug tied to the heavy posts. He moved along the battered old boards of the dock, his senses assaulted by the heavy smell of diesel fuel and fish. Only a few feet away from the tug, Rory was suddenly picked up by two of the men. They eagerly tossed him in the air over the low back end of the fishing tug.

Rory landed hard on the steel deck on his side. His breath was knocked from his lungs and his head snapped - banging against the steel plating. He fought to stay conscious - he heard the men laughing - and he could feel the fishing tug move up and down in the water as the men boarded behind him. Closing his eyes, he lay still to make it look like he was unconscious again as he tried to get his breath back.

"What a wimp," one of the men said as he stepped up near Rory. He kicked Rory in the center of his back.

Rory was expecting it but still cried out in pain. He felt the air shoot out of his lungs again.

Someone grabbed the chain around Rory's legs, turned him around on the rough deck and pulled him away from the back edge of the Great Lakes fishing tug before turning him back around again.

Fighting the blackness with everything in him, Rory lay deadly still, his eyes closed as the cries of seagulls filled the air far above the tug.

"Let's cast-off," yelled someone from the bow of the tug. A few moments later, a deep growl penetrated through the tug as the Volvo 290 hp engine started up.

"I'll get the bowline, you get the stern," another voice said.

Rory was slowly regaining his breath. He wondered how many men he would have to deal with now. They hadn't secured his chains to anything this time so he had an opportunity to move. But he was cautious and only moved enough to take a look to his right.

Six feet away was a man with a stocky build. He was coiling a rope on the deck, his back to Rory.

Rory could feel the back end of the tug sink lower as the engine growl increased. He saw a tall wooden pole slip by just beyond the man's head. They were moving away from the dock. Rory glanced towards the front of the tug. Beyond the 36 feet of open deck space, he could see the wheelhouse and two men inside. With the man to his right, two men in the wheelhouse and one at the bow to cast off the line, it looked like his odds had doubled, from eight men down to four. Rory was about to move against the man closest to him when he saw Frost coming along the side of the wheelhouse on the left. Rory closed his eyes and pretended to be out.

"Keep an eye on our passenger here, Butchie. I'm going below to see why the engine is chugging a bit," Frost said.

"Right."

As Rory lay there, his brain started to analyze the situation. This didn't look good. His arms and legs were chained in shackles, with a connecting chain between the two hampering his movements. And he had four trained men to overcome. He wasn't sure what he could do yet, but his brain burned with anger at Brecc and his cronies. He hated bullies. And Brecc was the worst kind of bully. A world-class bully sanctioned by governments who turned a blind eye in order to protect freedoms. And what was worse, Brecc was stealing Jane's freedom to protect freedom. That was dead wrong. He had to find some way to get back to her.

Chapter 47

RORY FELT THE 71-foot Great Lakes fishing tug moving up and down as it encountered larger swells. That meant they were moving into deeper water, heading towards the center of Lake Erie. Rory caught a glimpse of those swells of black water behind the tug and he felt a sliver of panic start to rise in his throat. Just after he had learned to swim when he was a youngster, Rory had nearly drowned when he had stepped into a deep drop-off in the black waters of the Spanish River in Northern Ontario. The rolling black water behind the tug reminded him of that near-death experience. He had to ignore it, he told himself. He had to concentrate on finding some way of taking over the boat and getting back to land, to get back to Jane. But what could he do? Rory kept his eyes half closed, watching the man closest to him, watching for an opening.

Butchie pulled out a cigarette and lit it up.

Rory watched as Butchie walked a few steps to the stern and stood with one foot on the low steel railing that ran around the stern of the tug, taking deep drags on his cigarette.

Using small movements of his head, Rory scanned the area around him, looking for some way to get free and fight back. Nothing looked promising. He glanced back at Butchie. The man was blowing smoke rings and ignoring the prisoner lying on the deck behind him. That was good. Now all Rory needed was something to hit him with or...that's when Rory spotted the handgun Butchie had slipped into the back waistband of his jeans. A plan formed in his mind quickly. But the plan made him look back at those black swells again and he had to fight the rising panic. He pushed the black water from his mind...just take it one step at a time he told himself.

Rory glanced back towards the wheelhouse.

The men inside were looking forward as the fishing tug moved to deeper waters.

Frost was still somewhere below, working on the engine. That was good as Rory assumed he would be a tougher opponent to overcome.

It was now or never.

Careful to keep the chains from rattling, Rory slowly pulled his feet in towards his butt, getting ready to act. His eyes settled on the swells of the black water behind the tug and he felt that sliver of panic start to rise in his throat again. Pushing the feeling back down, he set his feet under him. Taking it slow to stay balanced against the rise and fall of the tug, Rory slowly rose to a standing position. Glancing over his shoulder, he could see the other two men were still looking dead ahead. It was now or never. Taking a quick hop to get momentum, he began a power-shuffle towards the back end of the tug.

The chains rattled.

Butchie was turning.

Rory pushed off the deck with both feet, turning in the air as he jumped As he was passing Butchie, Rory was able to get his hands up high enough to slip the chain over Butchie's head and then downward, snagging the man around the neck. Rory's feet landed on the top edge of the low steel railing. He pushed hard backward, pulling Butchie off the deck with him.

Butchie gasped in surprise.

Rory sucked in a big gulp of air but almost lost it from the shock of hitting the cold, black water. Rory could feel the push of the tug's propeller as they sank, their bodies just missing the sharp whirling blades.

Butchie started fighting, throwing elbows and trying to punch back over his head.

Rory pulled hard on the chains and maintained the pressure. He had to get this over with quickly before the weight of the chains carried him too deep.

Butchie fought desperately, clawing at the chain and trying to pull it away from his throat.

Rory grit his teeth and pulled harder, crushing Butchie's windpipe.

Butchie made a bubbling and gurgling sound in his throat, then sagged as the life went out of him.

Rory had to move quickly, the weight of the chains pulling him deeper into the cold, black water. Slipping the chains up over Butchie's head, he pushed the man's upper body forward while reaching for the man's handgun in the back waistband of his jeans.

The butt of the gun slipped through his fingers.

Rory felt fear.

His body started dropping past Butchie's body because of the weight of the chains.

Butchie's body seemed to be floating away.

Rory rolled his feet upward, wrapping them around the body at the last minute. Using his legs, he pulled Butchie's body closer.

Rory twisted his body and reached for the handgun again.

He got it.

Unwrapping his legs, he let the body go, now concentrating on getting the weapon aimed at the proper angle.

The chains made it difficult.

He sank deeper and fought off the rising fear of the dark, black water.

Pulling the trigger, the bullet smashed through the lock at his wrists. The chains holding his hands loosened.

Rory let himself roll back in the black water.

He fired.

And missed.

He fired again.

The lock at his feet blew apart.

Rory worked to shuck the chains off.

Then he stuck the gun firmly into the back waistband of his jeans, pushed his shoes off and looked up.

Was that up?

He began swimming hard for the surface.

He hoped.

His lungs were burning.

All the exertion had burned up most of his oxygen.

Rory swam higher in the cold, black water.

Or was he?

Fear raised its ugly head again and he pushed it back down, thinking of Jane sitting in that chair.

His lungs were burning.

The black water became a little lighter above him.

His legs kicked harder and his hands pulled at the cold water.

Rory burst through the surface and found himself carried up the side of a four-foot swell. His lungs pulled in air and water, making him cough. Out of the corner of his eye, to the right, he saw the fishing tug turning back towards him. He caught a glimpse of one man on-board lifting an arm in his direction.

Rory dove fast.

The man was aiming a gun.

Bullets hissed and cut through the cold, black water, inches from his face.

Rory kicked hard and swam underwater as far as could.

He had to resurface for air.

He did it fast, taking a deep breath and looking for the fishing tug.

Not fast enough.

The men on the tug had guessed correctly and were almost on him.

Rory jackknifed under the water again and swam directly towards the dark hull instead of away.

Bullets hissed around him, the slugs seeking his body.

A moment later he dove deeper again and the hull of the tug began passed over him, offered him temporary protection. At the midway point, Rory swam at an angle away from the underside of the hull to avoid the churning blades cutting through the water. As the tug passed by, Rory tried to figure out what to do next. He didn't have much air left.

The hull of the fishing tug began a turn to the left. They were either going to swing back to him or circle the spot, waiting for him to come up. Either way, they would win eventually when he tired out.

His only hope was a surprise attack.

Rory swam hard for the surface, pulling the handgun from the back of his jeans just as he broke from the black water. He immediately saw the open stern of the fishing tug and two men on the deck.

One man was looking in his direction. The other was saying something back towards the wheelhouse. The man talking was Frost.

Rory raised the weapon and fired before the man looking at him could act.

The man clutched his throat and toppled forward over the railing and into the black water.

Frost turned quickly, raised his weapon and began firing.

Bullets splashed around Rory.

The fishing tug was moving up and down with the swells and Frost tried to adjust his aim.

Rory unloaded towards the fishing tug, hoping to hit something as the cold, black water moved him up and down as well.

Frost kept firing at Rory.

Rory kept firing in the direction of the tug.

The fishing tug exploded in a large orange fireball, incinerating Frost.

Rory was knocked underwater. He fought hard against the cold blackness that threatened to swallow him, desperately clawing his way back to the surface. He finally broke through, choking from the water he had swallowed. He had lost his weapon and was now at the mercy of any of the men who might have survived.

The fishing tug was a mass of fire and black, rolling smoke.

Rory wiped water from his eyes as he surmised he must have hit one of the six fuel tanks on board. It didn't matter though. There were other matters more important to think about right now. Rory moved up and down with the swells.

Fear of the black water tried to raise its ugly head again, but Rory tamped it back down.

He had someone else to think about.

The fishing tug began slipping under the swells. In moments, all that was left were a few burning embers on the surface, moving up and down in a macabre dance of death.

Off to his right, Rory caught sight of the shoreline in the distance. As the waves moved him up and down, he realized it was Port Dover he was looking at, which was about 30 minutes west of his cottage. That was good. Well, somewhat good. There was all this black, cold water between here and there.

He pushed the thought down again and began the long swim back to Jane.

Chapter 48

RORY SAT IN the stolen SUV on the shoulder of the road, watching the entrance to the compound from a distance. He had to find a way to get inside. All he could think of right now was coming back at night and scaling the fence. But without a detailed floor plan of the buildings inside, he had no way of knowing exactly where Jane was. He would have to be awfully fortunate to find her before they found him. Calling his office or a military contact to get detailed plans might trigger some alert through their spy network inside and probably trip him up as well. This was one of the few times he felt helpless and without a direction to move in.

A loud engine rumble from behind attracted his attention and just as he turned his head, the heavy draft from a passing transport truck rocked the SUV. Then another one passed. And another. Rory realized they were not transport trucks, they were fuel tankers. And they kept coming. The SUV rocked from the heavy draft as each one drove past. Rory recognized the logo on the side of the trucks. It was from the nearby refinery.

By the time they were all past him, Rory counted two dozen.

And they were headed directly for the compound. Obviously, someone in the compound wanted to refill the fuel bunkers.

But that didn't make much sense. He doubted they would need much more than two or three tankers. The convoy of fuel tankers eventually stopped at the front entrance, lining up one behind the other.

Rory had an idea. It didn't matter why they needed all those fuel tankers, it only mattered that they were headed into the compound. He put the SUV in gear and pulled out, heading for the back of the convoy. Stopping right behind the last tanker, he put the car in park and stepped out. Closing the door softly, he checked for on-coming traffic and then walked along the driver's side to the cab. Stepping up on the running board, knocked hard on the glass before stepping back down onto the pavement.

The driver inside rolled down his window and looked down, "Yeah? What do ya want, pal?"

"You've got a heavy leak back here," Rory said as he jerked a thumb towards the back of the man's tanker. "Just thought you'd want to know." He started walking back and could hear the driver swearing as he opened the cab door.

"I can't believe this," grumbled the driver as he stepped down from the cab, leaving the door open and walked towards the back of his tanker truck. "I promised the wife I'd be home early. We got a barbecue and my two sisters are coming with their families–"

Just as the man stepped around the back, Rory knocked him unconscious with one punch. "Tell your wife I'm sorry, but you'll be a little late," Rory said as he caught the man before he dropped to the pavement. Rory quickly dragged him to the driver side of the stolen SUV, opened the door and piled him into the passenger seat. Rory got back in and backed the car quickly onto the shoulder where he left it. He jumped out and headed to the back of the tanker, picked up the man's ball cap where it had fallen.

Pulling the bill of the cap down low over his eyes, Rory sauntered back towards the open door. He stepped up into the cab. The vehicle was still running.

The tanker in front of him had pulled ahead a full truck length.

It had been some time since Rory had driven a large truck and he fought to get it in gear, grinding the transmission. The truck bounced as he finally got it in a gear and he pulled forward. He slammed on the brakes at the last minute, almost piling into the tanker in front of him. He waited for an angry trucker to come back and give him an earful but nothing happened. Rory kept pulling ahead every time another tanker went inside the compound.

There was only one tanker truck left in front of him. Rory felt a chill when he realized the guard at the gate was checking each driver's credentials and face against a tablet the guard was holding in his hand. He cursed under his breath. The guards near the security shack carried submachine guns over their shoulder. This could be over in a heartbeat.

Chapter 49

RORY SCRAMBLED TO think up a plausible a story about relieving the other driver. He began checking the inside of the cab quickly for papers or identification for the other driver. If he knew the man's name, maybe he could bluff his way through. But there was nothing. The driver must have had what he needed in a pocket. And he was back in the stolen vehicle. The diesel engine of the tanker ahead of him rumbled louder, jerked to a start and pulled ahead through the gates. Rory's truck was being waved forward. He had no choice but to pull up to the gate and stop for the check. He pulled ahead to a stop and rolled down the window, wondering if he would be shot or brought back to the lake.

The guard stepped up onto the truck running board and held up his tablet, "Look this way, Calvin."

Rory's mind whirled as he tried to think up a story. He was about to say something–

"Okay," the guard said as he pointed, "pull through the gates and follow your buddies around to the left." He stepped back down and backed away from the truck, waving Rory forward.

Rory's mind was only half on getting the truck in gear. How in the world had he been able to pull that off? He certainly wasn't a twin to the driver he had left back in the stolen SUV. As he drove through the gates, Rory's antenna went up. Had they recognized him and were they now trying to trap him inside? That was the only explanation. He looked at each side mirror, looking to see if they were following him.

Nothing.

He looked to the left and the right.

No one was coming for him.

This didn't make any sense.

Looking ahead again, he saw the black, glass building just off to the right. Maybe he could–

A guard just ahead signaled him to turn left.

He saw a line of tankers off to his right though. Crap! This was it. They *were* separating him. Now what?

Turning the wheel to the left, Rory looked for a way out. But as he straightened the wheels out, he realized there was a line of tankers to the left as well. The convoy was being split into two groups and he was being moved in the direction of a large building to the left of the black, glass building. His muscles relaxed a bit but he stayed on high alert as he drove to the left. He was ready to fight if he had to.

His driving was a bit slow and he ended up falling far behind the other line of tankers as they disappeared around the building on the right. He glanced into the side mirrors on both sides. He couldn't see anyone in his field of view behind the truck. He glanced around quickly but didn't see any guards nearby. He considered stopping the truck against the side of the building and make a run for the glass building. But that would probably alert them within five or ten minutes to an intruder not just intent on delivering fuel. No, he would just have to play it by ear from here.

He stepped on the gas, speeding up. By the time he got around the corner, most of the tankers were parked side-by-side in a line.

One of the tankers was over near a set of gas pumps and the driver was hooking up a large hose to the side of the tanker. He was surrounded by the several other drivers who had gotten out of their trucks as well as a number of guards. Rory surmised he was going to pipe his load into the underground tanks for the gas pumps as well. And he had no idea how to do that. He hoped he would be a fast learner or this infiltration was over.

Rory pulled in beside the other tankers, turned the engine off and got out. He walked over to the group, keeping the bill on his ball cap low over his eyes.

One of the guards was talking into a microphone on his shoulder. "And I'm telling you I have two dozen tankers filled with gasoline. No. I said two dozen...that means 24. Yes, I can count. I *know* that we don't normally get that many. Look, my iPad shows orders for a dozen tankers to be parked by the fuel bunkers and gas pumps on this side. The other 12 were to be parked next to the bunkers and pumps to the east of the main building. That's what I've done. No, I have no idea why. But–" The man shook his head as he looked at the other guards.

"How long we going to be?" one of the drivers asked.

One of the other guards snapped at him, "Just be quiet."

"Look, we gotta get back and get ready for other loads, pal."

The driver with the hose was now over by the valve that fed the gasoline into the underground bunker and he was arguing with another guard, "And I'm telling you this bunker is already full."

"It can't be," the guard yelled back as he looked down the filler tube. "Why else would you be here?"

Rory approached one of the guards as the others argued. "Wouldn't have a washroom I could use, would you?" He lowered his voice, "If I have to stay around these other whiners and moaners, I better get comfortable."

The guard looked at him for a minute and then smirked and nodded. "This way," the guard said as he walked away.

Rory followed him into a large building that looked like a maintenance garage. There was the distinct odor of gasoline, grease and cleaning solvent.

The guard pointed diagonally across the room to a door, "Washroom over there on the right. Make it quick and get back outside with the others."

Rory nodded and started walking quickly towards the washroom door, a man in need of relief.

He heard boot steps moving away behind him and he turned after a few moments to see the guard stepping back outside.

Rory slowed his walk towards the washroom and quickly surveyed the room he was in.

There was a door far to the left and another door directly opposite the one he had come in. That one was marked exit. That door directly across should be in the right direction to take him to the glass building and Jane Doe. Rory took another look back at the door he had come in. It was open a crack and he could see the guard standing just outside, his back to Rory. It was now or never. He walked as quietly as possible across the room to the door marked exit. But as he reached for the doorknob he cursed under his breath. It had a security lock with a keypad for a code to be punched in. He twisted the doorknob anyway, hoping for a miracle. It was locked. Rory looked up and realized there was a security camera over the door. He cursed again. He was forgetting this was a secure facility. They were sure to be watching him.

He was about to head over to the door on his left when he heard a click.

His blood ran cold.

Slowly reaching for the doorknob, Rory found it turned freely this time.

He pulled the door open.

There was no one waiting on the other side.

What in the world was happening here?

Rory looked up at the security camera again.

There was only one answer. They had let him into the compound. And now they were letting him inside this building. They would probably funnel him towards a force of waiting guards. Or maybe the same black-garbed attack teams from the hospitals. Like a fly being lured into a Venus flytrap, Rory was being led to his own death. Well, at least he was getting closer to Jane.

Rory took a deep breath and stepped through the doorway.

Chapter 50

THE OPERATIONS CONTROL CENTER continued to be a hub of frenetic activity as the staff at the desks and workstations worked diligently, busy siphoning, translating, analyzing and cataloging the amazing amount of data that was flowing again.

In the middle of the activity, Bartlett Foxen was bent over, looking over a worker's shoulder at one of the larger workstations, intently watching the data racing across the man's array of computer screens.

The worker's fingers were a blur as he began keyboarding a series of codes. After a few moments, he gave Foxen a thumbs up over his shoulder.

Foxen patted the man on the back and straightened up. He finally felt good again. They would soon begin transferring the appropriate information to each military or government agency they had as clients, which meant everything was back on track as needed. He smiled to himself; *everything* was back on track. He moved across the floor and climbed the stairs to the hallway. At the top of the stairs, he paused for a moment and took one last look over the operations control center, feeling immense satisfaction. Then he headed into the hallway for the Light Dome next door.

Brecc was still standing and watching the screens in the operations control center as Foxen entered. "We are back to normal, sir," he said as he closed the door behind him.

There was no reply or acknowledgment. Brecc simply stood there watching the activity below.

Foxen looked over at the woman in the chair. The beam of light shimmered upward through her nude body and gave her a warm, sculptured look.

Brecc finally spoke without turning, "Are you telling me *everything* is back to normal?"

"Yes, sir. I contacted Mr. Stratis and got him started again. We just confirmed through the system that the special project is back on track. *And*...the indicators show we are close to cracking the financial codes already."

Brecc smiled as he continued watching the data flashing at immense speeds across the screens, "Perfect."

"The coffers should soon begin filling again," Foxen added. He felt his cell phone vibrate and he pulled it from the holder in his belt. A text message popped up and he read it. "Excuse me, sir, there is a matter that needs my attention in the hard drive room."

Brecc didn't bother answering.

Foxen slipped out of the viewing room and headed for the engineering center. They were responsible for the remote access and operations of the two floors above them that held all the storage devices. Those storage devices held all the intercepted information that was being collected from around the world. It was a long walk but he finally reached the secure entrance where he punched his security code into the keypad. When he stepped inside, no one was waiting for him as he had expected. That angered him. His time was important. He went looking for the lead engineer who had texted him the message. He found it strange that all the equipment was running but he didn't see anyone. Every workstation and every office was unoccupied. He walked back around a second time, yelling but getting no answer.

The place was empty.

That didn't make any sense. It only made him angrier. He was determined now to find the lead engineer and fire the jackass. He returned to the door where he had entered but the doorknob wouldn't turn. He jiggled and twisted it a number of times but it was locked. That didn't make any sense at all. There was another door on the other side of the engineering center but he found it locked as well. Why couldn't he get out? Cursing, he pulled his cell phone. He hit speed dial.

Nothing happened.

He slapped the stupid thing.

It was offline. Cursing a blue streak, Foxen began looking for a land line. He saw one at a workstation and grabbed it.

Dead.

He went into an office and tried another land line.

Equally dead.

He checked the computer that worked with the large LCD monitor on the wall they used for internal meetings. The application wouldn't run. This made absolutely no sense. He was trapped inside the engineering center with no way to call or get out. What in the world was happening here?

Chapter 51

BACK IN THE LIGHT DOME, Brecc continued to watch everything in the operations control center below, his own feeling of satisfaction growing–

"Mr. Brecc? We have a problem, sir."

Brecc turned sharply at the intrusion and saw a young woman had entered the Light Dome, "What are you doing in here? And why are you talking to me about some problem? Talk to Foxen. That's what I pay him for–"

The young woman shrank back but meekly said, "I'm afraid I can't find him, sir. And this is important, so...."

Brecc looked around the room behind him.

Other than Jane in the chair, there were only two men in lab coats in the room.

"Where is Foxen?" Brecc yelled in a loud, authoritative voice.

Both men looked at each other, then shrugged their shoulders. "I heard him say something about a problem, but I'm not sure where he went," answered one of the men meekly.

Brecc grumbled under his breath before turning to the young woman again, "*What* is so important that you're in here bothering me?"

"I have a report that shows a number of gasoline tankers have just arrived inside the compound–"

"What are you talking about? I know for a fact the bunkers are full. Send the two tankers back. Is that so hard?"

"S-sir...there are twenty-four gasoline tankers–"

"Twenty-four? We would *never* need that much. Just call the refinery and tell them they've made a mistake," Brecc grumbled.

"Sir...I checked and we *do* have internal purchase orders showing a large quantity of gasoline being ordered from the near-by refinery. And I *did* check with the refinery and they said their paperwork showed the same quantity to be delivered, with a bonus payment for *immediate* delivery," the young woman explained.

"Who would be so stupid as to order materials we don't need?" thundered Brecc.

"I'm...I'm not...sure...sir. No one seems to know who ordered it and why. And I can't find anyone in purchasing. We usually only require one for each–"

"Didn't I just say that?" Brecc interrupted her sternly.

"Yes, sir."

Brecc looked angrily around the room, "And where is Foxen!"

"As I said...."

Brecc marched across the room and into the hallway with the young woman running behind him to keep up. Minutes later he burst into the purchasing offices. But where there should have been a dozen purchasing assistants working away busily, every desk was empty. The place was like a morgue.

"Where is everybody?" Brecc yelled. He looked back at the young woman.

"That's just it, I... I don't know sir." She took a hurried look at her watch, "It's...it's not lunch yet...."

"I'm very aware of that," Brecc grumbled as he glared around the empty room.

"S-sorry, sir."

"You're useless. Go find Foxen," Brecc commanded her.

The young woman ran off down the hallway, very happy to get away from the well-known temper of Maxwell Brecc.

Brecc strode across the empty office with his fists clenched, heading for the office of the head purchasing agent. "I'll fire everybody in this place," he grumbled. He only found another empty room. Brecc cursed and headed back for the door to the hallway. It was closed. Brecc twisted the doorknob. It wouldn't open. He twisted the doorknob again. Then he shook it, cursing. Brecc stepped back from the door, "What in the world is going on around here?" He pulled a cell phone from his pocket and found he had no service. "How in thunder can we have no service?" he yelled into the empty room around him. He turned and looked for a land line. But each phone he picked up was inexplicably dead. With his rage rising, Brecc careened around the room, looking for one of the LCD monitors hooked up to the internal communication system.

Chapter 52

RORY MOVED ALONG the wide hallway, the odor of gasoline, grease and cleaning solvent dissipating. It was replaced by the scent of fresh paint, hand sanitizer and the light fragrance of perfume. There were a number of open doorways ahead, spaced evenly on both sides of the hallway. He took a deep breath and tried to walk business-like as if he belonged here. Passing the first doorway on the right, he saw it was a small office with several cubicles inside. It looked like it had been recently renovated. He kept to the center of the hallway, passing several other open doorways and he could see people inside each space. Everyone was busy with paperwork or keyboarding something into a computer. So far, no one paid any attention to him.

He reached a corner where the hallway turned left. Rory slowed his pace and did his best to lean out to see if anyone was around the corner. So far, so good. He moved quickly around the corner and down the hallway, trying to tread lightly to avoid bringing any kind of attention to himself. He passed a few more open doorways and still, no one paid any attention to him.

Then someone stepped out of an office in a hurry and bumped into him. It was a security patrol guard with a rifle sling carrying a machine pistol over his right shoulder, "Sorry, pal–"

"That's okay," Rory said as he tried to bluff his way past. Then he saw the man's embarrassed grin turn into suspicion.

The guard's hand went for the weapon over his shoulder.

Rory reacted instantly the only way he could in close quarters, by bringing his head down into the man's face.

The man grunted with pain as he staggered back. Blood flowed from his broken nose. But he was a hardened professional, still trying to shrug the sling forward to grab the machine pistol.

Rory moved forward, pushing the weapon back over the man's shoulder with his left while slamming a fist into the man's throat.

The guard fell, clutching his throat and gagging.

Rory reached down for the weapon.

But the man fell over on his back, pulling the weapon with him as he desperately fought to breathe through a crushed larynx.

"Hey? Why are you guys fighting–?"

Rory turned.

A short woman was standing behind him at the corner of the hallway. Her eyes were filled with alarm and a moment later she reacted, turning her head and yelling back down the hallway, "Carl, we have an intruder!"

Rory started running as soon as the woman disappeared back around the corner. Twenty feet down the hallway, he heard a man yelling at him from behind.

"Stop where you are. Someone stop that man."

Heavy boot steps began running down the hallway after Rory.

Rory kept running, expecting someone to shoot, but it didn't happen.

A man stepped out of an office up ahead to see what was happening.

Rory lowered his shoulder and bull charged into him.

The man yelped as he was knocked backward, careening off the edge of the door and crashing back into the office, overturning several chairs on his way to the floor.

Rory kept running, passing more offices and cubicles. There was a glass door up ahead on the right. That had to be an exit.

"Stop or I shoot!"

That voice was older and Rory knew from the tone that he would. He slowed down and lifted his arms in the air only a few feet away from the glass door.

"Stay right there, pal," instructed the older voice. Boot steps sounded as the man marched towards Rory.

Rory counted to three and then bolted for the door, ducking as he pushed it open.

A bullet exploded into the door frame just over his head.

Rory found himself running inside a large stores area. There were shelves lined with various parts on either side of him, but they were open and offered no real place to hide. A workbench ran the entire length of the wall ahead of him. Reaching the end of the shelves, Rory looked to the left and to the right. There was a doorway on the left. He ran for it.

The door behind him slammed open against the wall with a loud bang.

"Stop!"

Rory heard the shot and a ricochet sounded off the metal bench to his right. Reaching the door, he grabbed the doorknob and then realized it was another security door. He was trapped.

Rory cursed. These people were security anal. He turned to look for a place to hide.

Boot steps pounded from between the line of shelves, heading directly for him.

There was a soft click behind Rory.

He turned and tried the doorknob.

It opened!

Rory ran through, not looking a gift horse in the mouth. At least he would survive the guards coming after him. He pulled the door shut to delay his pursuers and then ran hard down another hallway.

As he passed a door on the right, he heard it click several times.

He stopped running and stepped back to the door. It looked like another security door but there was no keypad on this side. This had to be an exit to the outside. He could hear several soft clicks from the doorknob again. *Someone* wanted him to go through this door. He looked around and noticed a red security camera bulb in the ceiling back down the hallway. He was still being watched. His jaw clenched. Still tunneling the rat through the maze? Fine. He took a deep breath, twisted the doorknob and pushed the door open a crack. He could see outside like he had expected. He pushed the door fully open and cautiously took a look.

A wide grassy area and a roadway were dead ahead. And then, across another wide stretch of grass, he could see the large, three-story black glass building that served as the main building.

He was definitely being funneled in that direction.

Rory stepped outside into the sun but kept the door open as he looked in both directions. He saw a couple of vehicles pass by in the distance on the right, but other than that, everything was quiet. He looked at the black, glass building again. That had to be the place where Jane was being held. It made sense. But why would they funnel him directly to her? Only one way to find out. *Here I come, Brecc.*

Letting the door close behind him, Rory hustled across the grass and pavement between the two buildings. Reaching the expanse of grass on the other side of the road, he spotted a security door with a with a keypad just to the left and he headed for it. Reaching it, he looked up that the security camera staring down at him. Okay, Brecc, are you going to let me in or not?

There was a soft click at the door.

Rory reached down and turned the doorknob. It was unlocked. He looked back up at the camera. "Here comes the rat through the maze," he whispered and he pulled the door open.

There was no one on the other side.

Rory stepped through the doorway and let the door close behind him.

There was a stairway to the left.

Chapter 53

IN THE COMPOUND'S ARMORY, Conrad Blayze felt the buzz of his cell phone. He pulled it out. It was a text message from Foxen. That seemed strange. Usually, when they were inside the compound, he and Foxen would communicate directly. He read the message:

ASSEMBLE ALL MEMBERS of Response Tactical Team One and Response Tactical Team Two to the rear of the main building on the east side. Wait there for further instructions.

BLAYZE READ THE MESSAGE a second time. He assumed it was the next part of plan B. Remove family and friends of their target. But it was unusual for him to head up both teams. Then again, Frost hadn't returned yet and he wondered if there'd been a problem with Steele. Tapping away on his cell phone, he quickly composed a text message to Frost and then hit send. He cursed when the message didn't go anywhere. He hit speed dial to call instead but it wasn't working either. Blayze felt his jaw tighten as he slipped the phone back in its case, "Great, it's working for every-one but me." He turned to his men working on their weapons, "Listen up everybody. Gather your gear and get ready for a mission."

The men immediately went into action, eager to get started.

Blayze called out to one of his men, "Bowman. Tactical team two is in the shooting range. Go get them and bring them here on the double. Foxen's orders."

Within twenty minutes both tactical teams were moving around to the rear of the main building on the east side. Vehicles were being pulled into position by team members. As Blayze hustled alongside the building, he noticed a number of gasoline tankers parked not far away. That didn't make any sense. Then again, if he was assembling the two teams back here, maybe they were part of the mission. He'd find out soon enough.

Chapter 54

RORY CLIMBED THE CONCRETE STAIRS slowly, trying to keep as quiet as possible. He had no weapon and they knew he was in here because they had let him in, but he didn't want to make it too easy. Maybe he could catch somebody off guard, waiting anxiously for him to appear. He stopped at the first landing and listened.

Nothing. Everything was quiet.

He began moving up the stairs again. At the next landing, he approached the exit door.

The door flew open.

Rory froze.

A large, heavy set guard came hustling through the door. He stopped dead in his tracks, surprised that he had almost run over someone.

Rory tried to act like everything was normal and gave the man a nod and took a step to go around him and through the slowly closing door.

The guard moved to the side, a sheepish grin on his face, "Sorry about that–" The grin fell when he realized Rory was an intruder and he took a step back to get some distance, reaching for the submachine gun slung over his shoulder.

Throwing a left hook, Rory connected solidly with the man's jaw.

But the bulky man only staggered back two steps, his weight absorbing most of the blow. He reached for the submachine gun again but the stock caught between the closing door and the door jamb.

Rory lowered his head and hit the man with a tackle, driving him back into the edge of the door.

The big guard grunted in pain but he reacted quickly, throwing a short, hard right.

The punch caught Rory below the ribs and lifted him to his toes. The pain was immense as Rory staggered backwards from the blow.

The big guard charged., growling.

Rory only had one move. He used his backward momentum to fall on his back, bringing his feet up and catching the charging guard in the midsection.

The bulky guard was taken by in surprise and his eyes widened as he was hoisted into the air.

Fighting to keep his knees from buckling under the man's weight, Rory strained hard to use the man's momentum to flip him over his head - it played out in slow motion.

The big guard flailed his arms, trying to find something to hold onto - then he screamed as he went head first over the stairs.

Rory's own momentum carried him over backward in a roll over the first stair and he desperately reached for something to stop his fall.

The big guard landed on his head with a loud thump and then his body tumbled down to the next landing, the final thump echoing off the walls.

Rory landed face down on the stairs, each knee taking a sharp, painful blow from the edge of the steps. His body slid down several steps and he managed to turn over, bringing his hands up, ready to continue the fight. He stopped sliding.

Everything was quiet.

Rory lifted his head and looked down the stairway.

The big guard lay motionless on the landing below, his neck bent at an impossible angle.

Rory struggled to his feet and moved down the stairs to grab the big guard's submachine gun. He picked it up and checked it. He cursed when he saw the box magazine was twisted. It wasn't going to work. He threw it down. Still weaponless, Rory started back up the stairs.

Chapter 55

INSIDE THE LIGHT DOME, Pollard felt the buzz from his cell phone. He pulled it out and read the text message. Foxen wanted him to assemble with the other staff in meeting room three. That was unusual. Someone was always present in the Light Dome and right now he was all alone. But the message was labeled as a top priority. And Foxen wasn't one to disobey or cross. Still...Brecc might not approve. He tapped in a reply to let Foxen know he was alone and pressed send. Nothing happened. That was strange. He tried to send a reply again. Still nothing. He tried to make a call. No service? That didn't make any sense. He had no choice, he had to go to meeting room three. Putting his cell phone back in his pocket, Pollard walked over to the large chair in the center of the dome. His eyes traveled over the woman's naked body. He felt excitement rise in his loins. He reached out and placed his hand on her right breast, feeling its softness as he whispered, "Don't miss me while I'm gone, sweetheart. Maybe one of these days, we'll take things to a whole new level. Hole new, get it?"

Jane's head rolled slowly to her right. Her eyelids opened halfway and her blue eyes seem to bore deeply into the man's eyes.

Pollard stepped back with a jerk. The smile dropped from his face. There was something about the half look that made him afraid. Very afraid. But that was crazy. She was heavily drugged and totally out of it. Pollard then gave a half laugh and rolled his shoulders, trying to relax. "I'll be right back, sweetheart," he said as he turned and left the Light Dome.

Chapter 56

RORY FOUND THE HALLWAYS EMPTY. He moved as quietly as possible towards the area where he last saw Jane. He passed several offices that were also empty. He wondered where everyone was. He passed a door that had the sign Medical on it. He had to find Jane but there was also the problem of helping her get rid of that device in her head. He decided to take a few moments to see what he could find. He reached down and turned the doorknob quietly. It was unlocked. Rory opened the door and peeked inside.

It was empty.

Rory slipped inside quickly.

There were several rooms off the main waiting area. One of them had a number of filing cabinets.

Rory moved over to them quickly and pulled the drawers open. The files inside were sparse. He imagined most of the records would be on a medical computer system. There was a keyboard and a computer monitor on the desk. Rory moved to it quickly and tapped the keyboard. The screen came on. The name of IntelliMax International rotated on the screen. Rory grabbed the mouse and tried to access the system.

It was frozen.

Rory tapped the keyboard several times to no effect. He looked for the computer tower but there was nothing. This was simply a workstation tied into the larger system. Rory cursed and decided to move on. Back in the empty hallway and moving as quickly as he could, Rory couldn't figure it out. Where was everybody?

He stopped at a corner and peered around.

Like all the others, this hallway was empty and quiet.

He stepped around the corner and moved cautiously past several open doors.

Every single office space he passed was quiet and empty. No staff. No guards. No one single soul in the entire place This didn't make any sense.

Rory reached a part of the hallway that looked familiar. He rushed up to a door on the right and opened it quickly. He was positive this was the room where they had prepared Jane!

He moved down the hallway quickly now, trying the doors on either side. But everything else was locked. Rory twisted every doorknob hard in frustration. He decided to head for the end of the hallway, determined to find Brecc–

Rory heard a soft click as he passed a door on the left and he froze.

Everything was quiet. No one stepped into the hallway.

Rory stepped back slowly and looked at the painted letters on the door; OCC Room. He had no idea what that was–

The doorknob softly clicked several times.

Just like before, someone wanted his attention. And that someone wanted Rory to go inside. He slowly reached down and turned the doorknob. It was definitely unlocked. But it *wasn't* just a second ago. Rory set his jaw; they were still funneling the rat through the maze. He took a deep breath and opened the door just a crack.

No one jumped out at him.

He pushed open the door and stepped through to find himself on a small landing at the top of a set of stairs. He realized he was looking down over the massive room he had seen from the large domed room. Brecc had called it the operations control center. That's what the letters were on the door. But when he first saw this room, it was a hub of activity. Right now, it was quiet and *totally* empty of people. What was going on?

Rory let the door close behind him as he listened intently.

But the only sound was the door softly closing behind him.

A moment later, he walked slowly down the stairs to the room below. Reaching the bottom of the stairs, he prepared himself, waited for someone to jump out and attack. It didn't happen. Why would they lead him in here?

Rory looked around as he moved between a couple of workstations. The streams of data and graph were still running across the screens high on the walls. But they appeared to be running a lot slower than when he first saw them. The wall on the far side, dead ahead, had the words IntelliMax International scrolled across it. He turned, putting the stairs to his left and looked at the far wall. The upper half was black and shiny. Rory assumed the black material was some type of one-way glass. That had to be where Brecc had been looking down into this room. He took a step, looking up at the black material with anger, wondering if Brecc was watching him right now. Then he realized...if he had this right, on the other side of that black glass, Jane would be strapped into that chair!

He had to get up there.

He turned and headed back for the stairs–

"Hello, Rory."

Rory stopped dead in his tracks.

The voice was loud, slightly metallic and seemed to echo from a deep well. But there was one thing that was unmistakable. That was Jane Doe's voice. He turned and looked around the room. A flicker of light from the black, shiny material stretched across the upper wall on his left caught his attention. Rory took a step in that direction, wondered if it was his imagination –

There was another flicker of light again.

Rory narrowed his eyes, watching the flickering now come in quick bursts of color. That's when he realized the material wasn't just one-way glass as he thought. It was also a large computer monitor stretching right across the entire wall–

The monitor sprang to life and an image appeared. The image took up the middle third of the wall.

Jane's face was staring down at him. She still had the black helmet and the millions of colored threads of light were still flashing like brilliant lightning around the upper half of the room, making her look like a strange, exotic Medusa.

Chapter 57

THE IMAGE OF JANE DOE flickered several times on the black screen. Her eyes were closed and her head slowly rolled to the side.

Rory took a step as he looked up and whispered, "Jane."

She reacted, her eyelids fluttering and her head slowly coming back. The image stabilized again and Jane opened her eyes, giving him a sleepy half-smile, "Sorry about that. I think my body just wants to give up the fight and go to sleep." The image flickered once more and she shook her head softly, "And the drugs still interfere somewhat with my controlling things...but...I'm not going to...."

The voice *was* drug-tinged and it made Rory think back to their conversation with Doctor Tomlinson. The army doctor had been right. Jane *had* built a tolerance for the drug they were using. They still hadn't given her a large enough dose to knock her out completely

Jane's eyes started to close and then they snapped open. "Sorry," she whispered again in a soft voice.

"Just hold on," Rory urged her, "I came back to get you—"

"I know you did. I'm the one who let you into the building. I'm the one who led you here, Rory."

"*You* did...?"

Jane nodded her head slowly, "I'm sure the military won't appreciate my repositioning all their satellites in my attempt to find you."

Rory was stunned. Could she really do that?

"I was worried. I found you getting into that tanker...." Her voice trailed off, as she was falling asleep.

"And you exchange my picture for the driver I replaced," Rory said, finally understanding.

Jane nodded, her eyelids blinking several times, "Yes. Sorry I couldn't control all the guards as well once you got inside. But I wanted to say thank you. And goodbye."

Rory took a step forward, "I'm not leaving here without you. Just sit tight–"

"No, I won't be leaving with you," she said firmly.

"Jane–"

"I also brought you here, because I need you to do something for me. Can you–?"

Rory started to object again when another image appeared to the left of Jane.

The image showed Foxen walking around inside a large room. He tried to open a door but it wouldn't budge. He walked to another door and growled in frustration as he tried to open that one well.

Another image appeared on the right side of Jane's image.

It was Maxwell Brecc. And he was mad. He appeared to be looking into a computer screen somewhere in the building. "Is there anybody out there," he yelled. "This is Maxwell Brecc and I am currently trapped inside an office. I need someone to–"

"Hello, Mr. Brecc," Jane said. "Please sit patiently while I finish my conversation with Rory."

Brecc looked highly insulted, "Who is this? Do you know who you're talking to–?"

"Oh yes," Jane said firmly. *"This* is the Echelon Mind speaking. And I know exactly who *you* are."

Brecc was shocked speechless. He knew the voice from her days of crying and begging in a drugged stupor when they had first started. He staggered back a step. "It...it can't...be...."

Rory shook himself out of his own shock, "What's going on Jane? We can still get out of here together. Just lead me to where you are–"

"No, Rory," Jane said sadly. "I was able to reverse what they've been doing to me. They're no longer controlling everything through me. In fact, I'm now in control of this entire facility. And I can even reach out to the outside world through their various connections. I can do a lot more than just control a few satellites."

"Jane, just lead me to you," Rory pleaded.

"I've spent time searching for my identity, Rory," Jane added. "But it appears Mr. Brecc has used my own abilities to wipe everything clean. I've penetrated every database for law enforcement and news organization I could find. I searched for missing persons, checked news accounts, ran facial recognition software on any person reported missing or involved in any crime or an accident and...nothing. It's as if I never, ever existed."

"They said you had all these mathematical degrees," Roy said quickly. He tried to remember what Brecc had said, "A Bachelor of Science degree...an MBA...a Ph.D.–"

"I heard that part...it was like voices in the distance as I started to wake up," Jane told him. "But I researched that as well...all gone."

"But...someone is probably still looking for you–"

"No," Jane countered. There was immense pain and anger in that single word. "Brecc's method of operation not only involves removing any traces of my identity...it also involves removing *every* loved one who remained behind that might look for me. And by removing I mean *kill*."

That stunned Rory. How was that possible?

Jane took a deep breath and continued, "I've been able to access the medical records on what they've done to me. But the original scientists who created the device and the doctor who developed the procedure to implant it are somewhere in South America. I've had to reach out and penetrate several hospitals to use their medical diagnostic software to analyze my situation. Doctor Tomlinson was right. My brain cells are dying...." There was a catch in her throat. "And the odds of my surviving the removal of the device are very slim...if not impossible."

"We can't simply give up," Rory said in sympathy, "We can find the doctor–"

"There's no time for that," Jane countered.

"There's always time," Rory said firmly. "I won't just give up on you. I won't."

Jane smiled again, "I know. You were there for me. You don't know how much I appreciate that."

"It's just what we do," Rory said quietly.

"No," Jane said gently, "it's also about who you are. And that's why I brought you here. Right now, there is another young lady that needs your help. A young lady they kidnapped. Just like they did with me. They had plans to use her mind if they couldn't get me back. They haven't done anything to her yet and we can't let that happen. I need you to take her out of here–"

"You have no right," Brecc interrupted sternly.

Jane's face took on an angry look and she spoke forcefully, "You are no longer in charge, Brecc. I am."

"Brecc looked smug, "We will see about that–"

"Do you need proof? Clevon Sharp and Cyrek Stratis were ordered by you to board your Gulfstream G150 corporate jet one hour ago."

"What are you talking about? I did no such thing," Brecc protested.

"I was the one who sent the message on your behalf, and piloted the plane from here in the Light Dome," Jane said. "It rose to its service ceiling of 51,000 feet and then dove straight into the ground. Would you like to see a satellite image of their final moments?" The image flipped to a shot of a plane powering directly towards the earth. The name and logo for IntelliMax were very evident on the tail. A moment later, the corporate jet exploded in a fireball in a field of cucumbers. The image flipped back to Jane, "Satisfied?"

Brecc had a stunned look on his face and his mouth opened and closed like a fish.

"And just so you know, I have issued security instructions to clear this compound of all innocent personnel," Jane said. The image changed to show a shot of the front gate. A number of vehicles were leaving the compound.

"We can leave too, Jane," Rory said. "Do you hear me? Jane?"

But she wasn't listening. The image of the front gate changed to show another large room. It was filled with people in white lab coats. They were milling about, pulling at the exit door in futility as Jane spoke again, "However Brecc, you and Foxen, along with these people are *not* innocent. They are all a part of your organization and they all knew exactly what you were doing. That's why all of you are staying here with me."

Brecc's face was a mask of rage now, "Staying for what? When I get out of here–"

"You won't," Jane stated. "Excuse me, I'll be right back to you."

Brecc sputtered at her dismissive attitude but his first word was cut off as the image changed to another room, filled with more staff in white lab coats, milling about in confusion.

Pollard, the man who had shaved and abused Jane was looking into the onboard camera on a laptop as he tapped the keyboard several times, "Hello, hello. Is anyone there? We've been locked inside room three–"

"Yes, I'm here, Pollard," Jane said.

Pollard blinked as he squinted, looking at the image that had appeared on the laptop's screen, "Who is this? What's happening–?" His face took on a look of shock, "It...it can't be...?"

"Oh, yes. It's me."

Taking a faltering step back, a look of horror shot across Pollard's face and he shook his head, "No. It's not possible–"

Jane's voice was filled with hard, determined anger, "You wanted to take things to the next level, Pollard. Isn't that what you told me? I'm going to fulfill your wish. Unfortunately, it will be a level down. You are going to burn so hard, you're going to wish you were in hell."

The man staggered back, trying to put distance between himself and the retribution he could feel was coming.

"Do you hear me?" Jane said harshly.

Pollard shook his head, "Please, no-"

"Funny, I said the same thing but you wouldn't listen."

The image changed back to Brecc, who was yelling at the screen, "-hear me? You-"

"Yes, I can hear you," Jane said calmly.

Brecc shook his head angrily, "You can't keep us here forever. Once the military wonder why we aren't sending-"

"I don't plan on keeping you here forever," Jane said. "You see, I'm also the one who ordered the twenty-four gasoline tankers from the refinery that your staff told you about."

Brecc's eyes blinked several times, a look of confusion crossing his face, "So what? We don't need-"

"Twelve of those tankers are presently sitting to the west and the other twelve to the east of this main building," Jane explained. "Your teams of goons, the ones you sent after me, the ones who tried to kill the man who was helping me? They are presently standing next to each group of tankers, right where I ordered them to be."

Brecc shook his head, still trying to comprehend what was happening.

"This entire compound is computerized," Jane said. "And I have full control, thanks to your planning. Your underground gasoline tanks are full and have been opened...and the vapor level is nearing the 7% air/gasoline mixture needed for the explosion."

Chapter 58

RORY STOOD LOOKING UP at the image, confusion in his mind but alarm in his heart, "The explosion?" He shook his head, "Jane, what are you doing?" We can still all leave. There's still time–"

"No." Jane shook her head sadly, "It's too late for me. But you *can* help the person they've kidnapped and I'll stop it from ever happening again–"

"This facility is vital to our democracy," Brecc yelled loudly. "Mr. Steele, we need to stop this woman from destroying a compound that is geared toward protecting all of our loved ones–"

"The way you were going to protect the loved ones of the young lady you recently kidnapped," Jane snapped. "I found orders for your hit teams to kill *all* her loved ones and closest friends. To make sure no one ever came looking for your *asset*."

Brecc opened his mouth to protest.

"How many people did you kill in *my* family," Jane continued in an angry voice. "How far did you go? Did you kill all my friends as well, so *no one* would come looking for *me*!"

"We did what we had to do," Brecc insisted pompously.

"And I'll make sure you won't be able to do it again. *Ever*," Jane stated firmly. "As I already said, the remaining members of your hit teams are presently waiting behind this building and to the east as per their instructions. They will be incinerated along with everyone else–"

"Mr. Steele," Brecc said urgently. "You must work with me. You have to understand how vital this compound is. *We* are the main bulwark standing between the free world and terrorism. *We* are working closely with democratic governments around the world to protect–"

"No!" Jane yelled in rage. Her blue eyes speared into the monitor, "Keep in mind Brecc, that I have access to *all* the surveillance devices worldwide that you have used to spy on the world. And I have overridden all of the failsafe codes that filtered out any information regarding you and your company, IntelliMax International. *And* everyone who is behind this whole deception."

Brecc looked absolutely dumbfounded.

"Mr. Brecc is been less than truthful with us, Rory. He has held me captive for a number of years. This entire facility was built to use my mind to a greater capacity, that part is true. But that's just a front. While he continues to provide his government cronies with the spy data they crave in return for their support, he and Mr. Foxen have been running their own *special project* through my mind."

"You're crazy. Don't listen to her Mr. Steele," Brecc said. But his voice and demeanor lacked its normal bluster.

"There was a large independent bank that went bankrupt in the United Kingdom three months ago. It was attributed to dabbling in derivatives," Jane said. "But like many of the banks and financial institutions in the United States that folded, many people wondered where the money went. Brecc actually used *me* to decipher the international banking transfer protocols and siphoned the money into *his* accounts. The capabilities of my mind were used to restructure the records to hide that fact."

Rory looked at Brecc who had turned white.

"Entire countries are on the verge of bankruptcy because of Brecc and those with him. They have siphoned trillions of dollars from banks, manipulating the records and covering their tracks through cyberspace at every turn. They've also begun to move gold and any other commodity that props up money into their own control. It's a massive heist of wealth. And I'm the only one who knows," Jane continued. "But I have set matters in motion to return the money along with all the commodities."

"No! You can't do that," Brecc yelled frantically as he pounded his fists on the monitor in front of him.

"You and your cohorts planned to create a new world order by siphoning all the money into your own control. Because the real power in the world is money, isn't it Brecc? No government can operate without money. No army can go to war without money. No business can operate without money. And you would've had it all, right Mr. Brecc? Every single person on earth would have had to dance to your every whim. But I've taken it all...I've taken every...single...penny."

"You can't do that," Brecc shouted. "Who do you think you are—"

"I'm the woman you should never have crossed," Jane stated firmly.

"You bitch! I'll kill you. I'll kill you," Brecc yelled. He continued ranting and raving but the sound disappeared.

Jane's blue eyes were firm as she looked at Rory, "There are still a few billion dollars left in Brecc's account, accumulated wealth through interest that had nowhere to go. Except into your account, Rory."

That comment stunned Rory, "I...I don't understand...."

Jane's face softened. "I'm your client," she said. "And I'm paying my bill."

Rory felt tears forming. "You're more than a client," he whispered.

"I know. I could have used charities to disperse the funds, but I needed to be sure the person in charge would do the right thing. I know you will do that. I want you to use the money to help other people like you helped me. I know that's what you and your family do."

"Jane...."

"It's done," Jane said kindly. "Now go back up the stairs and once you're in the hallway, go right. Go to the fourth door on your left. That's where you will find the young lady they kidnapped to replace me. When you come out of that room with the young lady, turn right and go all the way to the door at the end of the hallway. Everything will be unlocked. You have seven minutes."

Rory was about to say something.

"Seven minutes," she repeated. "Goodbye...friend." Jane's image vanished.

So did the images of Foxen and Brecc.

"Jane," Rory yelled as he took a step towards the wall.

He yelled again.

The screen was black and dead and the room was quiet.

Chapter 59

RORY STOOD STILL, stunned by the sudden turn of events. His eyes moved over the black, shiny monitor, hoping to see the image of Jane Doe again. He had to talk her out of her plan – the wall flickered and an image appeared. It showed the interior of a small, dingy room. A frightened, raven-haired young woman, dressed in a red blouse and blue jeans, was sitting in a corner next to a single bed, hugging her knees. She was rocking back and forth.

That must be who I'm supposed to rescue. 'Go back out the door you came in, turn to the right and the fourth door on your left.' Seven minutes she said.

Rory backed slowly away from the image, hoping it would change back to Jane. He hoped she would reconsider staying. But it didn't happen. There was only silence and the image of the young woman rocking. Finally turning, Rory ran for the stairs and took them two at a time. Once he was back in the hallway, it only took him a minute to reach the fourth door on the left. It was unlocked. Rory turned the doorknob and stepped inside a stale smelling room.

The young woman stopped rocking immediately. Her voice was small as she shrunk back and her eyes filled with tears, "Please don't hurt me."

Rory just stood there for a moment as he was slammed back in time. This felt exactly like the first time he saw Jane back at the cabin. His heart ached for the young woman. And for Jane. Rory held his hand out and said in a soft voice, "I was sent here by a friend to help you. We don't have much time."

The young lady wiped the tears from her eyes as she looked at him, still uncertain.

Rory stayed patient, despite the dwindling time. He simply nodded his head once to reassure her that he was here to help.

She slowly took her arms from around her knees and stood up. But she just stood there, still uncertain, afraid.

"What's your name?" Rory asked gently.

"Erika," she whispered after a moment.

"Please Erika, we need to hurry."

Erika hesitated, her eyes blinking. Then she looked into Rory's silver-blue eyes and meekly stepped across the room and placed her hand in his. Rory gave her shaking hand a squeeze and then turned and led her out into the hallway. Everything was quiet. Rory could hear their footsteps echoing lightly as he and Erika moved down the hallway. He stopped at the door just before the room with the workstations. Behind this door was Jane Doe. Rory lightly placed his fingers against the door. He thought about all they had been through. And it all came down to this. His fingers curled into a fist and he banged it in frustration against the door.

"Are you okay?" whispered Erika behind him.

Rory looked at her and nodded, "I will be. It's just...hard to lose a friend...and you can't do anything about it."

Erika nodded, tears forming in the corners of her brown eyes.

"Let's go before we run out of time," Rory said finally. He urged Erika to run and they took off down the hallway. Reaching the door at the end, Rory cautiously opened the door and peered out.

They were at the side of the building and a large, black SUV was parked right there. Rory led Erika around to the driver side of the vehicle where he took a quick look inside.

No keys.

Rory was about to look for another vehicle when realized this one was a pushbutton start.

Jane had arranged for everything.

"Can we use this?" Erika asked.

"Yes, thanks to my friend," Rory whispered.

Erika was already running for the other side of the vehicle. She eagerly climbed into the passenger seat.

Rory got in and pushed the start button. The vehicle started immediately and the engine roared. Putting it in drive, Rory slammed the accelerator to the floor. The tires squealed as they accelerated into a half circle and then towards the far corner of the black glass building. The SUV swish-tailed as Rory took the turn at full speed. Straightening it out, he drove directly towards the main gates on the other side of the compound. Rory wondered how much time they had used up. Even when they topped 100 mph, time seemed to run in slow motion.

The main gates slowly began opening.

"Thank you, Jane," Rory whispered.

The SUV shot through the gates and down the roadway, away from the immense compound.

After a few minutes of hard driving, Rory slammed on the brakes and cranked the steering wheel hard to the left. The tires squealed and black smoke swirled into the air as the black SUV swished around hard on the pavement. They came to a stop, facing the compound back down at the end of the road.

"What wrong? What are we doing?" Erika asked in a weak, thready voice.

"I just can't leave her–"

"Who? Are we going back?"

Rory looked over at Erika.

Tears of fear filled her brown eyes.

He couldn't take her with him.

And he couldn't leave her here alone.

But he had to go back–

It was too late.

An explosion erupted on the western side of the compound, near the main, three-story black-glass building.

Rory's heart sank. It was the fuel bunker.

A second massive explosion erupted on the western side of the building. A massive fireball ripped right through the structure, shattering and melting black glass.

A third massive explosion happened seconds later on the eastern side. Another massive fireball ripped through the main building, devouring everything in its path.

The two fireballs from the loaded fuel tankers met in the middle of the main building, turning it into a cauldron of fire that reached skyward.

The combined explosions rolled to the edges of the compound and beyond, obliterating everything in its path. Tall masts, massive satellite dishes, large white radomes...all disappeared in the inferno that ate through the perimeter fence and reached beyond.

The black SUV was enveloped in flames and the shock wave pushed it backward down the road.

Erika screamed.

Rory instinctively threw his arm up to shield his eyes from the searing light.

The force of the blast moved the SUV backward in a hard slide for fifty yards where it finally rocked and came to rest.

Rory slowly lowered the arm shielding his eyes.

He watched as the entire compound was engulfed by an orange fireball.

Thick black smoke rose into a mushroom cloud, reaching into the blue sky over top of the thousand acre compound.

"Goodbye, Jane." Rory whispered as he choked back tears.